# VALNIR'S BANE

REINER HETSAU MADE a bad decision and now he's been condemned for the rest of his life, and that doesn't look like it's going to be very long. Sitting in the stockade, his only thoughts are of escape and a return to a simple life of card-sharking.

The appearance of Captain Viert changes all that. Reiner and a motley crew of fellow prisoners are given a simple choice: volunteer for an 'errand' or be executed right away. Now Reiner must try and survive a suicide mission, the purpose of which just gets darker and more sinister, the only people to watch Reiner's back are cutthroats and murderers.

Screenwriter Nathan Long delivers a tense, action-packed tale of dark heroism and adventure in the gothic fantasy world of Warhammer.

*More Warhammer from the Black Library*

## · GOTREK & FELIX BY WILLIAM KING ·

TROLLSLAYER
SKAVENSLAYER
DAEMONSLAYER
DRAGONSLAYER
BEASTSLAYER
VAMPIRESLAYER
GIANTSLAYER

## · THE AMBASSADOR NOVELS *
## BY GRAHAM MCNEILL

THE AMBASSADOR
URSUN'S TEETH

## · OTHER WARHAMMER ·

RIDERS OF THE DEAD by Dan Abnett
MAGESTORM by Jonathan Green
HONOUR OF THE GRAVE by Robin D Laws
SACRED FLESH by Robin D Laws
THE BURNING SHORE by Robert Earl
WILD KINGDOMS by Robert Earl

A WARHAMMER NOVEL

# VALNIR'S BANE

## NATHAN LONG

*To my mom and dad for their encouragement*
*To Emma and Will for their guidance*
*To Sue and Grey for their wisdom*

**A BLACK LIBRARY PUBLICATION**

First published in Great Britain in 2004 by
BL Publishing,
Games Workshop Ltd.,
Willow Road, Nottingham,
NG7 2WS, UK

10 9 8 7 6 5 4 3 2 1

Cover illustration by Adrian Smith.
Map by Nuala Kennedy.

© Games Workshop Limited 2004. All rights reserved.

Black Library, the Black Library logo, Black Flame, BL Publishing, Games Workshop, the Games Workshop logo and all associated marks, names, characters, illustrations and images from the Warhammer universe are either ®, TM and/or © Games Workshop Ltd 2000-2004, variably registered in the UK and other countries around the world. All rights reserved.

A CIP record for this book is available from the British Library

ISBN 1 84416 166 8

Distributed in the US by Simon & Schuster
1230 Avenue of the Americas, New York, NY 10020.

Printed and bound in Great Britain by
Bookmarque, Surrey, UK.

No part of this publication may be reproduced, stored in a retrieval system, or transmitted in any form or by any means, electronic, mechanical, photocopying, recording or otherwise, without the prior permission of the publishers.

This is a work of fiction. All the characters and events portrayed in this book are fictional, and any resemblance to real people or incidents is purely coincidental.

See the Black Library on the Internet at
**www.blacklibrary.com**

Find out more about Games Workshop
and the world of Warhammer at
**www.games-workshop.com**

THIS IS A DARK age, a bloody age, an age of daemons
and of sorcery. It is an age of battle and death, and of the
world's ending. Amidst all of the fire, flame and fury
it is a time, too, of mighty heroes, of bold deeds
and great courage.

AT THE HEART of the Old World sprawls the Empire, the
largest and most powerful of the human realms. Known
for its engineers, sorcerers, traders and soldiers, it is
a land of great mountains, mighty rivers, dark forests
and vast cities. And from his throne in Altdorf reigns
the Emperor Karl-Franz, sacred descendent of the
founder of these lands, Sigmar, and wielder
of his magical warhammer.

BUT THESE ARE far from civilised times. Across the
length and breadth of the Old World, from the knightly
palaces of Bretonnia to ice-bound Kislev in the far north,
come rumblings of war. In the towering World's Edge
Mountains, the orc tribes are gathering for another assault.
Bandits and renegades harry the wild southern lands of
the Border Princes. There are rumours of rat-things, the
skaven, emerging from the sewers and swamps across the
land. And from the northern wildernesses there is the
ever-present threat of Chaos, of daemons and beastmen
corrupted by the foul powers of the Dark Gods.
As the time of battle draws ever near,
the Empire needs heroes
like never before.

Norsca
Sea
Sea of Chaos...
Laurelorn forest.
The Wasteland.
L'Anguille.
Couronne.
Marienburg.
Arden forest.
Gisoreux.
Bordeleaux
Bretonnia
Brionne.
Quenelles.
Loren forest

f Claws
North of Here Lie The
Dreaded Chaos Wastes.
Erengrad.
Here Be Trolls...
Praag.
middle mountains.
Kislev
Kislev.
lenheim.
Wolfenburg.
Talabheim.
The Empire
Altdorf.
Karak Kad
Sylvania.
Nuln.
The
Moot.
Dracken
-hof.
Zhufbar.
ains.
Averheim.
Black
Water.
Black fire Pass.
Karak
Norn.

# CHAPTER ONE
## VICTIMS OF CIRCUMSTANCE

REINER HETZAU HAD not had a good war. When he had ridden north with von Stolmen's Pistoliers to join in the last push to drive the heathen horde back north of Kislev where they belonged, he'd hoped to return home to Altdorf with a few battle-scars to impress his various sweethearts and bedmates, a few trunks full of plunder and battlefield souvenirs to sell on the black market, and a few saddlebags full of gold crowns, won from his fellow soldiers in games of chance played behind the cavalry stables. Instead, what had happened? He had been wounded in his first battle and forced to sit out the rest of the offensive in Vulsk, a Kislev border town that fell further and further behind the front as the Grand Alliance forced the raiders deeper into the Chaos Wastes.

Then, while recuperating, he had single-handedly flushed out an evil sorceress disguised as a sister of Shallya and slayed her before she had succeeded in spreading disease and confusion throughout the army. But had they heaped praise and promotions upon him for this heroic act? No. Through the blind stupidity of his superiors, he was charged with murdering a clergywoman and perpetrating the very crimes he had stopped the false sister from committing.

Fortunately – or unfortunately – depending on how one looked at it, his arrest had coincided with the final offensive of the war, and the outcome had been so uncertain that little things like court martials and executions had been postponed while the conflict came to its blood-soaked climax. Reiner had cooled his heels in various cells for months, being moved from brig to brig as the vagaries of war demanded. At last, with the war half a year over, he sat in the garrison brig at Smallhof Castle, an Empire outpost just west of the Kislev border, awaiting execution by hanging at dawn in a cell full of the lowest sort of gallows trash.

No, it had not been a good war. Not a good war at all.

Reiner, however, was not the sort of fellow to give up hope. He was a gambler, a follower of Ranald. He knew that luck could be twisted in one's favour by an astute player with an eye for the main chance. Already he had succeeded in bribing the thick-witted turnkey with tales of treasure he had hidden before his arrest. The man was going to sneak him out of the brig at midnight in return for a cut of that fictitious cache. Now all he needed was one further accomplice. It would be a long, dangerous road to freedom: out of the camp, out of the Empire, into the unknown, and he would need someone to keep watch while he slept, to boost him over walls, to stand lookout while he liberated horses, food or clothes from their rightful owners. Particularly, he needed someone to push in the way of the authorities so that he could make his escape if they were trapped.

As the sun set outside the barred brig window, Reiner turned and surveyed his fellow prisoners, trying to determine which of them might be the most desirable travelling companion. He was looking for the right combination of competence, steadiness and gullibility – not qualities to be found in great abundance inside a prison. The others were all trading stories of how they came to be imprisoned. Reiner curled a lip as he listened. Every one of them proclaimed his innocence. The fools. In their eyes, not one of them deserved to be there.

The engineer in the corner, a brooding, black-browed giant with hands the size of Wissenberg cheeses, was shaking his head like a baffled bull. 'I didn't mean to kill anyone. But they wouldn't stop. They just kept pushing and pushing. Jokes and names and...' His hands flexed. 'I didn't swing to kill. But we were framing a siege tower and I held a maul and...'

'And yer a bloody great orc what don't know his own strength, that's what,' said a burly pikeman with a bald head and a jutting chin beard.

The engineer's head jerked up. 'I am not an orc!'

'Easy now, man,' said a second pikeman, as thin and wiry as his companion was sturdy. 'We none of us need another helping of trouble. Hals meant no harm. He just lets his mouth run away with him now and again.'

'Is that why you're here?' asked Reiner, for he liked the look of the pair – sturdy sons of toil with an alert air – and wanted to know more about them. 'Did your mouths dig a hole your fists couldn't fill?'

'No, my lord,' said the thin pikeman. 'Entirely innocent we are. Victims of circumstance. Our captain...'

'Blundering half-wit who couldn't fall out of bed without a map,' interjected Hals.

'Our captain,' repeated his friend, 'was found with a pair of pikes stuck in his back, and somehow the brass came to blame us for it. But as the coward was running from a charge at the time, we reckon it was Kurgan done for him.'

Hals laughed darkly. 'Aye. The Kurgan.'

There was a giggle from the shadows near the door. A fellow with white teeth and a curling black moustache grinned at them. 'Is no need to make stories, boys,' he said in a Tilean accent. 'We all in boats the same, hey?'

'What do you know about it, garlic-eater?' growled Hals. 'I suppose you're as pure as snow. What are you in for?'

'A mis-standing-under,' said the Tilean. 'I sell some guns I find to some Kossar boys. How I know the Empire so stingy? How I know they don't share with allies?'

'The Empire has no allies, you thieving mercenary,' said a knight who sat near the door. 'Only grateful neighbours who flock to it in times of need like sheep to the shepherd.'

Reiner eyed the man warily. He was the only other man of noble blood in the brig, but Reiner felt no kinship for him. He was tall and powerfully built, with a fierce blond beard and piercing blue eyes, a hero of the Empire from head to toe. Reiner was certain the fellow saluted in his sleep.

'You seem awfully keen for a man whose Empire has locked him up,' he said dryly.

'A mistake, certain to be rectified,' said the knight. 'I killed a man in an affair of honour. There's no crime in that.'

'Somebody must have thought so.'

The knight waved a dismissive hand. 'They said he was a boy.'

'And how did he run afoul of you?'

'We were tent-pegging. The fool blundered across my line and cost me a win.'

'A killing offence indeed,' said Reiner.

'Do you mock me, sir?'

'Not at all, my lord. I wouldn't dare.'

Reiner looked beyond the knight to a beardless archer, a dark-haired boy more pretty than handsome. 'And you, lad. How comes one so young to such dire straits?'

'Aye,' said Hals. 'Did y'bite yer nursie's tit?'

The boy looked up, eyes flashing. 'I killed a man! My tent mate. He...' The boy swallowed. 'He tried to put his hands on me. And I'll do for any of you as I did for him, if you try the like.'

Hals barked a laugh. 'Lovers' tiff was it?'

The boy leapt to his feet. 'You'll take that back.'

Reiner sighed. Another hothead. Too bad. He liked the boy's spirit. A sparrow undaunted in an eyrie of hawks.

'Peace, lad,' said the thin pikeman. "Twas only a jest. You leave him be, Hals.'

A tall, thin figure stood up from the wall, a nervous looking artilleryman with a trim beard and wild eyes. 'I ran from my gun. Fire fell from the sky. Fire that moved like a man. It reached for me. I...' He shivered and hung his head, then sat back down abruptly.

For a moment no one spoke, or met anyone else's eye. He's honest, at least, thought Reiner, poor fellow.

There was one last man in the room, who had not spoken or seemed to take any interest in the conversation: a plump, tidy fellow dressed in the white canvas jerkin of a field surgeon. He sat with his face to the wall.

'And you, bone-cutter,' Reiner called to him. 'What's your folly?'

The others looked at the man, relieved to turn to a new subject after the artilleryman's embarrassing admission.

The surgeon didn't raise his head or look around. 'Never you mind what ain't your business.'

'Oh, come sir,' said Reiner. 'We're all dead men here. No one will betray your secrets.'

But the man said nothing, only hunched his shoulders further and continued to stare at the wall.

Reiner shrugged and leaned back, looking over his cellmates again, contemplating his choices. Not the knight: too hot-headed. Nor the engineer: too moody. The pikemen perhaps, though they were a right pair of villains.

The sound of footsteps outside the cell door interrupted his thoughts. Everyone looked up. A key turned in the lock, the door squealed open, and two guards entered followed by a sergeant. 'On your feet, scum,' he said.

'Taking us to our last meal?' asked Hals.

'Yer last meal'll be my boot if y'don't move. Now file out.'

The prisoners shuffled out of the cell. Two more guards waited outside. They led the way with the sergeant into the chilly evening, and across the muddy grounds of the castle in which the garrison was housed.

Thick flakes of wet snow were falling. The hackles rose on Reiner's neck as he passed the gallows in the centre of the courtyard.

They entered the castle keep through a small door, and after descending many a twisting stair, were ordered into a low-ceilinged chamber that smelled of wood smoke and hot iron. Reiner swallowed nervously as he looked around. Manacles and cages lined the walls, as well as instruments of torture – racks, gridirons, metal boots. In a corner, a man in a leather apron tended brands that glowed in beds of hot coals.

'Eyes front!' bawled the sergeant. 'Dress ranks! Attention!'

The prisoners came to attention in the centre of the room with varying degrees of alacrity, and then stood rigid for what seemed like an hour while the sergeant glared at them. At last, just as Reiner felt his knees couldn't take it any longer, a door opened behind them.

'Eyes front, curse you!' shouted the sergeant. He snapped to attention himself as two men stepped into Reiner's line of vision.

The first man Reiner didn't know: a scarred old soldier with iron grey hair and a hitch in his walk. His face was grim and heavily lined, with eyes like slits hidden under shaggy brows. He wore the black-slashed-with-red doublet and breeks of an Ostland captain of pike.

The second man Reiner had once or twice seen at a distance – Baron Albrecht Valdenheim, younger brother to Count Manfred Valdenheim of Nordbergbruche and second-in-command of his army. He was tall and barrel-chested, with a powerful frame running a little to fat, and he had a lantern jaw. His reputation for ruthlessness showed in his face, which was as cold and closed as an iron door. He wore dark blue velvet under a fur coat that swept the floor.

The sergeant saluted. 'The prisoners, my lord.'

Albrecht nodded absently, his ice-blue eyes surveying them from under a fringe of short, dark hair.

'Ulf Urquart, my lord,' said the sergeant as Albrecht and the scarred captain stopped in front of the brooding giant. 'Engineer. Charged with the murder of a fellow sapper. Killed him with a maul.'

They moved to Hals and his skinny friend. 'Hals Kiir and Pavel Voss. Pikemen. Murdered their captain while in battle.'

'We didn't, though,' said Hals.

'Silence, scum!' shouted the sergeant and backhanded him with a gloved hand.

'That's all right, sergeant,' said Albrecht. 'Who's this?' He indicated the pretty youth.

'Franz Shoentag, archer. Killed his tentmate, claims self-defence.'

Albrecht and the captain grunted and moved on to the angular artilleryman.

'Oskar Lichtmar, cannon. Cowardice in front of the enemy. He left his gun.'

The grizzled captain pursed his lips. Albrecht shrugged and stepped to the blond knight, who stared straight ahead, perfectly at attention.

'Erich von Eisenberg, Novitiate Knight in the Order of the Sceptre,' said the sergeant. 'Killed Viscount Olin Marburg in a duel.'

Albrecht raised an eyebrow. 'A capital offence?'

'The viscount had only fifteen summers.'

'Ah.'

They next came to the Tilean.

'Giano Ostini,' said the brig captain. 'Mercenary crossbowman. Stole Empire handguns and sold 'em to foreigners.'

Albrecht nodded and stepped to the plump man who had refused to name his crime. The sergeant eyed him with distaste. 'Gustaf Schlecht, surgeon. Charged with doing violence to a person bringing provisions to the forces.'

Albrecht looked up. 'Not familiar with that one.'

The sergeant looked uneasy. 'He, er, molested and killed the daughter of the farmer his unit was billeted with.'

'Charming.'

The men stepped in front of Reiner. Albrecht and the captain of pike looked him up and down coolly. The sergeant glared at him. 'Reiner Hetzau, pistolier. The worst of the lot. A sorcerer who murdered a holy woman and summoned foul creatures to attack his camp. Don't know as I recommend him, my lord. The others are wicked men, but this one, he's the enemy.'

'Nonsense,' said the captain of pike, speaking for the first time. He had a voice like gravel under iron wheels. 'He ain't Chaos. I'd smell it.'

'Of course he isn't,' agreed Albrecht.

Reiner's jaw dropped. He was stunned. 'But... but then, my lord, surely the charges against me must be false. If you know I am no sorcerer, then it is impossible that I summoned those creatures, and...'

The sergeant kicked him in the stomach. 'Silence! You horrible man!'

Reiner bent double, retching and clutching his belly.

'I read your account, sir,' said Albrecht, as if nothing had happened. 'And I believe it.'

'Then... you'll let me go?'

'I think not. For it proves that you are something infinitely more dangerous than a sorcerer. You are a greedy fool who would allow the land of his birth to burn if he thought he could make a gold crown from it.'

'My lord, I beseech you. I may have made a few lapses in judgement, but if you know I am innocent…'

Albrecht sniffed and turned away from him. 'Well, captain?' he asked.

The old captain curled his lip. 'I wouldn't pay a penny for the lot of them.'

'I'm afraid they're all we have at the moment.'

'Then I'll have to make do, won't I?'

'Indeed.' Albrecht turned to the sergeant. 'Sergeant, prepare them.'

'Aye sir.' The man signalled the guards. 'Into the cell with them. All but Orc-heart here.'

'I am not an orc!' said Ulf as two guards stuffed Reiner and the rest into a tiny steel cage on the left wall. The other two led Ulf to the far side of the room where the man in the leather apron stirred his coals. The guards kicked Ulf's legs until he kneeled, then flattened his hand on a wooden tabletop.

'What are you doing?' asked the big man uneasily.

One of the guards put a spear to his neck. 'Just hold still.'

The man in the apron picked a brand out of the fire. The glowing tip was in the shape of a hammer.

Ulf's eyes went wide. 'No! You can't! This isn't right!' He struggled. The other guards hurried over and held him down.

The guard with the spear pricked his skin. 'Easy now.'

The torturer pressed the brand into the flesh of Ulf's hand. It sizzled. Ulf screamed and slumped in a dead faint.

Reiner swallowed queasily as he smelled the unpleasantly pleasant odour of cooking meat.

'Right,' said the sergeant. 'Next.'

Reiner suppressed a shudder. Next to him, Oskar, the artilleryman, was weeping like a child.

REINER WOKE WITH a sensation of cold on his cheek and searing agony on the back of his hand. He opened his eyes and found that he was lying on the flagstones of the torture chamber. Apparently he too had passed out when they had branded him.

Someone kicked his legs. The sergeant. 'On your feet, sorcerer.'

It was hard to understand the order. His mind was far away – detached from his body like a kite at the end of a string. The world seemed to revolve around him behind a wall of thick glass. He tried to stand – thought he had, in fact – but when he focused again, he found he was still on the floor, the pain in his hand rolling up his arm in waves like heavy surf.

'Stand at attention, curse you!' roared the sergeant, and kicked him again.

This time he managed it, though not without mishap, and joined the others who formed a ragged line before Albrecht and the captain. Each prisoner had an ugly, blistering, hammer-shaped burn on his hand. Reiner resisted the urge to look at his. He didn't want to see it.

'Sergeant,' Albrecht barked. 'Give the surgeon fellow some bandages and have him dress those wounds.'

The torturer in the leather apron produced some unguents and dressings which he gave to Schlecht. The plump surgeon salved and bound first his own burn, then started on the others.

'Now then,' said Albrecht, as Schlecht worked. 'Now that we have you leashed, we can proceed.'

Reiner snarled under his breath. They had leashed him indeed. They had scarred him for life. The hammer brand told all who saw it that the man who wore it was a deserter and could be killed on sight.

'I am here to offer you something you did not have an hour ago,' said Albrecht. 'A choice. You can serve your Emperor on a mission of great importance, or you can be hanged from the gallows this very evening and go to the fate that awaits you.'

Reiner cursed. Hanged this evening? He was to escape at midnight. Now the fiends had stolen even that from him.

'The chances of surviving the mission are slim, I warrant you,' continued Albrecht. 'But the rewards will be great. You will receive a full pardon for your crimes and be given your weight in gold crowns.'

'What good is all that when you also gave us this?' growled Hals, holding up the back of his ruined hand.

'The Emperor values your service in this matter so highly that he will command a sage of the Order of Light to remove the brands when you return successful.'

This sounded too good to be true, thought Reiner. The sort of thing he himself would say if he was trying to con a mark into some foolish course of action.

'What's the job?' asked Pavel, sullen.

Albrecht smirked. 'You mean to haggle? You will learn the nature of the mission once you have volunteered for it. Now, sirs, give me your answers.'

There was much hesitation, but one by one the others voiced or nodded their assent. Reiner damned Albrecht under his breath. A choice, he called it. What choice was there? Wearing the hammer brand, Reiner could never again travel easily within the Empire. It was early spring now. He might still wear gloves for a while, but come summer he would stick out like a sheep in a wolf pack. Never would he be able to go back to his beloved Altdorf, to the card rooms and cafes, the theatres and dog pits and brothels that he thought of as home. Even if he could somehow escape the brig, he would have to leave the Empire for foreign lands and never come back. And now that Albrecht had moved his execution to this evening instead of tomorrow at dawn, and thus foiling his only plan, even that unappetising option was closed to him.

Only by accepting the mission did he gain any chance of escape. Somewhere along the road he could perhaps slip away: west to Marienburg, or south to Tilea or the Border Princes or some other foul hole. Or perhaps the mission wouldn't be as dangerous as Albrecht made out. Perhaps he would see it through to the finish and take his reward – if Albrecht truly meant to give him one.

All that was certain was that if he declined the mission, he would die tonight, and there would be no more perhapses.

'Aye,' he said at last. 'Aye, my lord. I'm your man.'

# CHAPTER TWO
## A TASK SIMPLE IN THE TELLING

'VERY GOOD,' SAID Albrecht, when all the prisoners had volunteered. 'Now you shall hear your mission.' He indicated the grizzled veteran at his side. 'Under the command of Captain Veirt here, you shall escort Lady Magda Bandauer, abbess of Shallya, to a Shallyan convent in the foothills of the Middle Mountains. A holy relic lies there in a hidden crypt. Lady Magda shall open the crypt, then you will escort her and the relic back here to me with all possible speed. Time is of the essence.' He smiled. 'It is a task simple in the telling, but I have no need to remind soldiers of the Empire, no matter how debased, that the lands 'twixt here and the mountains are not yet entirely reclaimed, and that the mountains have become the refuge of Chaos marauders – Kurgan, Norse and worse things. We have word that the convent was recently pillaged by Kurgan, they may still be in the area. You will be sorely pressed, but for those who survive, and return the relic and the abbess to me, the Empire's munificence will know no bounds.'

Reiner heard little of Albrecht's speech. He had stopped listening after 'abbess of Shallya.' Another sister of Shallya? He had barely survived his last encounter with one such. Granted, that one had been a sorceress in disguise, but once bitten twice shy, as he always said. He wanted no more to do with that order. They weren't to be trusted.

Erich, the blond knight, seemed to have some objections to the plan as well. 'Do you mean to tell me,' he burst out indignantly, 'that we are to be led by this... this foot soldier? I am a Knight of the Sceptre. My horse and armour cost more than he has made in his whole career.'

'Bloody jagger,' muttered Hals. 'My spear's killed more northers than his horse and armour ever will.'

'Captain Veirt also outranks you,' said Albrecht. 'He has thirty years of battles under his belt, while you are, what? Vexillary? Bugle? Have you even blooded your lance yet?'

'I am a nobleman. I cannot take orders from a common peasant. My father is Frederich von Eisenberg, Baron of...'

'I know your father, boy,' said Albrecht. 'Would you like me to tell him how many young knights you have slain and maimed in "affairs of honour?" You deprive the Empire of good men and call it sport.'

Erich's fists clenched, but he hung his head. 'No, my lord.'

'Very good. You will obey Captain Veirt in all things, is that clear?'

'Yes, my lord.'

'Good.' Albrecht surveyed the whole group. 'Horses are waiting for you at the postern gate. You leave at once. But before you go, your commanding officer has a few words. Captain?'

Captain Veirt stepped forward and looked them all in the eye, one by one. His glance shot through Reiner like an arrow from a longbow. 'You have been chosen for a great honour tonight, and offered a clemency which none of you deserve. So if any of you attempts to abuse this kindness, by trying to escape, by betraying our company to the enemy, by killing each other or sabotaging the mission, I give you my personal guarantee that I will make the rest of your very short life a living hell the likes of which would make the depredations of the daemons of Chaos look like a country dance.' He turned toward the door and limped toward it. 'That is all.'

Reiner shivered, then joined the rest as the guards began herding them out.

IF NOTHING ELSE, Albrecht made sure they were well kitted out. They were led through the castle and out through the postern gate, where a narrow wooden drawbridge spanned the moat. On the far side, on a strip of cleared land flanked by a fallow field, a pack mule and ten horses were waiting for them – their breath white steam in the chill night air. The horses were saddled, bridled and loaded with regulation packs, complete with bed roll, rations, skillet, flint, canteen, and the like. Reiner's sabre was returned to him – a beautiful weapon, made to his measure, and the only gift his skinflint father had ever given him that was worth a damn. There was also a padded leather jerkin and sturdy boots to replace the ones taken from him in the brig, as well as a dagger, a boot knife, saddlebags full of powder and shot, and two pistols in saddle holsters – though not loaded or primed. Albrecht was no fool. A cloak, steel lobster-tail bassinet, and back-and-breastplate strapped over the pack completed the inventory.

Almost everybody seemed satisfied with their gear. Only Ulf and Erich complained.

'What's this?' asked Ulf angrily, holding up a huge iron-bound wooden maul that looked bigger than Sigmar's hammer. 'Is this a joke?'

Veirt smirked. ''Tis the only weapon we know you're competent with.'

'Do you ask a knight to ride a pack horse?' interrupted Erich. 'This beast is barely fourteen hands.'

'We go into the mountains, your grace,' said Veirt dryly. 'Yer charger might find the going a bit rough.'

'Looks tall enough to me,' said Hals, eyeing his horse uneasily.

'Aye,' said Pavel. 'Can you make 'em kneel so we can get on?'

'Sigmar, save us!' said Erich. 'Will we have to teach these peasants to ride?'

'Oh, they'll pick it up quick enough,' said Reiner. 'Just learn from his lordship, lads. If you ride like you've got a pike up your fundament, you're on the mark.'

Pavel and Hals guffawed. Erich shot Reiner a venomous glance and turned toward him as if he meant to pursue the matter. Fortunately, at that moment Albrecht came through the gate, leading a chestnut palfrey on which sat a woman dressed in the robes of an abbess of Shallya. Reiner's fears were somewhat allayed when he saw her, for Lady Magda was a stern, sober-looking woman of middle years – attractive enough in a cold, haughty way, but by no means the sort of dewy-eyed, waif-like temptress that had so recently been his ruin.

This woman looked like she measured out the charity of Shallya with an assayer's scale, and healed the sick by shaming them into health. She seemed as unhappy to be travelling in their company as they were to be in Veirt's. She looked them over with barely concealed disdain.

Only when Albrecht led her to her place beside Veirt did Reiner see her show anything like human feeling. As the baron handed her her bridle he took her hand and kissed it. She smiled down at him in return and stroked his cheek fondly. Reiner smirked. There was some fire in the cold sister after all. Still, the moment of affection gave Reiner pause. Why would Albrecht leave a woman he cared for in such disreputable company? It was curious.

When they were all mounted, Albrecht faced them. 'Ride swiftly and return quickly. Remember that riches await you if you succeed, and that I will kill you like dogs if you betray me. Now go, and may the eye of Sigmar watch over your journey.'

He saluted as Veirt spurred his horse and signalled them forward. Only Veirt, Erich and Reiner returned the salute.

As they started down the rutted dirt road between tilled fields toward the dark band of forest in the distance, it began to drizzle. Reiner and the rest all reached behind them to unstrap their hooded cloaks from their packs and pull them on.

Hals grumbled under his breath as the rain spattered his forehead. 'There's a good omen for you, and no mistake.'

It rained all night, turning the road to mud. Spring was coming to Ostland as it did every year, cold and wet. The party rode through the moonless night huddled in their cloaks, teeth chattering and noses running. The throbbing pain of his brand was now only the first in a long list of miseries that Reiner mentally added to with each passing mile. They could see little of the countryside. The woods were pitch black. Only when they passed open fields, where the previous week's blanket of snow was melting into grey slush, was there enough light for them to see any distance at all.

This was wild land. Smallhof was on the Empire's easternmost marches and there was much forest and few towns. It was relatively safe, however. The tide of Chaos had crested, then receded back east and north leaving the land desolate, even of the bandits and beasts that normally terrorised the local farms and towns. The few crude huts they passed were mere blackened shells.

Just before dawn, as Reiner was nodding and swaying in the saddle, Veirt called a halt by a river. A patch of tall pines clustered near it, and into this he led them. It was black as a cave within the spinney, but the ground was almost dry.

Veirt dismounted briskly. 'We'll rest here until dawn. No tents. And sleep in your gear.'

'What?' said Reiner. 'But dawn's only an hour away.'

'His lordship said time is of the essence,' said Veirt. 'You'll get a full night's sleep when we make camp tonight.'

'Another day of riding?' moaned Hals. 'My arse won't stand it.'

'Would you rather your arse was swinging by a rope?' asked Veirt darkly. 'Now get your heads down. Urquart, help me.'

While the company saw to their horses and made pillows of their bedrolls, Ulf and Veirt put up a tidy little tent for Lady Magda that included a folding cot. When it was finished and Lady Magda installed within it, Veirt laid down in front of it, blocking the entrance.

'Don't worry, captain,' said Hals under his breath. 'We don't want none.' He laughed and nudged Pavel. 'Ha! Get it? We don't want nun!'

'Aye,' said Pavel wearily. 'I get it. Now go to sleep, y'pillock. Blood of Sigmar, I don't know which hurts worse, my hand or my arse.'

REINER WOKE WITH a start. He had been having a vivid nightmare that Kronhof, Altdorf's most notorious moneylender, was drilling though his left hand with a carpenter's auger as punishment for unpaid debts, when someone in the dream had begun banging on an iron door. He opened his eyes and found himself in the pine spinney, but the pain in his hand and the banging continued. It took a moment to remember that he was a now a branded man, and another moment to realise that the horrible noise was Veirt, banging his skillet against a rock and shouting, 'Rise and shine, my beauties! We've a long day ahead of us.'

'I'll make him eat that skillet in a minute,' growled Hals, clutching his head.

Reiner climbed painfully to his feet. He wasn't sore from riding. He was a pistolier – born in the saddle. But lack of sleep made his bones feel like they were made of lead. They dragged at his flesh. The pain in his hand seemed to have spread to his head; while the rest of him was frozen, his head felt on fire. His eyes ached. His teeth ached. Even his hair seemed to ache.

Worse than Veirt's banging and shouting was his clear-eyed alertness. To Reiner's annoyance, the man seemed utterly unaffected by lack of sleep. Lady Magda was the same. She waited calmly outside her tent, hands folded, as clean and pressed as if she had just led morning prayers. Veirt chivvied them through a rushed breakfast of bread, cheese and some ale and then onto their horses. Last to mount up were Pavel and Hals, who lowered themselves into their saddles with much hissing and groaning, like men settling bare-arsed into thorn bushes. Less than half an hour after waking, they were on the road again.

The rain had stopped, but there was no sun. The sky was a featureless and uninterrupted grey from horizon to horizon, like a dull pewter tray hung upside down over the world. The party pulled their cloaks tight around them and leaned into a wet spring wind as they rode toward the Middle Mountains, which rose out of the seemingly endless forest like islands in a green sea.

As the day went on and they left the scrubby wastelands of the east behind, the forest grew denser and they came across a few villages, tiny communities carved out of the wilderness and surrounded by winter fields. But while these so typically Imperial sights should have cheered men so long from home, instead the convicts' faces grew longer and longer, for the villages were empty shells – sacked and burned to the ground, with rotting skeletons strewn about like children's playthings. Some still smoked, for though the war was officially over months ago, Chaos Warlord Archaon and his hordes having at last been pushed back beyond Kislev, fighting continued, and doubtless would for some time. The endless forest of Ostland could swallow armies whole, with scattered bands of marauders, lost or left behind by their fleeing compatriots, still wandered it, looking for food and easy plunder. Other northmen had reportedly fled into the Middle Mountains and stayed, finding the frozen heights to their liking.

Still reeling from its all-or-nothing fight, the Empire was too busy regrouping and rebuilding to send armies out to vanquish these scavengers, and so it was left to the beleaguered local lords to defend their people with the ragged remnants of their household guard. But here, in these forsaken hinterlands, no lord but Karl Franz held sway, and the villagers must fend for themselves or die. Most often they died.

In one village, decapitated heads rotted on spikes mounted on the palisade. Bodies decomposed where they had fallen because there was no one left alive to bury them. The stench of death rose from wells and barns and cottages.

At noon they passed a temple of Sigmar. The old priest had been crucified before it, his ribs pried back and his deflated lungs flapping in the wind like wings. Pavel and Hals cursed under their breath and spat to avert bad luck. Erich rode straighter in the saddle, his jaw muscles twitching. Franz shivered and looked away. Reiner found himself torn between hiding his eyes and staring. He'd never had much use for priests, but no man of the Empire could see such a thing and be unaffected.

After a lunch eaten in the saddle, a watery sun came out and the mood lifted a little. The forest receded away from the road and for a while they rode through a marshy area of rushes and clumps of snow that dripped into meandering streams. The men began to talk amongst themselves and Reiner found it interesting to see how the group sorted out. He was mildly surprised to see Pavel and Hals, a pair of Ostland farmers who had never left their homeland before being called to war, getting on well with the Tilean mercenary Giano. The typical insularity of the peasant, to whom even Altdorf was a foreign country, and who viewed all outsiders with mistrust, seemed to have been trumped by the commonality of all foot soldiers, and soon the three were laughing and exchanging tales of rotten provisions, terrible billets and worse commanders.

Behind them, little Franz and giant Ulf talked in low tones – a confederacy of the teased, thought Reiner. While bringing up the rear were Gustaf and Oskar, riding in glum silence and staring straight ahead – a confederacy of the shunned.

Veirt rode at the head of the party with Lady Magda. They were silent as well: Veirt constantly on the lookout for danger and Lady Magda, with her nose in a leather-bound volume, pointedly ignoring all that surrounded her. Reiner rode behind them, and much to his annoyance, so did Erich. It was inevitable, of course. Other than Lady Magda, Reiner was the only person of Erich's class in the party. He was the only prisoner Erich could acknowledge as an equal, the only one he would deign to talk to. Reiner would have been much happier swapping bawdy songs and barracks insults with Hals, Pavel and Giano, but Erich had attached himself like glue and babbled incessantly at his shoulder.

'If you were in Altdorf you must know my cousin Viscount Norrich Oberholt. He was trying to become a Knight Panther. Damned fine rider. Spent a lot of time at the Plume and Pennant.'

'I'm afraid I didn't mix much with the orders. I was at university.'

Erich made a face. 'University? Gads! I had enough learning from my tutor. Were you studying to be a priest?'

'Literature, when I studied at all. Mostly I was just there to escape Draeholt.'

'Eh? What's wrong with Draeholt? Excellent hunting there. Bagged a boar there once.'

'Did you?'

'Yes. Damned fine animal. I say, your name is Hetzau? I believe I met your father on a Draeholt hunt once. Jolly old fellow.'

Reiner winced. 'Oh yes, he's always at his jolliest killing the lesser orders.'

There was a rustle in the dead grass beside the road. Giano instantly unslung his crossbow and fired. A rabbit bolted out of hiding and sprinted across their march. Before Giano could do more than cry out in disgust, Franz raised his bow from his shoulders and an arrow from his quiver and fired in a single smooth motion. The rabbit turned a cartwheel and flopped dead in the melting snow, a clothyard shaft between his shoulder blades.

The entire party turned and looked at the boy with new-found respect. Even Erich nodded curtly. 'Neat shooting, that. Lad would make a good beater.'

Franz hopped lightly off his horse, removed the arrow and handed the rabbit to Giano, who had three more hanging from his pommel that he had shot earlier. 'One more for the stew,' he said with a smirk.

'Grazie, boy,' said Giano. 'Much thank yous.' He added the coney to his brace.

As Franz climbed back on his horse again, Reiner leaned in to Erich. 'Care to bet on who pots the next one?'

Erich pursed his lips. 'I never wager, except on horses. I say, have you seen the racers Count Schlaeger is breeding down at Helmgart? Damned fine runners.'

And on and on it went. Reiner groaned. Here he was, out in the world, freed from prison, his neck spared – at least temporarily – from the noose. But was he allowed to enjoy it? No. Apparently Sigmar had a nasty sense of humour.

Erich was talking about his father's annual hunt ball now. It was going to be a long trip.

Veirt finally called a halt in the lee of a low cliff just before sunset and the men fell to making camp. Reiner found it curious that the men all found roles for themselves without any apparent communication. Pavel and Hals groaned about how sore they were from riding while they fetched water from a nearby stream and hunted for wild carrots and dandelion leaves to add to the stew. Reiner saw to the horses. Ulf erected Magda's tent and then assisted the others with theirs. Franz and Oskar collected wood and started the fire. Gustaf flayed and deboned the rabbits with an intensity Reiner found disturbing, while Giano seasoned the stew and talked endlessly about how much better the food was in Tilea.

The stew was delicious, if a bit garlicky for Imperial tastes, and they slurped it down eagerly as they hunched close around the fire.

'Draw lots for tents,' said Veirt between mouthfuls. 'I'll not have anyone pulling rank or any fighting over who tents with who. Yer all scum to me.'

The men made their marks on leaves and put them in a helmet. There were five tents: a fancy one for Lady Magda, a small one for Captain Veirt, and three standard-issue cavalry tents, which slept four uncomfortably, as the old barracks joke went, so the nine men could sleep three to a tent. Luxury. But when the helmet passed to Franz, he passed it on without adding a lot.

'Can't write your name, lad?' asked Veirt.

'I'll sleep alone,' said Franz.

Heads came up all around the fire.

Veirt scowled. 'You'll sleep with the others. There's no spare tent.'

'I'll tent under my cloak.' He looked straight into the fire.

Reiner smirked. 'The army ain't *all* inverts, boyo.'

'It only takes one.'

'Soldier,' said Veirt, with soft menace. 'Men who sleep alone tend to be found missing in the morning. Sometimes they run. Sometimes something takes them. I will allow neither. I need all the men I have for this goose chase. You…'

'Captain, please,' said Hals. 'Let him sleep alone. The last thing any of us needs is some excitable lad with a hair trigger cutting our throats for rolling over.'

A chorus of 'ayes' echoed from around the fire. Veirt shrugged. It seemed that Franz's stock with the company, which had risen after his display of bowmanship, had fallen precipitously once again.

When the lots were drawn – with a blank leaf holding Franz's place – Reiner shared a tent with Pavel and Ulf. Hals, Giano and Oskar had another, and Erich and Gustaf had the third tent to themselves. Veirt took first watch, and the rest bedded down immediately, near dropping from their night and day in the saddle. Still, it took Reiner a while to get to sleep. He couldn't stop thinking about what an odd lot of madmen and malcontents the company was. He couldn't understand why Valdenheim had entrusted them with such an important mission, and with the life of a woman he obviously held dear. Why hadn't he dispatched a squadron of knights to be her escort?

Reiner at last drifted off into fitful dreams without having found a satisfactory answer to his questions.

# CHAPTER THREE
# IN THE DOGHOUSE

IN THE MIDDLE of the third day of their journey, with the ground rising beneath them and the Middle Mountains looming above, Pavel and Hals began to look about them with increased interest.

'This is the road to Ferlangen, or I'm a goblin,' said Hals.

'And there's the Three Hags,' said Pavel, pointing to a trio of mountains in the distance that looked from this angle like three hunched old women. 'My dad's farm ain't half a day south.'

Hals sniffed the air. 'I knew we was home, just by breathing. Lady of Peace, I could swear I smell my mother's pork and cabbage cooking in the pot right now.'

Gustaf chuckled unpleasantly and spoke for the first time that day. 'Don't get your hopes up, yokel. It's more likely your mother cooking in the pot.'

'Y'filthy clot!' cried Hals, trying clumsily to turn his horse toward Gustaf. 'You'll take that back or I'll have yer guts for garters!'

Captain Veirt interposed his horse between the men before Reiner even noticed him moving. 'Stand down, pikeman,' he barked at Hals, then wheeled to face Gustaf. 'And you, leech. If you open yer trap only for that sort of garbage, yer better off leaving it shut.' He stood up in his stirrups and glowered around at the whole troop. 'You'll not lack for fighting before we're done, I guarantee it. But if any man wants more than what's coming to him, come see me. I'll show you yer own spine. Am I clear?'

'Perfectly, captain,' said Gustaf, turning his horse away.

Hals nodded, head lowered. 'Aye, captain.'

'Right then,' said Veirt. 'Ride on. We've twenty more miles to make today.'

AT DUSK THEY rode through a ruined town. The houses, taverns and shops were nothing but blackened sticks. Drifts of ash-blackened snow clung to crumbled stone walls. Pavel and Hals stared around in blank dismay.

'This is Draetau,' said Pavel. 'My cousin lives in Draetau.'

'Lived,' said Gustaf.

'We sell our pigs in the market down there,' said Hals, pointing down a cross street. There was no longer any market.

Pavel trembled with rage and wiped at his eyes. 'The heathen bastards. Filthy, daemon worshipping swine.'

Beyond the edge of the town they saw an orange glow through a stand of trees and heard faint cries and the clash of arms.

'Weapons out!' barked Veirt, and drew his sword. The men followed suit. Giano wound his crossbow and Franz nocked an arrow on his string. Reiner checked that his pistols were primed and cocked.

'Von Eisenberg, Hetzau,' called Veirt. 'With the lady.'

Erich and Reiner jogged up so that they flanked Lady Magda. Veirt rode directly before her. Through a gap in the trees they could see that a small cluster of farmhouses were burning. The silhouettes of huge men with horns – whether sprouting from their helmets or growing from their heads it was impossible to tell – ran through the flames, chasing smaller silhouettes. Others drove off sheep and cattle. A few carried human prizes. Reiner and the others could hear the thin shrieks of women over the crackle of fire.

Pavel and Hals kicked their horses awkwardly forward. 'Captain,' said Hals. 'Those are our people. We can't just…'

'No,' said Veirt grimly. 'We've a job to do. Ride on.' But he didn't look happy about it.

Erich coughed. 'Captain, for once I agree with the pike. The village isn't much out of our line of march, and we might…'

'I said no!' bellowed Veirt, so they rode on. But before they had gone another quarter mile, Veirt struck his leg with his gloved fist. 'This is all the fault of those mealy-mouthed fools who surround the Emperor and fill his ears with cowardice disguised as caution. We are too extended, they say. The treasury is depleted, they say. We cannot afford to prolong the war. The fools! They can't afford not to!'

The squad looked at him, surprised. From their short association with him, they knew Veirt as a taciturn man, who kept his emotions to himself, but here he was raging like tap-room orator.

'It wasn't enough to push the hordes beyond our borders and into the mountains, and then return as if the mission were accomplished. It is as Baron Albrecht says. We must destroy them utterly. Otherwise it will be as you see – a little raid here, a little raid there, with our mothers and sisters never truly safe, the Empire never truly sovereign. Unless we want to endlessly fight for land we have called our own for centuries, we must seek out the barbarians in their own lairs and kill them to the last man, woman and child.'

'Hear hear,' said Erich. 'Well said. But then…'

'No,' said Veirt. 'The relic Baron Albrecht has commanded us to recover is more important. It could turn the tide at last. It could mean the end of the northern curse for all time. Once m'lord Albrecht has it, he and his brother Manfred will be able to retake Nordbergbruche, their ancestral home, from the Chaos filth that stole it while m'lords were fighting in the east. Then it will become a bastion against the scum that hide in the mountains, and Valnir's Bane will be the spear with which the Empire will at last drive out...'

'Captain,' said Lady Magda, sharply. 'This is a *secret* mission.'

Veirt looked up at her and visibly composed himself. 'Forgive me, lady. I let my tongue get away from me.'

Veirt returned his horse to her side and they got under way once more.

'Quite a speech,' muttered Reiner, dropping back a bit.

'Oh yes,' said Hals, grinning. 'Old Veirt's a firebreather all right.'

'You served under him?'

Pavel shook his head. 'Would that we had. There's one who wouldn't run in battle.'

Hals laughed. 'Not him. That's why he's here, trying to win his way back into Albrecht's good graces.'

'Veirt's in the doghouse too?' asked Reiner, surprised.

'Worse than the doghouse. His neck's on the block. Direct disobedience of orders,' said Pavel.

'He was under the command of Albrecht's brother, Manfred, at the battle of Vandengart. Manfred told him to hold his position,' continued Hals, 'but Veirt saw a troop of gunners being destroyed by some horrible norther beasties and couldn't stand it. He charged. Cost Manfred the battle.'

'Lost him nearly a hundred men,' added Pavel.

'But Veirt's pikes never broke,' said Hals proudly. 'Slaughtered every last one of those nightmares. There's a captain.'

'Aye,' said Pavel.

Reiner chuckled. 'A squadron of the condemned led by the condemned.'

'It's nothing to laugh at,' sniffed Erich. 'I had no idea. The man's cashiered.'

Reiner spotted more torches moving through the fields just north of the road. 'Captain. On your right.'

Veirt looked where he pointed and cursed under his breath. 'Right. We turn west. Von Eisenberg, on point.'

The company reluctantly turned off the road. With a last, longing look over his shoulder at the marauders, Erich nudged his horse forward until he was fifty paces ahead. They rode through fields and sparse woods in a large half-circle until the Kurgan torches were out of sight and all they could see of the burning farms was a faint orange glow on the underside of the low-hanging clouds.

At last Veirt turned them north again. A long finger of wood lay between them and the road. Veirt called Erich back until he rode only a few yards ahead, gave him a slotted lantern which emitted a narrow wedge of light but hid its flame from prying eyes, and they began to pick their way through the wood.

Though narrow, the centre of the strip of woods became thick and tangled with undergrowth, and their progress was reduced to a walk. The horses pushed through the brush as if breasting through a stream, and it was necessary to hack at the branches that dangled overhead to avoid being dragged off their mounts.

'Captain,' said Erich. 'May I suggest we go about and circle this briar patch?'

Veirt nodded. 'Turn around. Back the way we…'

'Captain,' said Lady Magda. 'I believe my horse's hoof is caught. I cannot turn.'

Veirt grunted and sheathed his sword in his saddle-mounted scabbard. 'A moment, lady.' He dismounted, took Erich's lantern, and squatted by Lady Magda's horse.

After a moment he stood. 'Urquart. Her hoof's wedged between two roots. I need your strength.'

The big engineer dismounted and joined Veirt. As they hauled at the roots, Oskar's head snapped up. 'Do you hear something?' he asked tremulously.

The others fell still and listened. There was something, almost lost in the creaking of leather and shifting of horses – a rhythmic murmering like a tide over a pebble beach, like... breathing. They looked into the blackness of the woods. On all sides of them, glowing yellow eyes reflected their lantern light.

Veirt cursed and waded for his horse, trying to get to his sword. The men drew their weapons and tugged on their reins, attempting to settle their horses, which were shying into each other nervously as they scented the hidden threat.

'Protect the lady!' called Veirt.

A horse whinneyed.

Reiner looked back. A black shape, the size of a wild boar, but leaner, was pulling down Franz's horse, its teeth and claws deep in the poor beast's haunches. The horse crashed on its side in the undergrowth and Franz was thrown clear. Before Reiner could even call the boy's name, more of the black shapes attacked, roaring and howling.

Reiner and Erich pulled their pistols from their holsters. Oskar reached for his handgun.

'No guns!' called Veirt as he retrieved his sword. 'Their masters might hear!'

'Masters?' thought Reiner. Boars had no masters. Then he saw that one of the charging monsters wore a studded collar. They were hounds! But such hounds he had never seen: huge, deformed things with twisted, overmuscled limbs and fat, fleshy goitres bulging from their distorted faces. Their fanged jaws dripped with yellow mucus.

Erich spurred his horse forward and took a hound's charge on his spear. The impact wasn't strong enough to kill the beast, for both hound and horse were slowed by the tangle of undergrowth. The hound twisted and fought, clawing and biting at the spear. Reiner rode up beside it and jabbed down at its back with his sword. It was like trying to pierce a saddle. The muscle was nearly as dense as wood. Even its matted fur was hard to penetrate. Reiner raised his sword again and stabbed down with both hands.

Behind him, Pavel and Hals jumped off their horses and faced a charging hound on foot like the pikemen they were. They planted their beast and took the leaping brute in the chest.

Giano fired his crossbow at another. It caught the hound in the eye. The beast howled and whipped its head around, trying to dislodge the annoyance. The bolt stayed put. The hound stopped and attempted to wipe the bolt away on the ground and instead drove it further into its skull. It vomited blood and died. Giano cranked his crossbow for another shot.

Ulf swung his huge maul at a slavering hound. He hit it square in the shoulder, knocking the thing flat, but overbalanced and fell himself.

Another beast leapt at Oskar's horse. Oskar flailed at it with his sword, but his horse, rearing and kicking, did more damage.

Captain Veirt shouldered through the brush toward the bedevilled artilleryman.

Reiner finally forced his blade through his hound's ribs and found its heart. The thing shuddered and slumped beneath him. He pulled his sword free and surveyed the battle, looking for Franz. There was a swirl of movement beyond the boy's horse. A hound leaping and bucking. There was something on its back. Franz! The boy was riding the beast, one hand on its collar, the other stabbing it over and over again with a dagger while the beast snapped at him over its shoulder. Reiner had never seen anyone look so frightened. The boy's expression might have seemed comical had his situation not been so desperate.

Gustaf was closest to the boy, but though he had his sword out and watched alertly, he made no move to help. Reiner cursed and kicked his horse toward the boy, but the animal was entangled in the brush and was having difficulty turning. Damn this wood! He jumped from the saddle and pushed toward the boy on foot, taking briar scratches with every step.

Erich withdrew his spear from the beast Reiner had killed, but sought no new target, instead holding his place at Lady Magda's side.

Pavel's spear snapped under the weight of the beast he and Hals had stopped, and he went down beneath it. Hals bellowed and stabbed the hound in the side, trying to drive it off his friend. Pavel threw his arms up to protect his face. The beast clawed his arm.

The hound attacking Oskar got its teeth into the artilleryman's boot and dragged him, screaming, from the saddle. Giano fired at it, but missed. Veirt surged forward and hacked at the beast, cutting deep into its shoulder. The hound turned and leapt on him. Veirt stuffed his mail-clad fist in its maw and stabbed it through the neck.

Nearby, Ulf swung his maul again and this time crushed his creature's skull. The brute dropped at his feet, oozing grey matter and noxious purple fluids.

Reiner charged Franz's beast, roaring, but missed as he checked his swing for fear of hitting the boy. At least he'd got the hounds attention. The hound leapt at him, shaking off Franz at last. Reiner barely got his blade up in time. He caught the thing on the breastbone with a jarring impact. It bowled him over and slammed him to the ground, knocking the wind out of him. Fortunately, it was caught on the point of Reiner's sword, and couldn't reach him with its teeth or claws. It would likely kill him anyway. Its entire weight was on the sword, and the pommel was pressing into Reiner's ribs. Reiner could hear them creaking. He couldn't draw a breath. The creature's foetid drool dripped onto his face.

Something leapt out of the darkness – Franz! The boy hit the beast in the shoulder and toppled it to one side, stabbing at it in a frenzy. The beast snapped at him, and rolled on top of him. The boy shrieked like a girl as the beast's teeth clashed an inch from his face.

Reiner struggled up, sucking air. He swung wildly at the creature's head. His blade whanged off its skull, stinging his hand, but doing little damage.

'Come on, you mangy beast!' He stabbed it in the shoulder, again doing nothing. The hound looked up at him, snarling, and crouched to spring, but as it did, Franz stabbed it in the neck, directly below the jaw. The hound yelped, and a river of blood drenched the boy's arm. The beast collapsed on top of him, crushing him.

'Get it off,' he gasped. 'I can't breathe!'

'Stay there a moment,' said Reiner, looking around. 'Safest place for you.'

The melee seemed over at last. Veirt stood over a dead beast. Oskar was getting unsteadily to his feet. His boot was shredded, but the flesh beneath it thankfully only scratched. Behind them, Hals was helping Pavel up.

Pavel clutched his face. The left side was red and slick. The hound the two pikemen had fought lay with a foreleg in the air, their spears sticking from its ribs.

'All right,' said Reiner to Franz. 'All clear.' He rolled the hound off the boy and helped him to his feet. His arm was crimson to the shoulder.

'Any of that yours?' asked Reiner.

'Mostly the hound's, I think,' said Franz.

Reiner chuckled. 'Game little scrapper, ain't you?'

Franz looked embarrassed. 'You came to help me. I couldn't just stand by while...'

Reiner was embarrassed in turn. 'Aye aye, enough of that.' He shot glances at Erich, still on his horse by Lady Magda, and Gustaf, who was untouched. 'I could wish all our fellows felt the same. Didn't swing once, did you?' he snarled at Gustaf.

'I'm a surgeon. Who would patch you up if I got hurt?'

'Leech!' called Veirt. 'See to the wounded.'

Gustaf sneered smugly at Reiner and hurried to Pavel, his field kit over his shoulder.

Reiner watched him go. 'There's a fellow I wouldn't mind finding dead in a ditch.'

Franz grinned. They looked up at the sound of raised voices.

'And where were you, then?' Hals was shouting at Erich. 'Standing right there with yer spear at the ready and not doing nothing while we was getting slaughtered. Pavel's lost an eye, y'snot-nosed jagger!'

'Don't you dare take that tone with me, you insolent peasant.' Erich raised his spear as if to strike the pikeman.

Veirt stepped in the way. 'Don't you try it, my lord.'

'Insolent or not,' said Reiner joining them, 'he isn't wrong. You hung back almost as much as the surgeon here.'

'I killed my one.'

'I killed your one,' Reiner countered. 'You could have at least tried for another.'

'We were ordered to protect the lady.'

'Ha! I wonder do you obey all orders so literally?'

'Do you question my courage, sir?'

'Less of it!' growled Veirt. 'All of you. These hounds don't travel far from their masters. Do you want raiders breathing down our necks?'

He spoke too late, for as the men grew silent, harsh voices and the sound of tramping boots reached them. They looked toward the road. Flickering torches and hulking shapes were pushing swiftly through the woods.

'Blood of Sigmar!' swore Captain Veirt. 'Tie off your wounds and mount up, on the double.'

Gustaf finished wrapping a bandage around Pavel's head and closed up his kit.

'What about me?' asked Oskar, plaintively pointing at his leg. 'Look at all this blood.'

'What blood?' asked Gustaf as he packed up his kit. 'I've had fleabites that bled more.'

The men hurriedly mounted their horses, but Franz's was dead, its throat ripped out by the monstrous beast, and the mule carried too much to take a rider. No one looked eager to share a saddle with him.

'I don't need a knife in the ribs if he gets the wrong idea,' said Hals.

Reiner sighed and offered Franz a hand up. 'Come on, lad.'

Franz grabbed his kit from the dead horse and swung up behind Reiner, but sat far back on the saddle.

'Hold tight,' said Reiner. 'It might be a wild ride.'

'I… I'll be fine.'

There was no time to argue. Before they had all turned their horses, huge almost-human figures crashed out of the darkness, roaring and swinging enormous weapons.

# CHAPTER FOUR
## A BREATH OF FRESH AIR

THERE WERE A few moments of nightmarish confusion as the men savagely spurred their horses away from their pursuers and the company plunged into the darkness of the tangled woods. Trees seemed to spring out before them and roots rise up to trip them, and Reiner swore he felt the raiders' hot breath on his neck, but at last they burst out into the open fields and the horses stretched into a headlong gallop. Pavel and Hals, who had never ridden faster than a trot before, didn't like this at all, and clung to their horses' necks with death-grip terror, but by Sigmar's grace they didn't fall, and the company soon left the raiders behind.

Veirt took no chances. He kept up a punishing pace for a good hour until they had left the environs of the farming village far behind and reached an area of low hills and deep, wooded ravines. They filed into one of these, walking the horses down the centre of an ice-rimed stream for nearly a mile, until Veirt found a flat, pebbly stretch of riverbank and told them to put up their tents.

It was a sorry camp. Veirt allowed no fire, so they dined on cold rations while Gustaf cleaned and bound their wounds and a light snow melted on their horses' sweating flanks. Pavel's sobs and his cries of, 'It can't be gone! I can still feel it!' as he held his hand over his missing eye were not an aid to digestion.

Reiner's newfound friendship with Franz didn't change the boy's mind about tenting alone, and while the others bundled into their sturdy tents, he curled up best he could under his cloak, propped up at one end with his short sword and at the other with his scabbard.

For the next two days it got colder and colder as Lady Magda led them higher into the foothills of the Middle Mountains and the rain of the flatlands became wet, clinging snow. It was as if each gain in elevation turned back time, as if spring were becoming winter instead of summer. Gustaf had them smear their hands and faces with bear fat to prevent frostbite, a disgusting but effective trick.

Veirt, a native of Ostland, seemed to blossom in the cold, growing cheerier and more voluble the more bitter it got, telling stories of forced marches and desperate last stands, but Giano, from sun-baked Tilea, hated it. His usual cheery disposition soon became replaced with angry snappishness and long, whining reminiscences about the beauty of his homeland and the warmth of its sun.

Pavel's empty eye socket grew red and choked with pus. He developed a fever that had him screaming and gibbering in the night and waking the others up, which did nothing to lighten the general disposition of the group. During the day he couldn't sit astride his saddle, so Ulf knocked together a simple stretcher out of saplings and twine that dragged behind his horse. Gustaf bound him into it and packed him in snow to keep him from burning up. Though it pained him, Reiner begrudgingly allowed that Gustaf did his job well, even changing the dressing on

Pavel's eye at every meal stop. Hals was unusually quiet during his friend's sickness, his normal flow of insult and wit frozen with worry.

The tiny mountain villages they passed through were all deserted, and most destroyed. Axe-scarred skeletons lay between the houses, picked clean by crows, and it was obvious by the many tracks of unshod hooves that Kurgan raiders passed back and forth through the area constantly. Reiner expected the villages to be picked as clean as the skeletons, but Hals, who, being a peasant, knew the tricks of peasants, showed them how to find hidden caches of food and liquor under dirt floors and at the bottoms of wells.

They made camp outside one such village two nights after the fight with the beasts and, armed with Hals's knowledge, went searching for hidden food to supplement their meagre rations.

Reiner, Franz and Hals were prying up the flagstones in a cottage kitchen when they heard a woman's scream. Fearing that Lady Magda was being attacked, they dropped the stone and ran out to the steep, twisting track that served the little settlement as a high street. The scream came again, from a shack further up the hill. They ran to it.

Hals was about to kick the door in, but Reiner stopped him, and motioned for him and Franz to circle around the tiny, tumbledown place. 'Block the back door,' he whispered. 'If it has one.'

Reiner waited at the front door as the others crept through the muddy yard. The cry came again, but muffled this time, and then a male voice. 'Hold still, curse you!'

The voice sounded familiar. Reiner stepped silently to an unglassed window and looked in. It was dim inside, and hard to see, but Reiner could just make out a pair of legs in torn woollen hose lying on the floor, and another pair in breeks lying on top of them. A male hand fumbled at a belt buckle. He couldn't make out the man's face, but he recognised the body. He'd been looking at it for days.

'Schlecht!' he roared. He ran to the door and kicked it in.

Gustaf looked up from where he lay on top of a wild-eyed peasant girl on the dusty wood floor. Her skirts were rucked up around her waist and he had his knife under her jaw. Splotches and smears of blood surrounded her.

'You filthy swine,' growled Reiner. 'Get off of her.'

'I… I thought she was a raider,' said Schlecht, pushing hurriedly to his knees. 'I was… I was…'

The back door burst in and Franz and Hals entered.

'What's all the…' Hals broke off as he took in the tableau. Franz went pale.

'You rotten little…' Hals stepped forward and kicked Gustaf in the face.

The surgeon fell off the girl, and Hals pulled her to her feet. There were bloody cuts on her chest. It looked as if Schlecht had carved his initials there. Reiner shuddered.

'Here now, lass,' Hals said softly. 'He can't hurt you now. Are you…?'

The girl wasn't listening. She screamed and lashed out, striping Hals across the cheek with her nails, and dashed for the door. Reiner didn't get in her way.

Hals turned back to Gustaf, who was sitting up groggily. 'You filth,' he growled. 'I knew what you were the minute I laid eyes on you, and I'm ashamed of myself that I didn't kill you then.' He kicked Gustaf in the face again and raised his sword.

'No!' cried Gustaf, crabbing backward. 'You daren't! You daren't! I'm your surgeon. Do you want your friend to die?'

Hals checked his swing, knuckles turning white on the hilt.

'He's right,' said Reiner, though he hated to say it. 'We need him. All of us. We've the whole trip to do again, with who knows how many raiders in the way. We'll need someone to patch us up.'

Hals's shoulders slumped. 'Aye,' he said. 'Aye, yer right.' He raised his head and glared at Gustaf. 'But when we get back, don't expect to live long enough to spend yer reward.'

Gustaf sneered. 'Do you think it wise to threaten the man who will tend to your wounds, pike?'

Hals rushed the surgeon again, but Reiner held him back. 'Ignore him, lad. Don't give him the satisfaction.'

Hals snarled, but turned toward the door. He motioned to Franz. 'Come on, lad. Let's get a breath of fresh air. It stinks in here.'

The two soldiers walked out. Reiner joined them, turning his back pointedly on Gustaf.

As the sun reached noon the next day, they saw the whitewashed stone walls of the Convent of Shallya on an outcrop above them. It shone like a pearl.

'Don't look pillaged from here,' said Hals.

Pavel, whose fever had broken that morning, and who sat swaying and fragile on his horse, grinned. 'Pillaged or not, we're here at last,' he said. 'Now we can get this whatsit and go home. I just hope the trip back don't cost me my other eye. I won't be able to see all me gold.'

'It is an hour's ride from here,' said Lady Magda. 'The path is narrow and winding.'

Oskar shielded his eyes against the noon-day glare. 'There is smoke. Coming from the convent.'

Veirt squinted where Oskar pointed. 'Are you certain?'

'Aye captain,' said the artilleryman. 'Campfire or chimney it might be.'

'Could be the nuns,' said Hals.

Veirt gave him a withering look.

The revelation of the smoke lengthened their trip up the mountain to two hours, for they went at a walk, with Giano and Franz spying ahead on foot, scouting each bend in the path for enemies. There were none, though they found evidence of recent passage: gnawed bones, prints in the snow, a discarded jar of wine shattered on a rock.

Reiner caught Hals looking uneasily at these traces, and smirked. 'A messy lot, these nuns.'

About three-quarters of the way up, the trail was joined by a much wider path winding around the mountains from the south, and on this wider path were countless snow-filled foot and hoofprints going in both directions, indicating that large groups of men and horses travelled it with some regularity.

Veirt eyed these signs with grim interest. 'Must be a nest of them further up.'

'Not in the convent?' quavered Oskar.

'You only saw one column of smoke?'

'Oh yes, of course.' Oskar looked relieved.

At last they reached the narrow shelf of rock upon which the convent was built, a sort of landing before the wide path continued up the stepped hills into the mountains. There was evidence that the forces that travelled up and down the path often made camp on the ledge – scorched circles of old campfires, bones, rubbish.

The convent's white walls extended from the cliff edge, which looked east toward Smallhof and Kislev, to the face of the mountain, cutting off the tapering end of the shelf. But the appearance of gleaming perfection that the walls had given at the base of the hill proved an illusion up close. They had been shattered and blackened in many places, and the great wooden gates hung off their hinges in a jumble of charred timber. The convent buildings rose in three steps behind the gates, with the spire of a chapel of Shallya highest and furthest back. Even from a distance Veirt's men could see that entire place had been gutted, walls burned, roofs caved in, garbage scattered about. The thin column of smoke still rose, seeming to come from the third step.

Giano made the sign of Shallya as he looked at the wreckage and muttered under his breath.

'It appears that Baron Albrecht's information was correct,' said Erich.

'Aye,' said Veirt.

Reiner looked to Lady Magda, expecting a reaction, but the sister seemed made of iron. She gazed at the wreckage with tight-lipped stoicism. 'The crypt we must enter is beneath the chapel,' she said. 'So we must get beyond whoever has lit that fire.'

'Very good, my lady,' said Veirt, and turned to the men. 'Dismount, you lot. Ostini, Shoentag, have a look and report back.'

As the men dismounted – much to the relief of Pavel and Hals, who rubbed their aching backsides vigorously – the mercenary and the boy tip-toed through the gate and disappeared. While they were gone, the party found a hidden corner in which to tie up the horses and then refreshed themselves with a drink of nearly frozen water from their canteens. Reiner could hear the ice sloshing around in his. Veirt ordered Ulf to set up Lady Magda's tent, and suggested to her that she wait while they saw to any difficulties, but she refused. She seemed as eager as the rest of them to get this whatever-it-was and return to civilisation. She declared that she would come with them.

Franz and Giano returned shortly.

'Six,' said Giano. 'Big boys, and with the big swords, hey? Northers?'

'Kurgan,' corrected Franz. 'Same as we faced at Kirstaad. They look to be foot troops. No horses I could see. No fresh droppings.'

'Two walking around,' continued Giano, making a circling motion with his fingers. 'Four in garden, eating.'

'You sure that's all of them?' asked Veirt.

Franz and Giano nodded.

'Right, then.' Veirt hunched forward. 'We take out the two on patrol as quiet as shadows, got it? Then everyone with a bow or gun will find good vantage on the four in the garden and put as much iron into them as we can. These lads are tough as your boot. If we have to come to grips with 'em I want 'em well peppered, you mark me?'

A chorus of 'Ayes' answered him.

'Right then; commend your souls to Sigmar and let's be at it.'

# CHAPTER FIVE
# HEROES DON'T WIN BY TRICKERY

THEY ADVANCED CAUTIOUSLY through the forecourt, weapons at the ready, Lady Magda and Pavel, still too weak from his fever to fight, at the rear. There were burned stables to the left and the remains of a dry storage to the right, shattered oil jars and empty sacks of grain lying among jumbled timbers. The main convent building faced them, a two-storey structure clad in white marble where the nuns had once taken their meals, and where the library and offices of the abbess and her staff were housed. Its walls still stood, but black smears of soot above each smashed-in window gave evidence of the destruction within. The walls were daubed with vile symbols that Reiner was glad he didn't understand. Decaying corpses in nuns' robes were scattered around the yard like rotting fruit fallen from some macabre tree. Oskar shivered at the sight.

They crept up wide curved steps that led to the level of the convent dormitory, where the nuns and novitiates had slept. The building was fronted by a small plaza. Neither had fared well. The dormitory, a wide, half-timbered, three-storey building, had lost its left wing to fire, and the right was sagging badly. The plaza seemed to have been used as a latrine and dump by the raiders, and was filled with rotting food, broken and burnt furniture, rusting weapons and excrement. It smelled like a charnel house that had caved into a sewer.

Giano stopped them on the last step before the plaza and they crouched down. He pointed up to the next level: a ruined garden, reached by another set of curving steps, and surrounded by a balustrade that looked over the plaza. Over a row of high burnt hedges, they could see pikes pointing up to the sky, with long-haired skulls spiked on top like totems. 'They making the camp there,' he said. 'Behind hedgings. Patrol walk around edge.'

Veirt nodded. 'Right. Ostini – no – Lichtmar and Shoentag, I want you up in the dormitory. There should be windows in the third floor that overlook the garden. If not, get on the roof. You cover the boys at the fire. Ostini, you join 'em once we've finished off the patrols.'

'Surely it won't take seven of us to kill two men?' said Erich.

'They are hardly men,' said Veirt. 'And I hope seven of us are enough to take them out one at a time. Now here is what I want to see.'

As Veirt laid out his strategy they saw the first of the raiders pass. He was an intimidating sight, a shaggy-haired giant in leather and furs, a head taller than Ulf, and unnaturally thick with muscle. Fetishes and charms dangled from braids in his beard, and the scabbarded sword that hung from his belt looked taller than Franz – and probably outweighed him too.

After waiting for the second raider to pass they hurried to their positions – Oskar and Franz running low for the dormitory door, and the rest heading for the steps that led up to the garden. Pavel, armed with one of Reiner's pistols, stayed behind with Lady Magda.

There was a smashed statue of Shallya directly below the balustrade that edged the garden. A blow from above had sheared it off from shoulder to hip, so that what remained was a sharp shard that pointed at the sky, while Shallya's serene face looked up from the rubble at the base of her pedestal. Giano touched his heart with his palm when he saw it.

'Heathens,' he muttered. 'Desecrate the lady. Blasphemy.'

Reiner smirked. 'A mercenary who venerates Shallya?'

'Always I fight for peace,' said Giano proudly.

'Ah.'

While the others pressed against the wall on either side of the steps where they wouldn't be seen, Reiner and Giano tip-toed up to the garden level. On its east side, it overlooked the cliff, and here the balustrade was lined with tall columns. These had once been topped with statues of Shallyan martyrs looking off toward the heathen wastelands, but the raiders had pulled them down, and the columns were empty.

Reiner eyed them uneasily. Veirt had asked him and Giano to climb the first two, and he didn't like the idea. It wasn't that they were hard to climb: they were wreathed with sturdy, if thorny, rose vines, which made for easy hand and foot holds. It was that they sat on the very edge of the cliff, and though Reiner wasn't terribly afraid of heights, clinging to a column by one's fingers and toes above a four hundred foot drop to jagged rocks would give any sane man qualms. It might have been his imagination, but the wind seemed to pick up just as he began his climb.

At last, well after Giano was already perched on his, Reiner pulled himself on top of the pillar. He swallowed. The top had looked wide enough when he was on the ground, but now seemed to have shrunk to the diameter of a dinner plate. He crouched down, knees trembling. Fortunately the briars were thick around the capital, so unless someone was actually looking for them, they were hidden from the ground. What was going to make them conspicuous was the blanket.

With a look to make sure the raider guards were out of sight, Reiner pulled his blanket from his pack, unrolled it and – holding firmly to a twist of vine – flipped one end over to Giano. The mercenary seemed to have no fear of heights. He reached out over the chasm and caught the blanket without a quiver. He gave Reiner a grin and the circled thumb and forefinger.

Reiner's pulse beat against his throat. If the raiders spotted anything, it would be the blanket, drooping between the two pillars like festive bunting. At least the sun was at such an angle that the thing cast no shadow over the walk.

He had little time to agonise. Just as he and Giano set themselves, the first of the raiders came around the high hedge and started toward them. Reiner crouched lower in the briars and gripped the blanket with both hands. He watched as the raider walked along, gazing idly out over the cliff at the endless forest below, then reached the steps and turned to walk along the balustrade that looked over the plaza, oblivious to the men above and below him.

Now was the moment. Reiner and Giano exchanged a look, then jumped off the pillars as one, holding the blanket out wide between them. They landed perfectly, catching the raider's head in the blanket while he was in mid-step and pulling back hard. The giant slammed flat on his back, gasping as the air was knocked from him, and before he had time to recover and cry out, the rest of Veirt's men had raced up the steps and leapt on him: Ulf sitting on his chest and pinning his arms, Gustaf and Hals holding his legs, and Veirt grabbing his head through the blanket and cramming the butt of his pistol into the man's mouth as he fought for air.

Erich raised his sword, but hesitated, for, though pinned, the Kurgan was so strong he jerked the three men that held him down this way and that and nearly threw them off. 'Hold him still, curse you,' he hissed.

Reiner pulled the bag of pistol shot from his belt and cracked the giant over the head with all his strength. The fight went out of his massive limbs, and Erich brought his blade down like an executioner's axe. The blow severed the raider's head from his body. Veirt wrapped it up in the blanket and pressed it against the giant's spouting neck. 'Now get him out of here before he bleeds all over the place.'

This was easier said than done. Ulf caught the warrior under the arms, and Gustaf and Hals lifted his legs, but he seemed twice as heavy as he should be, and they could barely inch him along. Beyond that, there was no stopping the blood. Though Giano tucked a second blanket under the raider's neck as they moved him, the flagstones of the walk were still spattered with bright red drops.

'Clean that up,' whispered Veirt, but it was too late. They could hear the second guard coming. Reiner and Giano ran to their columns again and started climbing while Veirt mopped at the bloody pavers with his cloak. Ulf, Gustaf and Hals, grunting with effort, tried to muscle the headless corpse down the steps, but Ulf lost his footing and went over backwards, tumbling down to the plaza with the body crashing on top of him as the rest ducked out of sight.

Reiner heard the second Kurgan call a question. He came around the hedge with his massive sword drawn and looked around suspiciously. He was as big as his companion, but bald, and with eyebrows so shaggy that he had braided the ends. He wore a mail shirt and a bearskin cloak. Reiner and Giano froze halfway up their pillars and edged around out of his line of sight like squirrels. The raider crept forward, wary. Reiner held his breath.

The raider barked another question, then stopped as he spotted the smeared blood on the flagstones. He backed up, shouting a warning to his comrades over his shoulder.

Raised voices answered him from behind the hedge.

'Kill him!' cried Veirt, and raced up the steps with Erich, Hals and Gustaf behind him.

The Kurgan turned to face them, which opened his back to Giano and Reiner. They leapt at him, daggers drawn, as he met Veirt and Erich's charge sword to sword. Reiner's dagger turned on his mail, but Giano's struck home and the raider roared in pain. He backhanded Giano and Reiner with his free hand while slashing at the others with his blade.

Giano was knocked to the ground, but Reiner hit the balustrade and came within an inch of tumbling over it into the void. Only a painful grab at a thorny vine stopped him. Pulling himself back to safety, Reiner heard the sound of running feet, and over it, the thrum of a bow and the crack of a gun, as Franz and Oskar fired from the dormitory windows at their suddenly moving targets.

Reiner helped Giano to his feet and they ran forward to help. The bald raider was surrounded by Veirt and the others, roaring like a cornered bull. Hals had his spear in his guts, and Veirt and Erich were laying into him like woodsmen felling a tree, but still the northman fought on. As he looked for an opening, Reiner saw Ulf, still dazed from his tumble, struggling back up the stairs, and behind him Pavel, hurrying across the plaza, pistol in hand, puffing like he'd run ten miles instead of ten yards.

The raider caught Erich a glancing blow on the shoulder and knocked him flat, then chopped through the haft of Hals's spear and pulled the head out of his innards. He used it to block Veirt's sword and returned the blow with a slash that sent Veirt's helmet clattering down the steps and dropped the grizzled captain to his hands and knees.

Reiner, Giano and Ulf rushed in to fill up the gaps. Reiner parried the raider's blade with his sabre. It was like trying to stop a battering ram with a fly whisk. His whole arm went numb with the force of the blow.

Giano too was knocked back, but not before he jabbed his sword into the crook of the giant's arm and cut something vital. Blood soaked the northman's leather wrist guard and his sword drooped to the ground. Ulf grabbed his other arm, shouting, 'I've got him! Kill him!'

Reiner drove his sword deep into the raider's chest. The man roared in pain and swung Ulf like he was a child. He crashed into Reiner and they went down in a heap.

'Hoy,' said a quiet voice.

Reiner looked up. The raider was turning to find the speaker, and came face to face with the barrel of the pistol in Pavel's shaking hand.

Pavel fired. The back of the raider's head exploded in an eruption of brains and gore. He dropped like a felled ox.

'Nice one,' said Hals.

Their relief was short-lived. Before Reiner and Ulf could do more than stand, four more raiders rounded the hedge at a run, axes and swords in hand. One had an arrow in his shoulder, evidence that Franz could hit more than rabbits.

Veirt stood and drew his pistol. 'Fire!'

Reiner and Erich drew as well and all fired in unison. Only two of the shots hit and only one was telling, ripping a raider's throat out. He fell to his knees, hands to his neck, guzzling his own blood. The others kept coming, and there was no time for another volley. Reiner tossed away his spent piece and mumbled a prayer to Ranald that the dice would roll his way.

Hals snatched Pavel's spear from him and pushed his friend down the stairs, crying, 'Get out of the way, y'old fool.'

Erich, Veirt, Giano and Ulf squared up to meet the charge, while Gustaf, as Reiner expected, hung back.

Just before the two sides met, a shot rang out and one of the raiders stumbled. Reiner saw Oskar and Franz running from the door of the dormitory. Oskar's gun was smoking.

Then there was no more time for looking around. With an impact like ships colliding, the two sides came together. Erich and Ulf, the biggest of the men, took the charge full on, and held, while Veirt, canny old warrior that he was, ducked low and slashed at the shins of his man. Reiner and Giano dodged left and right and swung at the raiders' backs as they ran by.

The three raiders took these attacks without flinching. Even wounded and outnumbered two to one, they looked to Reiner to be the winning side. They slashed at the circling men with a fearless ferocity that was frightening to behold. Reiner wondered how the Empire had ever prevailed against monsters such as these.

Ulf quickly found himself in trouble, forced away from the others by a raider with tattoos winding around his bare arms. He was overmatched, and gave ground with every exchange, the haft of his wooden maul splintering under repeated hacks from the norther's sword. But just as he was about to break through the engineer's defences, the Kurgan slipped on Reiner's discarded pistol and his leg skidded out from under him. Ulf took advantage, shattering the northman's shin with a scooping swing. The raider fell to one knee and Ulf darted in, aiming for his skull. But even unable to move, the raider was a danger. He parried the blow with his sword and gashed Ulf across the chest.

'Ulf!' cried Franz. 'Fall back! Back away!'

Ulf jumped back, bleeding, and Franz and Oskar, who had been hanging fire, shot the kneeling Kurgan point blank. Franz's arrow caught him in the throat. Oskar's ball smashed through his groin. He collapsed sideways, clutching himself, crimson to the knees in seconds.

There were two left, and one of them, the one with Franz's arrow in his shoulder, went down almost immediately, Veirt's long sword slipping neatly through his ribs, but the last – the leader by his size and power – fought on, roaring like a mountain cat. Though he bled from a hundred cuts, he only seemed to get stronger – and to Reiner's disbelieving eyes – bigger.

Reiner blinked and shook his head, ducking a wild slash from the man's axe, but when he looked again, the illusion remained. The raider seemed to be bursting out of his armour. The leather bands around his biceps snapped as he backhanded Veirt to the ground. The links of his chain mail shirt strained and popped. A weird glyph on his powerful chest seemed to glow as if lit from within. His pupils enlarged to fill his whole eye.

'What happens to him?' asked Giano, uneasily, as the raider's armour dropped from him like a shed skin.

'He is touched by his god,' said Veirt, recovering. 'His battle rage is upon him.'

'Well, I'm a mite peeved myself,' said Hals, and jabbed the monstrous warrior in the ribs. The spearhead snapped off as if he had jammed it into a stone wall. The raider kicked the pikeman back so hard he crashed into a pillar and collapsed. Giano swung his sword at the warrior's now naked back. It glanced off as if he wore field plate. Erich and Veirt hacked at him with similar results. Erich parried an axe blow on his sword and was knocked to the flagstones, a finger-deep notch in the edge of his blade.

This was ridiculous, thought Reiner. They outnumbered the raider ten to one and still they couldn't finish him? There had to be something sharp enough to pierce the inhuman warrior's skin. He frowned, thinking hard. The change had made the raider bigger and stronger, but he didn't seem any smarter – in fact he grew more bestial by the moment. 'Back toward the plaza!' Reiner shouted. 'I've an idea!'

The men looked to Veirt.

'Do it,' he rasped. 'We're not winning this way.'

He and the others backed toward the steps, following Reiner. The raider pressed after them, slashing mindlessly.

'Hals, Ulf,' called Reiner. 'Kneel at the balustrade with Hals's spear between you.'

'But the head's broken off,' said Hals.

''Tisn't the point I want,' said Reiner. He scooped up a handful of loose rocks, and as Hals and Ulf knelt, holding the broken spear between them, he hopped up on the balustrade, looking down into the plaza to make sure he had positioned himself correctly.

'All right,' he cried. 'Scatter!'

Giano and Veirt jumped back, but Erich hesitated.

'You heard him,' bellowed Veirt. 'Get away!'

Erich leapt to the side, and before the transformed northman could go after any of them, Reiner shied a rock at him. It hit him in the chest. He looked up.

'Come on, you dirt-eating heathen!' shouted Reiner. He hurled another rock. It caught the Kurgan on the bridge of the nose. He howled.

'You overgrown ox!' shouted Reiner. He bounced another rock off the warrior's forehead. 'You motherless son of a goatherd! I've stepped in things that smelled better than you.'

With an ear-splitting roar, the mutated marauder charged Reiner, axe swinging. At the last possible second, Reiner dived to the side and crashed to the flags. The raider hit the balustrade at thigh level and toppled forward. Hals and Ulf helped him along, raising his legs with the broken spear and flipping him over the rail to the plaza below.

There was a horrible wet crunch and an animal cry of agony cut short. Reiner stood, holding his mouth. He'd bitten his tongue when he landed and it was bleeding. He looked over the balustrade with the rest. They gasped. He smirked. His plan had worked. The Chaos marauder was impaled on the sheared-off statue of Shallya, the sharp wedge of marble jutting up through his shattered ribs like a white island rising from a red swamp.

'Sigmar's hammer,' said Hals, rubbing his chest where the raider had kicked him. 'He didn't half deserve that.'

'Bravo,' said Giano. 'But he might have missed. Why not just…?' He pointed to the cliff-edge balustrade.

'Because, unlike you,' Reiner said, rubbing his jaw, 'I have some regard for my own skin. A slip here and I bite my tongue. A slip there and…' Reiner swallowed at the very thought.

'Ah, yes.'

Veirt clapped Reiner on the back. 'Smart work, lad. Very smart.'

Erich sniffed. 'Hardly one for the bards, though. Heroes don't win by trickery.'

'That's why there are so many dead heroes,' Reiner retorted.

'Well, I thought it was fine,' said Pavel coming up the stairs. 'Never would have thought of something like that in a hundred years.'

The others nodded in agreement. Franz grinned and gave him the circled thumb and forefinger. Erich glowered and turned away.

Lady Magda appeared at the top of the stairs. 'If the danger has passed, it is time to enter the chamber.'

# CHAPTER SIX
## YOU WILL OBEY ME

THEY MOVED THROUGH the garden that fronted the Chapel of Shallya with wary vigilance. Franz and Giano had only seen six marauders, but there might well be more. In the centre of the garden they found a cooking fire burning inside a circle of planted spears and pikes, each with a grisly trophy affixed on top. Lady Magda's face was set as she surveyed the whitening skulls of those who had once been her sisters. The smell of roasting meat rose from the fire. Nobody looked too closely at what was cooking.

It was evident that a much larger force had camped here in the recent past. The remains of other fires were dotted around the garden, and heaps of rotting garbage were piled in the corners. The rose bushes and decorative borders had been trampled, the statues smashed and the fountains used as latrines. At one side a crude forge had been built, and broken and half-repaired weapons and pieces of armour were strewn about it.

But none of the vandalism the party had seen prepared them for the horrors wreaked upon the chapel. The white marble walls were blackened with smoke and the tile roof had caved in, leaving the interior open to the sky. And there were worse things than mere destruction. The raiders seemed to have reserved their most imaginative blasphemies for this shining symbol of charity and mercy. The statues in the alcoves around the white marble walls had been pulled down and replaced with naked nuns tied to stakes and left to die. Eldritch runes, so evil that it was difficult even to look at them, had been smeared on all the walls in blood, and the simple wooden dove-wings carving, the symbol of the Shallyan faith which was mounted over the door, had been hung upside down and covered with the most obscene blasphemies.

Inside, among the charred ruins of the roof beams were the bound bodies of more nuns, who had been abused most cruelly before they died. The beautiful tapestries illustrating the miracles of Shallya had been torn down and burned, and worst of all, upon the sacred altar some perverse ceremony had been performed. Strange symbols and arrows had been burnt into the stone floor in a circle around the dais, pointing toward all the compass points. Blood had been dribbled in unsettling designs, and on the altar itself, inside a thicket of melted candles and piled skulls, the body of the abbess, in life a plump, middle-aged woman, lay splayed, bound and naked, with runes carved into her flesh with a knife, and a huge sword driven down through her abdomen and into the stone table beneath her – a feat of strength Reiner could hardly credit. Shadows seemed to move around her. It took Reiner a moment to realise that these were rats, eating her extremities.

A sob exploded from Giano's throat and he rushed forward. 'Lady of peace, no! It no can be allow! We must clean! We must fix!'

'Ostini!' shouted Veirt. 'Leave off. We've other business!'

But the Tilean had jumped up on the altar and was knocking away the candles and rats and cutting at the ropes that held the abbess. 'Cursed rats! Defilers!'

Veirt marched to Giano and yanked him off the altar by his belt. 'I said, leave off!'

Lady Magda's face was grim and pale. She made the sign of Shallya over the abbess, then turned toward an arch in the right wall without a backward glance. 'This way,' she said.

The archway led to a stone stair which spiralled down into darkness. While torches were kindled, Veirt ordered Oskar to stand guard outside the chapel, then the rest started down the stairs. Veirt led the way, followed by Lady Magda. Erich brought up the rear.

At the bottom of the stairs they stepped out into an intersection of three short hallways. It was obvious that the raiders had found their way here as well. The bodies of a few nuns who looked as though they had died defending the catacombs lay butchered on the stone floor, and the large and intricately decorated bronze doors which glinted orange in the torchlight at the end of each hallway had been smashed open and hung from their hinges, revealing shadowed rooms beyond. The rats were feasting. Giano shuddered.

'The convent's mausoleums,' said Lady Magda. 'Where are buried all the abbesses who have led us down through the ages.'

Hals shivered and made the sign of the hammer. 'Graves?'

Lady Magda shot him a look. 'After the horrors through which we have just passed you are frightened of the long dead?'

Hals stuck his chin out. 'Course not. Just don't like it, is all.'

Magda started down the middle hallway to the desecrated mausoleum at the end. The men followed, weapons at the ready.

Veirt chewed his lip. 'Do y'think they found the Bane?'

'Impossible,' said Magda. 'The door to the chamber is cunningly hidden and impenetrable unless the correct incantation is spoken.'

They entered the mausoleum, a cramped, narrow room. The side walls had been lined with marble memorial plaques engraved with the names and dates of birth and death of generations of abbesses. The Kurgan vandals had pried most of the plaques off, then pulled the bones out of the holes they covered and scattered them, looking for loot. Hals stepped fastidiously around the remains, mumbling prayers under his breath.

The back wall was a finely painted frieze of Shallya holding a golden chalice to the lips of a dying hero as a host of Shallyan nuns looked on. Though age had dulled it, and the Kurgans had defaced it with axe and fire, it was still beautiful, with much gold leaf and intricate detail. Reiner could see every hair of Shallya's tresses.

Veirt looked around, confused. 'Is this it?'

'Stand well back,' said Lady Magda, 'and I will show you.'

Veirt backed to the door, motioning his men behind him. Lady Magda faced the painting and began to speak in a language Reiner half-recognised from his studies at university as an archaic ancestor of his own. Her hands moved constantly as she chanted, describing precise patterns in the air. At last she spread her arms wide, and with a grating of stone on stone, the entire back wall swung slowly out on a hidden hinge, crushing the scattered bones and shards of marble on the floor to powder until it touched the left wall.

As the torchlight found its way through billowing bone dust to the area behind the secret door, Reiner could see that it was larger that the mausoleum, much larger. Wide stairs led down to a vaulted central chamber that seemed almost as big as the chapel upstairs, and dark archways opened into further rooms all along the perimeter.

A weak voice came from inside. 'Abbess? Is... is that you?'
'Who's there?' Lady Magda peered through the dust.
Small forms in Shallyan robes lay like drifts of grey snow around the door. More nuns, skeletal, with gaunt faces and black lips.
One still lived. A gangrenous wound had blackened her left arm up to the shoulder and it smelled of death. Pink pus bubbled from her lips. It looked as if she had tried to eat the leather of her slippers and belt to stay alive. She raised her head as if it weighed as much as the chapel. Her dull, sunken eyes blinked. 'Praise Shallya, we thought they had killed...' She paused as she saw Magda approaching, and her eyes widened. 'Magda...' she croaked. 'You...'
Lady Magda knelt and covered the holy woman's mouth with her hand. 'Don't speak, sister. There is no need. I know what you desire.'
Magda drew her eating knife from her belt, and before any of the men even knew what she was doing, sunk it into the sister's neck just below the jaw, piercing the artery, then did the same on the other side. The woman's blood flowed out of her like water.
'Lady!' cried Veirt, shocked. The others murmured under their breath, confused.
Magda ignored him, whispering a prayer over the dying siter and moving her hands in ritual patterns. When she was finished, and the sister had breathed her last, she turned to the captain. 'I apologise. Her wound was too far gone. It was the only mercy I could give her.'
Veirt looked at her levelly for a long moment, then bowed his head. 'I understand, m'lady. Sorry to have spoken.'
'It matters not. Come, let us finish our business here and leave this unhappy place.'
Veirt and Lady Magda entered first, kicking up puffs of dust with each step as they walked down the stairs to the central chamber. The others followed, quieted by the sister's

actions. Reiner heard Hals mutter to Pavel under his breath. 'That's a cold one, and no mistake, mercy or no.'

Pavel nodded and Reiner had to agree as well.

Magda stopped in the centre of the main chamber. 'These are the convent's holiest treasures, acquired over the centuries. Gifts and relics and tomes of forgotten wisdom. Here also lie many heroes and martyrs who gave their lives in the defence of Shallya and the Empire.'

Giano, Hals and Pavel looked around with greedy eyes, but were quickly disappointed.

'It's just a lot of old books,' said Hals.

Reiner smirked. Though he was as fond of coin as any man who made the dice his life, he had been a student as well, and the 'old books' Hals scoffed at were greater treasures in his eyes than jewel-encrusted swords and chalices of gold ever could be. Reiner longed to be able to flip through them all and feast on the old knowledge, the stories out of the mists of time, the strange histories that were contained there. What a treat. The books were stacked all over, surrounding a few legitimate treasures: statues, paintings, suits of armour, the finger-bones of Shallyan saints displayed in reliquaries, iron-bound chests that could have held anything from manuscripts to gold crowns.

'Which is Kelgoth's crypt?' asked Veirt.

For the first time since he had met her, Reiner saw uncertainty in Lady Magda's eyes. She pursed her lips. 'It has been many years since I entered this place. I believe it is one of the three along the far wall, but I cannot be sure.'

Veirt sighed and looked around at the men. 'All right, you gallows birds, if we want to get out of these mountains before sundown we need to find this relic quick. You will help the lady search, but you will not slip any bits and pieces into your pockets, or I will pull off your fingers one by one, do I make myself clear?'

The men nodded.

'Right then, listen first,' said Veirt. 'What you're looking for is a battle standard.' The captain's voice suddenly trembled with emotion. 'The Griffin's Wing. The Heart of Kelgoth, known since the battle of Morntau Crag as…'

'Valnir's Bane!' said Erich in a reverent whisper. 'By the hammer!'

'Never heard of it,' grumbled Hals.

Erich sneered. 'Ignorant villain, it is one of the great lost relics of the Empire. A banner so pure and powerful that the mere sight of it could give an entire army the courage of a griffin.'

'Legend has it,' continued Veirt, 'that at Morntau, the daemon Valnir shattered the hammer of Lord Daegen Kelgoth and pierced his heart with a sword of flame. But with his dying breath, Kelgoth snatched up the Griffin's Wing, his family's sacred banner, and plunged the halberd on which it was mounted into the daemon's mouth, slaying it. Kelgoth died as well, but the day was saved and his name has inspired generations to valour.'

'Never heard of him either,' said Hals.

'I don't remember hearing that the banner was lost,' said Reiner, who vaguely recalled the legend from his tutor's lessons. 'I thought it was destroyed.'

'It was neither lost nor destroyed,' said Lady Magda brusquely. 'It was hidden away. Returned to the tomb of the hero who wielded it. For its power was too strong a temptation to ambitious men, who used it against their fellows rather than evil.'

Reiner raised an eyebrow. 'And you've noticed a change for the better in man's nature of late?'

'Hardly,' said Lady Magda. 'But desperate times require desperate measures. When we bring it to him, Baron Albrecht will use the Bane to instil in his troops the courage to turn back the Chaos tide and save these mountains from the foul clutches of Chaos.' She glared around at them all. 'Now may we begin the search?'

The men nodded and turned toward the crypts.

'The banner is described as pure white,' called Veirt as they spread out. 'With a griffin rampant emblazoned upon it in gold and silver thread, flanked by the hammer and the chalice and crowned with the jewelled circlet of the Lords of Kelgoth.'

'If you find it,' added Lady Magda, 'do not touch it, but call to me. It is too powerful and dangerous for the uninitiated to hold.'

The men began peeking into the crypts. Those of Shallyan martyrs were plain, with simple coffins and pious verse engraved on the walls. The crypts of heroes were more elaborate, with sarcophagi carved into the likenesses of their occupants and frescos of battle scenes painted on the walls.

Reiner and Franz investigated an arch in the back wall. Reiner raised his torch. A crowned 'K' was carved over the lintel.

He smirked. 'Promising.'

They stepped inside. The dust was so thick that it was difficult to make out the episodes of heroism depicted on the walls. A sarcophagus sat on a granite pedestal in the centre of the narrow room, but an old pike was propped against it, and it was draped with a filthy, dust-covered blanket, so it was hard to see what the hero beneath looked like.

'Pull that mess off and let's have a look at him,' said Reiner.

Franz pushed the pike aside and the blanket came with it, flopping to the floor in an eruption of dust. The boy yelped and jumped back, shaking his hand.

'What's the matter, lad?' asked Reiner.

'Something stuck me.' Franz sucked his palm. 'A splinter or something.' He looked at the stone casket, shaped like a knight in full plate armour, bare-headed, with long hair that flowed over the pedestal upon which he lay. 'Is it him, do you think?'

Reiner circled the stone knight. 'I see no banner.'

'You fools!' cried Lady Magda from the archway. 'You are stepping on it!'

Reiner looked down. His boots were on the dirty blanket. Magda hurried forward and pushed him off it. 'Step away! Step away, you imbeciles!' She stooped and snatched up the pike. A wince of pain twisted her face for an eyeblink as she raised it. The blanket came up too, and now Reiner could see that it was attached to the pike by a cross bar. He raised an eyebrow. It *was* a banner, but it couldn't possibly be *the* banner. In the shadowy crypt it was impossible to tell what colour it was, but it was certainly not white.

With shaking arms and clenched jaw, Lady Magda backed out of the crypt with the pike. Reiner and Franz followed her into the central chamber. Veirt and the others gathered around her as she shook the dust from the cloth, raising their torches to shine light on it.

'That can't be it,' said Veirt, frowning. 'It's all wrong.'

Reiner had to agree. The banner was dull red, emblazoned with a manticore rampant in black and dark green, flanked by a twisted sword and a skull, and crowned with a circlet of thorns. It made Reiner uneasy to look at it. He felt as if he needed to wash.

'It is,' insisted Magda. 'Look again.'

Veirt held his torch closer and the men leaned in. Reiner forced himself to examine it. Close up, he could see that the brown-red of the banner was dried blood, and that the black and green of the manticore, as well as the skull, sword and thorns, were clumps of crusted blood and mould and hairy mildew. Buried beneath this filth and gore Reiner could make out the faint raised outlines of the original design: the embroidered griffin, flanked by the hammer and chalice, and crowned by the circlet Veirt had described. The broken blade of the halberd was caked in dried blood which had run halfway down the haft.

Veirt recoiled in disgust. 'It has been tainted. The blood of the daemon has corrupted it. We should burn it.'

'Nonsense,' said Lady Magda. 'It only needs cleaning. Come, we must return to Baron Albrecht. There is no time to be lost.'

'But, lady, 'tis profane,' protested Veirt. 'Sigmar knows what would happen if an army marched under this... this foulness.'

'What does a common foot soldier know of such things?' Lady Magda retorted. 'You may have won a commission, captain. But you are still an unlearned peasant. Now do as Baron Albrecht commanded you to and accompany me back to Smallhof.'

Veirt's jaw set. His fists clenched at his sides. Reiner could see that there was a war raging within him between his duty and his instinct. At last his shoulders slumped. He hung his head. 'Forgive me, lady. But I cannot. I am indeed the peasant you name me, but I have fought the hordes and their evil sorceries for nearly as many years as you have lived, and I've learned that once touched by Chaos, a thing can never be truly cleaned.' He shifted uncomfortably. 'Now please give me the banner. We will burn it in the garden.'

'Dare you order me?' said Lady Magda, haughtily. 'Without the banner, the battle for Nordbergbruche may be lost. Will you face Baron Albrecht and tell him that, because of a feeling, you destroyed that which would have assured him victory?'

Reiner stared at her. Though no physical transformation had occurred, Lady Magda had changed. Gone was the quiet, stern holy woman. In her place stood some high priestess of old, eyes blazing with righteous wrath. She looked wild, powerful and dangerous, and as unsettled as he was by her sudden sinister metamorphosis, he also found her uncomfortably attractive. Her body, under her habit, which he had thought a touch overstuffed, suddenly looked voluptuous and wanton. She looked like she was used to getting her way and taking what she wanted, and Reiner had always had a weakness for that sort of woman.

'Lady,' said Veirt quietly. 'I am well aware of Baron Albrecht's plans, having helped form them, but no good could come from any venture undertaken under this debased banner. I will destroy it and accept what punishment he sees fit to mete out.'

'You dirty ranker,' burst out Erich. 'What about us? We face death if we fail in this mission. You condemn us to die for your backward superstitions.'

Veirt glared at him. 'Would you rather hundreds, maybe thousands, of your comrades died if we succeed?'

'We only have your word for it that anything would happen. Your word against the lady's.'

Reiner raised an eyebrow at this. If Erich couldn't feel the blood-soaked banner's evil influence he must have a head of solid granite.

Veirt ignored the novice knight and held out a hand to the sister. 'Give me the banner, lady. I beg you.'

'I will not,' she said, drawing back.

'Then I'm afraid I must take it from you.'

'Touch her at your peril!' shouted Erich.

As the lancer struggled to draw his sword, Veirt grabbed the haft of the banner and tried to tug it from Lady Magda's grasp, but with an angry cry, she shoved at his chest with her fingers.

Veirt stood a head and a half taller than the woman and must have been double her weight, but at her touch he stumbled back, gasping, and sat down heavily on the stone floor. To Reiner it appeared that the old warrior had tripped over something. Lady Magda had hardly touched him, and even with all her strength he doubted she could have budged him an inch.

Reiner and the others gaped at Veirt, who sat on the floor, clutching his chest and sucking air.

Hals knelt. 'Captain, are you hurt? Has the witch hexed you?'

Lady Magda raised the banner. Reiner could feel it behind him like a great eye watching over his shoulder. It felt as if it was pulling at him, forcing him to turn and face it.

'Leave him be,' said the woman. 'He has disobeyed the command of his lord. He is a traitor to Baron Albrecht and the entire Empire. From now on you will take your orders from me.' She pointed to Veirt. 'Now slay this traitor and escort me back to Smallhof.'

Reiner moaned. He had come to like the grizzled old bear and knew he was in the right, but orders were orders. Lady Magda was in command now. And it was for the good of the Empire. He drew his sword as the others were doing and turned to face Veirt.

'Just... just a minute... lassie,' said Pavel. It sounded as if he was pushing each word out through his teeth with his tongue. 'Baron Albrecht... put us under... command of Captain... Veirt. And until... he says otherwise... I take my orders... from him.'

Reiner paused in raising his sword and looked at the one-eyed pikeman. The ranker's brow was beaded in sweat and his arm shook as he forced his dagger to stay at his side.

'You will obey me!' cried Lady Magda. 'I am your leader now.'

Now Hals shook his head, less like he was disagreeing, and more like a bull trying to shake off flies. 'Sorry lass,' he said, straining to speak. 'I... don't think y've... got a... commission.'

Reiner frowned, trying to focus on what Pavel and Hals were saying. It was what he felt himself, so why was he still raising his sword to kill Veirt? Why was he, who had never followed an order in his life without making sure it was in his own best interest, blindly obeying a woman who had no official authority over him at all? He might have a weakness for commanding women, but he was no love-struck pup either. He hadn't let his little head rule his big head for years. What was causing him to act like a flagellant following a firebrand priest?

The banner. It had to be. Though the daemon's blood had corrupted it, it still gave its bearer a supernatural aura of authority, a presence so commanding that it could bend men's will and make them do whatever he – or in this case she – ordered, no matter how much it went against their natural inclinations.

Reiner tried to lower his sword, but to his chagrin, even knowing that he was being manipulated, found it hard to fight the banner's power. It took every iota of will to force his arm down. The feelings of pride and patriotism that so rarely moved him, that he sneered at in the stiff-necked knights and mindless boobs who thought the Empire wasn't just the centre of the world, but the world entire, were welling up in him and making him want to kill. He wanted to strike down Veirt for the glory of the Empire. He wanted to slay all that questioned Lady Magda or doubted her motives. He wanted to...

'No!' Reiner slapped his own face, hard. The pain broke the banner's spell, only for a moment, but it was enough. He made eye contact with Hals and Pavel and was strengthened by their rage. Beyond them, the others were frozen in tortured poses, all fighting the urge to kill Veirt. Little Franz stood shaking, his short sword frozen over his head. There were tears in his eyes. Reiner shook the boy's shoulder.

'Fight it, lad.'

But Franz remained frozen.

'I won't!'

The bellow made Reiner turn. Ulf, his face twisted with rage, flung his upraised maul across the room. It knocked a suit of armour to the floor with a clanging clatter. Franz jerked at the noise like a waking sleeper.

Feeling stronger now, Reiner turned to Lady Magda. 'We won't follow you. You aren't our captain.'

'Then you are traitors,' said Erich, drawing his sword and stepping in front of the holy woman.

'You're the traitor,' growled Hals, unsheathing his short sword. Pavel pulled a dagger.

'The captain,' said Franz. 'He's bleeding.'

'What?' Reiner turned.

Veirt lay flat on his back. Blood was seeping from under his breastplate.

'Captain?' said Reiner, stepping forward.

He heard running feet behind him and spun back around. Lady Magda was racing, with very un-nunlike haste, for the secret door, the banner in her hands.

'Stop her!' called Reiner.

Only Franz, Hals and Pavel had recovered enough to respond. They started forward with Reiner, but Erich jumped in front of them, brandishing his sword.

'You'll go through me first,' he said.

Franz tried to dart around him, but Erich kicked the boy in the hip and sent him sprawling into the clutter of treasures. Pavel and Hals shifted left and right, feinting with their daggers. Reiner grunted, annoyed. Was there ever a more thick-headed knight? He picked up a book from a chest and threw it at Erich's head. The knight blocked it easily, but the century of dust that covered it exploded in his face and he doubled up, choking and cursing. Reiner shouldered him to the floor and ran with Pavel and Hals for the steps.

Lady Magda stood just outside the chamber, mumbling and motioning with her free hand.

Dread dragged at Reiner's guts. She was closing the crypt door. She meant to trap them in there forever, like the poor dead nuns. He bellowed over his shoulder. 'Franz! Ostini! Cut her down.'

It was too late. Before the boy or the mercenary could ready their weapons, the door began to grind closed and Lady Magda ran away toward the spiral stair.

Reiner cursed and redoubled his speed, bounding up the stairs three at a time. Hals and Pavel were right behind him. They put their shoulders to the closing door and pushed, but their combined weight had no effect. Their boots skidded back through a gravel of crushed bone and marble.

'Urquart!' called Reiner. 'Bring a chest! Something big and bound in iron.'

Gustaf, Franz and Giano reached the door and pushed as well. The six of them slowed it a little, but it continued to close. Reiner looked over his shoulder. Ulf was waddling forward carrying a heavy oaken chest, his face beet red with strain.

'Hurry, you great ox!' Reiner looked to Franz, who was pushing mightily, but pointlessly. 'Leave off, lad. Go after her. Warn Oskar. Tell him to gun her down.'

'Aye,' said the boy, and dashed through the narrowing gap. But almost instantly Erich ran out after him, sword in hand.

'Deserter!' shouted Reiner after the lancer. 'Will you leave us to die?' He cursed. 'He'll kill the boy.'

'Go on. Catch him up,' said Pavel. 'We'll hold this. Don't you worry.'

Reiner looked back. Ulf was humping the chest up the broad stairs, one agonising step at a time. He bit his lip. 'You'd better.'

Reiner ran through the closing door and down the passage to the spiral stair, expecting at any moment to trip over Franz's body. He stumbled up the uneven, wedge-shaped steps and burst out into the ruined chapel.

Lady Magda, surprisingly, was still in sight. She had only just reached the great arched door that led to the garden. Must have had some trouble getting the unwieldy standard up the twisting stairs, thought Reiner.

In the centre of the chapel Erich had caught up to Franz, who was dodging and ducking to avoid the knight's slashing sword, and shouting at the top of his voice. 'Oskar! Stop her! Stop the lady!'

Reiner ran for Erich, drawing his sabre. 'Coward!' he cried. 'Picking on boys again? Face me if you want a fight.'

Erich looked up, but unfortunately so did Franz, and Erich, trained in close combat, took advantage. His blade caught the boy a glancing blow on the top of the head and he hit the floor in a jumble of limbs.

Reiner cursed and slashed at the blond knight, but kept running for the door, yelling as Franz had. 'Oskar! Stop her!'

Erich caught up to him in the huge open doorway, stabbing at his back. Reiner squirmed to the side and fell across one of the massive bronze doors that lay twisted on the ground. He rolled aside as Erich's greatsword slashed down at him, then hacked at the knight's knees.

Erich leapt back and Reiner jumped up. They squared off, each too wary of the other to run after the sister.

Oskar was trotting across the garden from his post at the plaza stairs, long gun in his hands. Lady Magda was running right for him.

'Oskar!' Reiner called. 'Stop her! Gun her down!'

'Hey?' said the artilleryman, confused.

'Stop her! She's betrayed us all.'

Oskar looked at the oncoming woman, a puzzled frown on his face. 'Lady?'

The holy woman raised the banner and he stepped back, confusion becoming fear as he stared at it.

'Back away!' she cried. 'Bow down!'

Oskar shied away, throwing up his arms to shield his face from the banner. She swung it at him, knocking him flat, then disappeared down the steps.

Reiner cursed and moved to go after her, but Erich stepped in his way. 'No, traitor,' he said. 'You will not pass me again.'

Reiner grunted angrily. Even if he could beat the knight, which was an open question, it would take too long. Lady

Magda would be on horseback and away long before the fight was over. With a sigh, Reiner shrugged and backed away. 'Very well. You win.'

He turned and ran back into the chapel. Franz was picking himself off the floor, clutching his bleeding head. 'Did she get away?' he asked.

'We'll get her later,' muttered Reiner, helping the boy stand. 'No woman can outpace me on horseback. Come on. Down to the vault.'

Erich came through the door. 'Where are you going? Are you afraid to face me?'

Reiner sheathed his sword. 'I am going to try to save my companions. The men you left to die.'

'They are traitors.'

'*They* didn't turn on their captain.'

Reiner and Franz hurried down the stairs.

'You all right?' asked Reiner, looking at the gash in Franz's scalp.

'It'll heal.'

A loud metallic groaning echoed around them as they exited the stairs. They raced for the crypt. Ulf had placed the iron-bound chest between the massive door and the wall, stopping it from closing, but it was slowly being crushed, the iron bands bending and the wood cracking.

Ulf and Gustaf stood outside the door, taking Veirt in their arms as Pavel and Hals, still inside, handed the stricken captain out to them. 'Bring him upstairs,' said Gustaf. 'I'll need more light.'

Pavel, Hals and Giano climbed out over the splintering chest and joined them. Reiner heard footsteps coming down the hall and looked back.

Erich approached, sheathing his sword. 'Does he live?'

'As if you care,' said Reiner.

'I do care,' said the knight. 'He is a good man. Just confused in his thinking.' He seemed calmer, almost contrite.

'Stand aside,' said Gustaf, and he started for the spiral stair with Ulf behind him, carrying Captain Veirt. The rest followed.

Erich brought up the rear, behind Reiner. 'I have no wish to fight fellow soldiers of the Empire, but you must see that you are in the wrong.'

Reiner rolled his eyes. Halfway up the stairs there was a horrendous crack from below and a deep echoing boom as the crypt door at last crushed the chest and slammed shut. It gave Reiner the shivers.

As the party entered the chapel they heard a faint high screaming, inhuman and frightened.

'Lady Magda,' said Erich, alarmed. He drew his sword and hurried for the door.

'If that's the lady,' said Reiner. 'I'm a Kossar.'

He followed Erich out of the chapel and ran with him through the garden, then across the plaza to the forecourt. The screaming, which had trailed away into whistling sighs of pain, was further on. Erich and Reiner paused at the broken gates, then stepped out of the convent cautiously, looking all around. The horrible sound was coming from the hidden ravine where they had tethered the horses. They crept forward.

As they edged around the entrance to the ravine, Reiner jerked back, shocked. There was a lot of blood. The mule and the horses had been ripped to pieces, as if by some giant beast. Limbs and torsos were strewn about. One or two horses were still alive, lying on their sides with their entrails spilling out, weakly lifting their heads and wailing in animal agony.

'The lady,' gasped Erich. 'Some horror has slain her and all the horses.'

'Don't bet on it,' said Reiner. 'Her palfrey's missing.'

He turned and ran for the cliff face. Erich followed. 'Where are you going? We must find her.'

'That's what I'm doing.'

Reiner looked out over the cliff. The winding path that had brought them up to the convent zig-zagged away below him. Rounding one of its switchbacks was a figure on a palfrey, hair flying in the wind, and deep red banner fluttering above her.

Reiner groaned. 'Sigmar curse all sisters of Shallya.'

# CHAPTER SEVEN
# THE RIGHT THING TO DO

When Reiner and Erich returned to the convent garden, they found the others clustered around Veirt, who Ulf had laid upon a stone bench. Gustaf had taken the captain's breast-and-back off and was kneeling over him, unbuckling his leather jerkin, which was soaked in blood.

'What was it?' asked Franz, looking up at Reiner.

'Some terrible beast has slain all the horses,' said Erich. 'Fortunately, Lady Magda has escaped unharmed with the banner.'

'Or,' said Reiner dryly, 'Lady Magda has slaughtered all the horses so we can't follow her, and escaped with the banner.'

Erich glared at him. 'Are you mad? Whatever killed the horses ripped them limb from limb. Lady Magda could never do that.'

'Don't be so sure,' said Gustaf. 'Look here.' He pulled open Veirt's jerkin to reveal his chest. The men hissed in surprise. A tremor of superstitious fear shivered through

Reiner for, though Veirt's back-and-breast was without a dent or scratch, and his jerkin unmarked, deep gashes had opened his chest to the bone and shattered his ribs. It looked like some monstrous animal with enormous claws had mauled him. The wound bubbled with each of Veirt's shallow trembling breaths. Franz choked and looked away.

'Surely you can't be suggesting that Lady Magda did this?' said Erich as Gustaf began determining the extent of the damage. 'She barely touched him. This looks like the work of a… mountain lion, or a…'

'A manticore!' said Hals with superstitious awe. 'Like the one on the banner.'

'Yes,' said Erich. 'A manticore.' Then, 'No! If you are suggesting…'

Reiner raised an eyebrow at Hals. 'That she killed the horses and cut down the captain with unnatural strength given her by the banner? I'd believe that before a mountain lion.'

Erich's face was turning red. 'And… and if she did, can you blame her? Veirt turned against her. You all did. You were sworn to bring her here, protect her, and return with her and the banner to Baron Valdenheim, and instead, the moment she finds what we came for, you, a motley collection of peasants and gallows trash, decide you know more of the lore of Shallya and the Empire than a noble lady of learning. You doubt her word, and when Veirt lays hands on her, do you jump to her defence? No. You…'

A wet gasp returned their attention to Veirt. With a hacking cough that sprayed blood across Gustaf's knees, the captain's eyes opened. He looked around at them all without any sign of recognition, then saw his chest. His eyes focused. 'Damn the woman. And damn Albrecht too, for listening…'

Reiner knelt beside him. 'What are you trying to say, captain?'

Veirt turned glazed eyes to him. He seemed to be looking at him from a far shore. 'Count... Manfred. Tell him his brother...' He coughed again, spraying Reiner with red spittle, then forced another word out. 'Tre... tre... treachery!' Blood welled up from his mouth like a spring. His head sank back until it touched the marble bench, but his eyes never closed.

The men stared down at him for a long moment, as if unable to comprehend what they were seeing. Pavel and Hals made the sign of the hammer and touched their hearts. Only Gustaf seemed unmoved, cleaning and putting away his knives and supplies like a scribe tidying his desk at the end of his day.

At last Ulf broke the silence. 'So, what now?' he asked.

They all exchanged wary glances. It was a simple question, but a dangerous one. What *did* they do?

More importantly, Reiner wondered, what did *he* do. Where did self-interest lie? What course of action was most likely to keep his skin intact? Did he go back to Albrecht? Did he follow Veirt's last order and look for Albrecht's brother, the count? Did he try to hunt down Lady Magda and stop her? Did he go it alone? Or did he stick with his newfound companions?

'We must follow our duty, of course,' said Erich. 'We must do our best to catch up with Lady Magda and escort her back to Baron Valdenheim as we were ordered to do.'

'Yer off your head, jagger,' said Hals. 'She'd do for us in an eyeblink. The captain's dead. She got her precious banner. I say our job's done, and there ain't nothing waiting for us but the hangman's noose when we get back. I say we go our separate ways and every man for himself.'

There were many nods and grunts of assent from the others.

'Suits me,' said Gustaf.

But Erich was having none of it. 'Do you abandon your duty so easily? You pledged to see this mission through. You cannot just walk away with it half done.'

Hals pulled off his right glove and showed Erich the brand – still red – on the back of his hand. 'I made no pledge. I submitted to blackmail is all. I'm off.' He turned to Pavel. 'What you think, boyo? Marienburg? I hear they pay honest gold for steady pikes.'

'Sounds as good a place as any,' said Pavel.

'In Tilea is summer now,' Giano said wistfully.

'They'd never find me in Nuln,' Gustaf muttered under his breath.

'I've relatives in Kislev,' said Ulf. 'Somewhere.'

Reiner shook his head, coming to a decision at last. 'You're making a mistake, lads. I think we're better off sticking together.' Or rather, he thought to himself, I'm better off if all of you protect me.

The others turned to him.

Erich smiled, smug. 'Come to your senses, have you, Hetzau?'

'This is wild country,' said Reiner, ignoring him. 'Raiders everywhere, wild beasts, unnatural things. I don't fancy going it alone. I don't know about you, but I wouldn't last a night. Until we're back in civilised lands, I think we need each other.'

'Makes sense,' said Hals.

'As to where we go,' continued Reiner, 'that's another question. I am inclined to believe Captain Veirt was right in thinking that the banner is tainted. I think…'

'You have no proof of that,' said Erich.

Reiner paid him no mind. 'Whether or not Lady Magda knew so before we found it, she certainly didn't think twice about using it once she knew its true nature.' He scratched his head. 'The real question is, what will Baron Valdenheim do with it once she brings it to him? Will he burn it as any sane man would, or will he let her convince him to use it to further his ambitions?'

'What makes you think she'll bring the banner to Valdenheim at all?' asked Franz. 'She might head straight north and deliver it into the hands of some daemon-worshipping chieftain.'

Reiner shook his head. 'That woman owes fealty to no one. She worships none but herself. I saw it in her eyes. She wants power in the realms of men, not in some deathless otherworld. Did you not see Albrecht with her when we started this journey? The way he looked at her. He may rule his army with an iron fist, but she has him wrapped around her little finger. Whatever his ambitions are, you can be sure they were hers first, and my guess is that Lady Magda's ambition is to be the wife of Baron Albrecht Valdenheim, and for Baron Albrecht Valdenheim to become *Count* Albrecht Valdenheim, and that she means to use the banner to accomplish these things.'

Ulf frowned. 'But Albrecht's older brother is already Count Vald... Oh. Oh, I see.'

'This is the merest conjecture,' complained Erich. 'You build castles out of air. Even if Lady Magda intends to use the banner for some unjust purpose, which I don't for a second suggest is the truth, you have no evidence that Baron Albrecht has any malicious intent.'

'Don't I?' asked Reiner. 'Then tell me this. If this banner is so important, and is meant to be used in the defence of the Empire, why didn't Albrecht send a battalion of pike and a squadron of lancers to accompany Lady Magda here? Why didn't he send handgunners and greatswords instead of a tiny band of condemned men?' Reiner smirked. 'Because he didn't want anyone to know what he was about. Because he intends to murder us all when we complete the mission in order to ensure our silence.'

'You speak treason, sir,' said Erich.

'Fluently,' said Reiner. He sighed and rubbed his eyes. 'My fear is, that if Baron Albrecht and Lady Magda suspect we live, and that we know what they intend, it will not matter how far we run, or where we hide. They will hunt us down and kill us wherever we go. And with the hammer brands on our hands, we will be that much easier to find. We will never be safe.'

'There's still Marienburg,' said Hals. 'Like I said before. And Tilea, and the Border Princes. The hammer brand means nothing there.'

'Aye,' said Reiner. 'That's true. But how long would it be before you were longing for home? Before you were homesick for Hochland ale and Carolsburg sausages? How long before you wanted to hear your mother's voice?'

'That's all lost to us, y'torturer,' said Hals bitterly. 'We're branded men.'

'Perhaps not,' said Reiner. 'There is one way I can see that we might get out of this with our skins and maybe even win the reward that was promised us.'

Giano's ears perked up at that. 'And how is this?'

Reiner shrugged. 'Follow Veirt's last order and warn Count Valdenheim of his brother's intrigue.'

There was a murmur of approval at this, but Hals laughed. 'And what makes you think Count Manfred is going to take the word of a bunch of murderers and deserters – for you know that's what they'll name us – over that of his brother and a reverend priestess of Shallya? What if he has us killed? Or throws us back into the brig?'

The others nodded, and turned to Reiner.

'Aye,' he sighed. 'There is that. And I've no answer for you. But there must be one honourable count in the Empire?'

'You'd know better than us, my lord,' sneered Pavel.

'It's a risk, I'll warrant you, but what's the alternative? Do you want to spend the rest of your life in foreign lands? Or living the life of an outlaw here, hiding your hands and skulking from place to place, with the law of the Empire always sniffing at your heels like a wolfhound? Do you want to never go home again? I say Manfred is the best of a lot of bad choices.'

'Not to mention that it's the right thing to do,' said Franz.

Reiner smirked. Hals and Pavel burst out laughing. Giano giggled.

Hals wiped his eyes, 'Oh laddie, you shame us all.'

Reiner looked around. 'So are we decided? Do we seek out Manfred?'

The men answered with 'Ayes' and grunts of approval, but Erich, who had been standing with his arms crossed at the edge of the circle at last spoke up.

'No, we are not decided,' he said. 'You've a smooth tongue, Hetzau, but I remain unconvinced. The *right* thing to do...' He shot a withering glance at Franz, 'Is to follow the orders we were given by Baron Albrecht and complete the mission. And as the ranking officer now that Veirt is dead, that is exactly what I command you to do.'

Pavel and Hals laughed again, and the rest glared at the lancer mutinously. Reiner groaned. Things would move much more smoothly without this parade-ground popinjay gumming up the works, but he was the best sword among them, and if Reiner wanted to get back to civilisation he would need around him all the swords they had. 'The Empire's authority doesn't mean much this far from Altdorf, von Eisenberg. We could kill you where you stand and no one would ever know, but if you want to play at rank, I'm not entirely sure you outrank me.'

'I am a novitiate knight of the Order of the Sceptre!' said Erich, drawing himself up.

'Aye,' drawled Reiner. 'Doesn't that mean that you polish the boots and fetch the beer?'

The men laughed.

Erich was turning red. 'I was to win my commission after my first battle!'

Reiner gaped in mock surprise. 'So you've yet to blood your lance? And you want to lead us? Laddie, my father may not have had the coin to buy me a position in an order, but at least I've seen battle. I was wounded at Kiirstad.'

Erich sputtered, but it was a charge he couldn't answer.

Reiner shrugged. 'My preference is that we have no leader. We're all worldly men – most of us anyway. Why don't we put the decision to a vote? All who want to return to Baron Valdenheim, step left, all who want to seek out and warn his brother the count, step right.'

'Vote?' bellowed Erich before anyone could move. 'There is no voting in the army. One does as one's commander orders. This is not the council of elector counts.' He glared at Reiner. 'If you mean to flout my authority in this way, then we will decide who commands here in the proper way. We will settle the matter on the field of honour.'

And with that he pulled off his left glove and threw it at Reiner's feet.

# CHAPTER EIGHT
# THEY STILL COME

REINER STARED AT the glove with his stomach sinking. The last thing he wanted to do was fight Erich. Reiner had always been an indifferent blade, his strong suits in the area of martial endeavours being riding and shooting. He knew Erich was the better man by far. And yet fight him he must.

Though the temptation to just kill the knight when his back was turned was almost overwhelming, he would be a fool to do it. In the first place, he needed Erich's sword for the dangerous journey ahead. In the second, for all his talk of not wanting to be leader, Reiner thought himself the coolest, wisest head among the motley band, and wanted the others to listen to him and do as he suggested. Though some of them might at first applaud him for shooting Erich in the back, he knew that the more they thought about it, the less they would trust him, and the more they would be worried that they might be next.

No, if he wanted to get home in one piece he needed all the men he had, and if he wanted them to guard his back he needed their trust. He would have to fight Erich and, sadly, fight him cleanly. Reiner was certain that the traditions of honour were so deeply entrenched in Erich that if Reiner won the duel fairly Erich would reluctantly obey its stipulations and agree to be led by him. But if Reiner cheated, Erich would refuse to be bound by the outcome. The only difficulty was that the odds of Reiner winning the fight without cheating were slim to none.

Of course if Reiner lost, and Erich commanded them to return to Albrecht, then something else might be done, but he would worry about that if it happened.

He looked up at Erich. 'To first blood?'

Erich sneered. 'If that is all you are prepared to risk.'

'I will need your blade when I win. If you had any sense you would realise that you will need mine if you become leader.'

Erich flushed, embarrassed not to have thought of it on his own. 'And if I win you will submit to my command?'

Reiner nodded. 'I will. As will you if I win, yes?'

Erich hesitated unhappily, then nodded. 'You have my word.'

'Very well.' Reiner pulled his cavalry sabre and scabbard from his belt. 'I'm afraid I cannot match the length of your longsword, so you will have to match mine. Would you care to select the ground?'

'Fine.'

After a hasty colloquy they determined that Oskar's sword matched Reiner's in length, and Erich took a few practice lunges with it to get the feel. The novitiate knight felt it would be unseemly to conduct an affair of honour in a convent, so they marked out the lists just outside the convent's gates. Here also they laid to rest the body of Veirt, for it didn't feel right to leave him unburied among the horrors and desecrations of the convent garden. The ground was rocky and they had nothing to dig with so instead they covered him with loose rocks – though not before Reiner had emptied his pockets of all that was useful: gold crowns, a whetstone, a compass, charms and fetishes to ward off harm and bring luck. Finally, much to Pavel's disappointment, Reiner posted him as lookout, telling him to keep his one eye on the paths leading to and away from the convent.

At last they were ready. Reiner swallowed queasily as the scent of the blood of the butchered horses in the hidden canyon reached his nose. It was too reminiscent of a slaughterhouse for his peace of mind at this particular moment. He rolled his shoulders and circled his arms to warm up, all the while watching Erich doing the same on the opposite side of the ground. Gustaf waited to one side with his field kit at the ready, and Giano, whose people were credited with making the practice of duelling into the ceremony it had become, stood in the centre ready to act as master of the lists. The rest of the men, Pavel, Hals, Oskar, Ulf and Franz, stood around the edges of the ground, their faces a mixture of anxiety and eagerness.

'Gentlemen, please to come to centre?' asked Giano.

Erich strode forward confidently, sword in hand and stripped to the waist despite the freezing wind. A look at the blond knight's broad chest and chiselled midsection made Reiner glad he'd kept his shirt on. The comparison would have done nothing for his morale. He stepped to Giano with a tremor in his knees he hoped no one else could detect.

Giano bowed formally to both of them. 'Weapons and ground alright by both gentlemen? Then we beginning. To the first bleeding, hey? If one gentleman can no continue, the contest go to the man who still stand. If no can see who strike first blood, then fight one more, hey?'

'Fine,' said Erich, sneering down his nose at Reiner.

'Yes,' said Reiner, looking at his boots.

'Excellent. Gentlemen please to stand at ends of blades.'

Reiner and Erich stepped back and extended their arms and swords. Giano held them until their sword tips touched. 'Gentlemen are ready?'

Erich and Reiner nodded.

'Very good.' Giano let go of the tips of the sabres and leapt back. 'Then begin!'

Reiner and Erich dropped into guard and began to circle, eyeing each other alertly. Reiner tried desperately to remember all the lessons he had ignored on those interminable afternoons with his father's master of the fencing, when he would rather have been in the hayloft, learning a different sort of lunge and thrust from his second cousin Marina. Was he supposed to look into Erich's eyes to watch for what he intended next, or was it best to focus on his chest? He couldn't recall. He was so out of practice. All his life he had been able to talk his way out of fights, and when he hadn't, when some angry rustic had caught him with weighted dice or an extra ace in his hand, he had fought dirty, throwing furniture, beer, sand, whatever came to hand. He had no experience fighting within a set of rules.

Erich lunged forward, executing a lightning thrust. Reiner parried, but much too wide. Erich's blade dipped easily under his and slid directly for his heart. Only an undignified backwards hop saved Reiner from being cut to the bone.

'Easy, sir,' gasped Reiner. 'Do you mean to mark me or kill me?'

'My apologies,' said Erich, looking not one whit apologetic. 'I expected more resistance.'

Reiner danced back, sweating, as Erich advanced gracefully, pressing his advantage. Reiner parried and blocked like mad, stopping Erich's blade mere inches from his face and chest time and again. There was no question of him riposting. He was too busy defending. If he tried an attack, Erich would slip past his guard and it would be over. He had to hope Erich would make some error, or lose his balance. It didn't seem likely.

As he dodged this way and that, the faces of the men who surrounded them flashed by: Hals, leaning on his spear and watching with grim intensity, Ulf, his brow furrowed, Giano, eyes shining, Franz with his fingers over his mouth. The boy seemed almost more worried than Reiner himself.

Erich slashed again. Reiner stopped the blow, but it was so strong it drove his own blade back into his shoulder. As he jumped back Reiner felt his arm. No blood.

'Nearly had you there,' said Erich, grinning.

'Nearly.'

Curse the man, thought Reiner. The lancer was so calm, so sure of himself. He had yet to break a sweat, while Reiner was perspiring so much the hilt of his sabre was twisting in his hand.

Erich came in again, jabbing and slashing. His blade seemed to be everywhere at once. Reiner could see it as little more than a blur. He backed away in a panic and his boot heel caught on a lip of rock. He started to fall and threw out his sword arm to try to regain his footing.

Even a lesser swordsman than Erich might have taken advantage of such an opening. Erich lunged like a striking cat, blade arrowing straight toward Reiner's chest. There was no way Reiner could bring his sword to guard in time to stop it.

But then suddenly Erich was tripping himself, his sword arm flailing. Reiner watched amazed, while time seemed to slow to a crawl and his sword swung forward just as Erich's arm fell into its path. It was the slightest touch. A scratch from a rose thorn, and yet there was blood – a line on Erich's arm, a smear on Reiner's blade.

Erich caught himself and jerked back again instantly, but not to press his attack. He spun to point his sabre accusingly at Hals. 'You tripped me, you vermin! You stuck out your spear and tripped me.'

'I didn't, my lord!' said Hals, his face as innocent as a newborn's. 'You tripped over it, certain. But I never moved it.'

'Liar!' Erich turned back to Reiner. 'It doesn't count. He tripped me. You saw him.'

'I'm afraid I didn't,' said Reiner truthfully. 'I was too busy tripping myself.'

Erich's eyes narrowed. 'Wait a moment. I see what it is. You're in collusion, the two of you. You knew you couldn't beat me fairly, so you conspired to cheat.'

'Not at all,' said Reiner. 'At least I didn't. Whether Hals tripped you on purpose you'll have to take up with him.'

'I swear, my lord,' said Hals. 'By Sigmar, I swear. I was leaning on my spear. I didn't move it.'

Erich snorted derisively. 'We'll have to go again.' He motioned to Giano brusquely. 'Come, Tilean. Do the necessary.'

'Sir,' said Reiner. 'You *are* bleeding.'

'It wasn't a fair touch,' snapped Erich. 'I told you. The man tripped me.'

'I have only your word for it.'

'Over that of a peasant. Surely there can be no question.' Erich snatched up his shirt and pulled it on over his steaming chest.

Reiner turned to the others. 'Did any of you see? Did Hals trip him?'

They all shook their heads.

He turned to Giano. 'Master of the lists?'

Giano shrugged. 'I see nothing. The contest go to Master Hetzau.'

Erich threw up his hands. 'This is preposterous! You're all in on it! You never intended for it to be a fair contest.' He turned to Reiner. 'You are a cheat, sir. The leader of a band of cheats.'

Reiner clenched his fists, affronted. The one time in his life that he had fought a duel cleanly, and he was accused of cheating anyway. Of course he had little doubt that Hals had tripped Erich, but for once he'd truly had nothing to do with it. He put the blame squarely on Erich's shoulders. If the fellow hadn't made himself so disliked by one and all he would have easily won the day. 'I'm sorry, old man,' he said to Erich, 'But you agreed to abide by the outcome of the fight, and if you didn't trust the impartiality of the master of the lists you should have said something before we began.'

'This is intolerable!' Erich cried. 'I refuse to submit! We must go again! We must...'

'Hoy!' came a shout from the far end of the ledge.

They all turned. Pavel was running toward them, waving. 'Kurgan coming!' he called. 'A whole bloody column!'

Reiner and Erich cursed in unison and ran with the others for the cliff edge, their argument for the moment forgotten.

Pavel pointed down and to the right. 'There. See 'em?'

Reiner squinted into the frosty haze. Coming up the broad southern path, like a gigantic metal snake winding around the curves of the mountain, was a long train of Kurgan, their bronze helmets and steel spearpoints glinting in the late afternoon sun. They were led by a large squadron of barbaric horsemen, resplendent in outlandish armour and huge swords scabbarded over their shoulders. Huge hounds like the ones Reiner and the others had fought in the thorny wood paced alongside their mounted masters. There were also shackled slaves, shuffling in step under the cracking whips of overseers. Wagons loaded with plunder and provisions brought up the rear of the column. They had not yet reached the point where their path joined the narrow path Reiner and the others had climbed, but they were close. Too close.

'We'll never make it down in time,' said Hals.

'We'll have to hide somewhere,' said Erich.

'Yes, but where?' asked Reiner.

Franz frowned. 'In the convent? In the chapel?'

Reiner shook his head. 'What if they make camp there? We'd be trapped.'

'The hidden canyon?' suggested Oskar. 'Where we put the horses?'

'No, lad,' said Hals. 'All that fresh meat? Those hounds'll sniff it out in a second.'

'If their masters don't first,' Pavel said with a shiver.

'We'll have to go further up,' said Reiner. 'Further into the mountains.'

'Are you mad?' asked Erich. 'Run pell mell into unknown territory with an enemy at our back?'

'Have you another suggestion?'

'There would be no need for suggestions if we had gone after Lady Magda an hour ago as we should have.'

'He didn't ask for complaints, jagger,' muttered Hals.

Reiner turned away from the cliff and started for the box canyon. 'We'd best collect what we can from the packs, but don't carry too much. We may have occasion to run.'

The others followed after him. Erich sniffed, disgusted, but followed as well.

STEPPING QUEASILY AMONGST the scattered horse parts, the company salvaged what they could from the saddlebags, tied the contents up inside their back-and-breasts, and slung them over their shoulders. Pavel and Hals hung theirs off spears they took from the garden of horrors to replace the ones they had lost fighting the Kurgan warriors. As quickly as they could, they started up the wide path that rose from the convent's ledge and wound further into the mountains. The Chaos column was less than half a league behind them.

Reiner took some comfort from the fact that, because of the slaves' slow pace, the column was moving at half march. Reiner's companions would outdistance them easily, but he was less than heartened to see that on this path too were signs of heavy traffic. What if they met another force coming down and found themselves trapped in the middle? Speed wouldn't matter then.

It was less than an hour from nightfall. A cold wind bullied them along and blew high clouds across the lowering sun. The path was alternately bathed in red-gold sunshine or plunged into cold, purple shadows as the trail wound along steep cliffs and through tight defiles. Maddeningly, it didn't divide. Through all its twists and turns it remained a single line, with no branches or crossings, and though they found a few places where two men could hide, or even three or four, there was no place large enough to conceal them all, or far enough from the path that the hounds wouldn't scent them.

After they'd gone a few miles Reiner sent Giano back down the path to see if the Chaos troops had made camp at the convent. He returned just as the sun touched the horizon, mopping the sweat from his brow.

'They still come,' he said between breaths. 'Pass the convent. And more fast than we think. They push slaves hard.'

Reiner frowned. 'Are they gaining on us?'

'No, no, but best we keep moving, hey?'

The nine companions marched on into the dwindling twilight. Reiner was becoming nervous. The wind was getting colder, and the clouds thickening. The men were slowing with fatigue. *He* was slowing. It had been a long day, and they had all received some hard knocks in the fight with the Kurgan. Pavel, still not recovered from his fever, was leaning on Hals and sweating like he was in the desert. Ulf was limping. They needed to find a safe place off the path to make camp.

Reiner cursed Veirt for dying. The old bear would have found a way out of this mess in an eyeblink. If he hadn't died, the duel would never have happened. He would have put Erich in his place with a single glare and they would have been off down the mountain long before the Kurgan host came into view.

Though he put on a brave front for the men, Reiner was in a panic. He didn't know what he was doing. The only reason he had taken command was that following Erich would have led to disaster. Of course, he seemed to be leading them to disaster at a brisk trot himself.

Half an hour later, as the purple twilight was thickening into murky blue, the trail finally divided. It had been hugging a steep mountainside, but then widened into a broad, boulder-strewn shoulder that rose at its far end into a razor-backed ridge. The path split around this, the left way swinging wide and angling down the ridge's outer slope, the right rising up into the cleft 'twixt it and the mountain. To Reiner's annoyance, both were wide enough to accommodate a marching column. The men examined the ground of each in the dim half light.

'Plenty of hoofprints up this side,' called Hals.

'Here too,' said Oskar.

Reiner groaned. Why couldn't it be a simple decision? Why couldn't he say boldly, 'This is the one, lads. Clearly this is the path less travelled.' Now he had to guess, take an even-odds gamble. He *never* made a wager at even odds. Gambling was for fools. Though laymen often called Ranald the god of gamblers, in reality, followers of the Trickster gambled as little as possible. Rigging the odds in one's favour was a holy duty, a sacrament. One never entered a game of chance without an edge of some kind: loaded dice, marked cards, an accomplice. Here there was no way to force an advantage. Here there was no mark to gull, no extra ace to palm. He had to roll clean dice with fate like some rustic peasant, and hope.

'What do you think, lads?' he asked. 'Which way looks more promising?'

'Both the same,' said Giano shrugging.

'This one might be a little sparse,' said Hals uncertainly. 'Then again it might not.'

'What if we wait at the fork?' said Franz. 'See which way they mean to go, then go the other.'

The company turned to stare at him. Reiner gaped. It was a good idea.

'But they'll see us.' said Oskar.

'No. No they won't,' said Reiner, heart pounding with newfound hope. 'They'll have torches by now. We'll stay dark, invisible. And the path splits early enough that we'll know which way they're heading long before they're upon us.' He patted Franz on the shoulder. 'Good thinking lad.'

The boy beamed.

Reiner looked back down the trail. It was so dark now he could hardly see five yards. 'We'll sit right here. Wear your cloaks over your packs, and wrap your swords. We don't want any steel reflecting their torchlight. Might as well have a bite to eat while we wait.'

They huddled together at the blunt tip of the ridge, gnawing on nearly frozen bread and sipping from canteens they had to bang against rocks in order to break the skins of ice that stoppered them. Fast-moving clouds nearly filled the sky. The rising moons were only rarely visible. Finally, almost an hour after full dark, the Kurgan host arrived. The men heard them before they saw them, a faint rumble like a far-off avalanche that never stopped: the sound of boots and hooves on stone, chains dragging through gravel, the crack of whips and the guttural marching cadences of the raider infantry.

By the time the men put away their food and made ready to move, a dim orange glow began to rim the path where it curved around the mountain. The glow grew brighter and the rumble louder until at last the Kurgan column appeared around the bend. Three slaves on long leashes came first. They held aloft torches on tall poles that cast a baleful light upon the Kurgan horsemen that followed them. Reiner swallowed as he saw them. He heard Franz moan beside him.

Though it was difficult to judge scale at this distance, all of the mounted marauders looked enormous, larger even than the monstrous men they had faced in the convent, but in the centre of the first rank rode a veritable giant. Mounted on a barded warhorse that made the largest destrier Reiner had ever seen look like a pony, was a knight – if a daemon-worshipping northern vandal could be given so noble a title – in full plate armour, lacquered a deep blood red and chased with bronze accents. His head was entirely encased in an elaborate helmet, built to look like a dragon's head. The resemblance was heightened by the two double-headed axes that rose from behind his massive shoulders like steel wings. Each must have been as tall as a man. The very sight of him turned Reiner's blood to water. The knight seemed to radiate fear like a stove radiates heat. Reiner wanted to run and hide, to curl up and weep.

His retinue was only less fearsome by comparison. Had the evil knight not been there, the marauders alone would have been quite enough to make Reiner quake in his boots. They were massive, muscular northmen, most in horned helmets and armour of ringmail, leather and the occasional gorget or breastplate. Some rode bare-chested, their sinewy arms and knotted torsos seemingly impervious to cold. But all had the same fell look. Their eyes were hooded and hidden. Not a glint of light reflected from them, not even those who wore no covering helmet, and they stared dead ahead, looking neither left nor right, though Reiner's skin crawled with the feeling that their awareness was examining every part of him like the bean of some glowing eye. Every fibre of his being told him to run.

'Wait for it, lads,' he whispered, as jauntily as he could manage. 'Wait for it.'

The horsemen continued pouring around the curve five abreast until more than a hundred rode behind the knight, then came foot soldiers, a ragged group who walked rather than marched into the valley.

'Look at 'em,' sneered Hals. 'Not one of 'em in step. No discipline.'

Just as the ranks of slaves began shuffling into view and the head of the column had reached the widening shoulder, one of the fell knight's lieutenants peeled off from the squad of riders and faced about. As the others rode on, he raised his hand and began bellowing orders in a bestial voice.

'Do they set up camp?' asked Erich uneasily.

Reiner hoped that it was true, for it would give the party some time to find a way around them, but he wasn't so lucky. There was movement in the ranks: captains shouting at their companies, overseers roaring at their slaves, wagon masters calling to each other, and for a moment all seemed chaos and confusion.

Hals squinted at the reforming column. 'What are they about? Oskar, you've got the eyes. What are they doing?'

'They are... They are...' said the artilleryman as he tried to make it out.

But by then it was clear to everyone what the Kurgan force was doing. As the mounted lieutenant stood in his saddle, motioning and shouting, the column began to split to his left and right like a river breaking around an island, some going one way, some the other.

Reiner's heart sunk. He groaned. 'The cursed heathen. They're splitting up. They're taking both paths.'

'Myrmidia, protect us,' said Ulf.

Oskar was whimpering, high in his throat.

Reiner wanted to cut and run, but he forced his fear down with both hands and remained where he was.

Erich turned on Franz. 'Foolish boy, we could have been far away by now. Now they are upon us.'

'Lay off him, von Eisenberg,' said Reiner. 'He suggested it. I ordered it.'

'But which way do we go?' asked Gustaf, querulously.

'Whichever way he doesn't,' muttered Hals, and no one had to ask who 'he' was. They could feel the fell knight's presence growing stronger as he neared.

'We go the way the slaves go,' said Reiner, relieved to be able to give an order he had some confidence in. 'They'll slow the train.'

The slaves went right, and the company breathed a simultaneous sigh of relief, for the red knight and most of his retinue had angled left, followed by half of the foot soldiers. A smaller company of horsemen led the slaves and the rest of the infantry.

'Right, lads,' said Reiner, letting the tension out of his shoulders. 'That's decided. Off we go.'

The party stood and hurried up the right-hand path into the dark cleft. No, thought Reiner. Though he hated to admit it, they didn't hurry. They fled.

# CHAPTER NINE
## TRAPPED LIKE RATS

REINER AND THE rest ran up the path in almost total darkness, tripping and cursing, but not daring to light a torch. When the wind-whipped clouds allowed it, the light of Morrslieb and Mannslieb illuminated the mountain tops, but the two moons hadn't yet risen high enough to shine down into the tight crevasse through which the company stumbled. They might have passed any number of branching paths, but they were invisible, blending into the dark basalt of the cliff sides.

All around Reiner came the hoarse breathing of the men. He recognised Franz's light quick breaths, Pavel's thready wheeze, Ulf's deep inhalations. They were exhausted. Waiting for the Chaos army had refreshed them a little, but it had been no replacement for sleep. They must stop soon. Even in the midst of their panicked flight, Reiner felt his eyelids drooping. It was pitch dark anyway. He might as well walk with his eyes closed.

After that Reiner was often unsure whether he was walking or sleeping – whether he was walking in a dream, or dreaming that he was walking. He drifted in and out of consciousness so often that he had no sense of the passage of time. He had no idea how long they had been travelling when, just as they topped a rise in the path, the steep ridges that had hemmed them in for so long opened away from them and they found themselves standing on the lip of a deep valley carpeted with a thousand points of light.

Reiner frowned sleepily. The lights looked like stars, but stars belonged in the sky. Maybe it was a lake.

'Torches,' said Oskar.

Reiner shook his head, clearing the fog from his brain. They *were* torches.

He stepped back into the shadows, heart thudding, and surveyed the valley. The others did the same. As if on cue, the clouds parted again and the two moons shown down on the scene.

The curving walls of the valley were rusty orange stone, and terraced like some giant's staircase. There were holes in the walls on each level, and odd ramshackle structures clinging precariously to the steps: little shacks, wooden sluice runs, scaffolding – except where one of the terraces had collapsed and slid in a heap to the valley floor. The furthest third of the valley was walled off by thick stone battlements, beyond which the party could just make out a confusion of low buildings built around the glowing orange mouth of what looked like a giant cave. But the sight that drew all their eyes was what was in front of the battlements: a sprawling camp of leather tents and blazing campfires, wagons and horses, and laughing, drinking, fighting barbarians.

Kurgan.

'Sigmar preserve us,' whimpered Oskar.

Reiner clamped a hand over the artilleryman's mouth, for he had suddenly noticed, not twenty paces to their left, a stone watch tower carved out of the valley wall. Oskar grunted in protest. The others turned. Reiner pointed to the tower. There were no torches visible, but Reiner was sure he'd seen a hulking figure moving above the crenellations. He motioned the others to retreat. When they were out of sight, Reiner slumped against the rocky wall and closed his eyes. The others gathered around him.

He rubbed his face with his hands. 'Well, we're in a spot, and no mistake.'

'Trapped like rats,' quavered Oskar.

'Kurgan in front of us,' said Ulf.

'Kurgan behind us,' said Pavel.

'Kurgan up our bloody fundaments,' growled Hals.

Reiner chuckled mirthlessly. 'I suppose, Erich, this is where you tell me "I told you so".'

There was no answer. Reiner looked up. He didn't see the blond knight. 'Where's von Eisenberg?'

The others looked around. Erich wasn't with them.

Reiner frowned. 'Any of you hear him drop back?'

Everyone shook their heads.

'Any of you slip a knife in his back?'

Silence.

'I wouldn't blame you if you did, but I want to know.'

More headshaking and 'not I's' answered him.

'Then where's he got to?'

'Maybe he's having a piss,' muttered Gustaf.

'That one don't piss,' said Hals. 'He's perfect.'

'Probably found a little hidey hole back there in the dark,' said Pavel. 'And didn't see fit to tell us. He'll slip around the northers once they've passed.'

'Aye,' said Giano. 'Stupid schoolboy. All he want is to tattle tales to Valdenheim.'

'A lot of good that'll do him,' said Franz.

'Well, never mind about him,' said Reiner. 'He's made his decision. We have to make ours. This place, whatever it is, is obviously the destination of the fellows behind us.'

'It's a mine,' said Ulf. 'An iron mine.'

The others looked up at him.

'Myrmidia's mercy,' said Franz. 'The slaves. They're bringing them here for the mine.'

'And mining iron for weapons and armour,' said Ulf.

'Bad news for the Empire,' said Hals.

'But good news for us,' said Reiner. 'At least I hope so.' He turned to Ulf. 'Urquart, those holes in the walls. They're mineheads, yes?'

'Aye.'

'Then they'll be deep enough to hide in?'

'Oh, certainly.'

'Then here's the plan. We slip past the tower, sneak along one of those ledges, duck into a hole and wait there until tomorrow night. By that time, the enemy troops behind us will have made camp, and we can sneak back out and away from these damned mountains with none the wiser.'

'Hear hear,' said Franz.

'You make it sound so easy,' said Gustaf. 'What if we're seen passing the tower? What if another force comes up the path tomorrow night?'

'I'll take any suggestions,' said Reiner.

Gustaf grunted, but said nothing.

The party edged back to the lip of the valley, standing just within the shadow of the canyon walls, and looked up at the tower. The Kurgan guard appeared and disappeared at regular intervals as he paced the top of the tower.

'Now?' asked Franz as the guard turned away again.

Reiner looked at the sky, another armada of clouds was sailing in from the north east. 'A moment.'

The clouds ate the moons once again and darkness covered the valley.

'Now we go.'

The men tiptoed swiftly to the nearest terrace, each of which connected to the path as it sloped down the hill. There was a collapsed shack near the close end. They crowded in behind it and waited, listening for the guard to call a challenge. None came.

'Come on. Before the clouds pass,' said Reiner.

They crept along the terrace to the first entrance. It was boarded up. Reiner tugged experimentally on the planks. They creaked alarmingly.

'Let's try further on.'

But the next entrance was walled up with brick and mortar.

'Why would anyone go to the trouble?' asked Reiner, annoyed.

'Cave-ins,' said Ulf. 'Or sink holes. You saw the landslide. This wall was probably overmined and became unstable.'

Oskar gulped. 'Unstable?'

The third hole was boarded up as well, but the boards were so weathered and warped that they had pulled away almost entirely from their nails. A trickle of water ran out from under the barricade and had carved a channel in the terrace.

'This looks promising,' said Reiner.

He and Hals and Giano began pulling the boards away as quietly as possible and set them aside. Some were so rotten they crumbled in their hands.

At last they had cleared the opening, and the timber-framed entrance yawned before them. It was easy to see why it had been closed. Water dripped from above, and it was clear that it had eaten away much of the ceiling. An attempt had been made to shore it up with wide boards propped up by posts, beams and bits of scrap lumber – so many that the entrance looked like a forest of thin, limbless trees – but the water had seeped into all of these, and they were bowed and rotting. The floor of the tunnel was muddy and calf-deep in loose rock and earth which had fallen from above. Reiner didn't like the look of it at all, but the clouds were thinning. There was no time to find another.

'Come on, then,' he said. 'In we go. And each of you carry a board. We'll have to close it up again from the inside or they'll notice.'

The others trooped in, each with a board under one arm, picking their way through the thicket of supports, but Oskar hung back, looking at the gaping hole with trepidation.

'Come on, gunner,' said Reiner.

The artilleryman shook his head. 'I don't like holes.'

Reiner rolled his eyes, impatient. 'Nor do I. But in we must go.'

'I cannot,' whimpered Oskar. 'I cannot.'

'You'll have to. There's no help for it.' Reiner stepped toward Oskar, reaching out to him.

The gunner pulled back. 'No.'

Reiner shot a glance over his shoulder and clenched his fists. 'Oskar! Stop messing about!' he hissed. He grabbed for Oskar's elbow.

Oskar flinched away and kicked a discarded beam with his heel. It tottered on the lip of the ledge, then tumbled down to the level below.

Reiner groaned and looked back toward the tower. It was too dark out to see it. But he thought he heard a guttural voice call a question.

Reiner lost his temper. 'Curse you, you craven ninny!' he whispered hoarsely, 'Get in there!' He leapt forward, grabbed Oskar by the arm and flung him into the opening.

He regretted the action instantly, for the artilleryman flew into the first rank of props and knocked them hither and thither. One snapped in half. A shower of dirt and small stones rained down on the fallen Oskar and the ceiling groaned ominously.

'Sigmar blast it!' Reiner ran into the entrance, grabbed Oskar by the collar and dragged him through the supports to where the rest of the men had turned at the noise. The floor was clearer here, and the posts fewer. He stopped and looked back.

There was a crack, loud as a pistol shot, then another. First one post, then two more began to bend and fold, then another three.

'Back!' Reiner shouted. 'Back!'

The men ran into the darkness, Franz helping to drag Oskar further down the tunnel.

With a thunderous crash the ceiling above the entrance collapsed, deafening them. A cloud of dust, invisible in the utter darkness, blew around them, making them choke and cough. Sharp rocks spat at their shins and ankles.

At last, with a few final thuds and plinks, the avalanche ended and the men's coughing and retching dwindled off into silence. It was pitch black.

'Everyone here?' asked Reiner. He called out their names one by one and they answered. All but Oskar.

Reiner sighed. 'Strike a light, someone.'

Hals got a taper going and they looked around for Oskar. He was still on the floor, clutching his knees and looking around him wildly. As the flame grew brighter he looked beyond them to the sloping mound of rock and mud that blocked the entrance. He cried out, an animal sound, and scrambled forward on his hands and knees. As the men watched, non-plussed, he began to scrabble at the rocks with his bare hands. 'Dig! We must dig! We must get out! No air! There is no air!'

The rocks were impossible to shift. Oskar began pounding on them, bloodying his hands and shrieking wordlessly.

The men grimaced and turned their heads, but Reiner had had enough. 'Sigmar's balls!' he blasphemed, stepping forward, 'Will you shut *up*!' He spun Oskar around by the shoulder and punched him as hard as he could in the jaw.

Reiner's knuckles flared with pain at the contact, but the result was extremely gratifying. Oskar flopped bonelessly to the ground and lay there, silent at last – out cold.

Reiner turned to the others, sucking a bleeding knuckle. They beamed appreciatively at him. He tried to think of something witty to say, but he couldn't. Exhaustion suddenly overcame him. His knees nearly gave way.

'Well,' he said wearily. 'I think this day's gone on long enough. Let's make camp.'

# CHAPTER TEN
# LET THE WIND BE YOUR GUIDE

WORN TO A frazzle though he was, Reiner still had some difficulty getting to sleep. He might have sneered at Oskar's panic, but he had punched the artilleryman because he'd felt it spreading to his own heart as well. He too had been overcome with an overwhelming sense of doom when the roof collapsed. And of guilt. He had done this. If he hadn't lost his temper and thrown Oskar into the posts it might not have happened. He had trapped them. Anything that happened to them now would be his fault. If they couldn't find another way out? His fault. If something crawled out of the dark, unexplored tunnel and devoured them? His fault. If the air became so sour they couldn't breathe? His fault. If they starved to death? If they went mad and ate each other to stay alive? His fault.

But at last even guilt couldn't keep him awake. Exhaustion dragged him down like a mermaid pulling him beneath the waves, and he slept the sleep of the dead until, sometime later, the scratching and squeaking began. He ignored it for as long as he could, drifting in and out of dreams where it was his old dog scratching at his door, a harlot of his acquaintance combing her hair on the creaking bed in his apartment back in Altdorf, a tree branch rubbing against the roof of his tent on the march up from Wissenberg, but finally images of rats and giant insects and bloodsucking bats forced him to open his eyes and look around.

There was nothing to see, of course. It was still as black as an orc's armpit. He could tell by the snores that the rest were still asleep. With a grunt of annoyance he fished around in his pack until he found his flint and steel, then struck a spark onto his tinder paper and lit a taper.

His moving around woke some of the others and they sat up blinking in the unaccustomed light as Reiner raised the taper and looked for the source of the scratching.

It was Oskar again, whining and clawing dispiritedly at the pile of stone. Reiner winced. The gunner must have been at it for hours. His fingernails were gone, ripped away, and the tips of his fingers were bloody shreds.

'Oskar,' Reiner called.

The gunner didn't respond. Reiner stood and stepped to him. Oskar's lips were moving. Reiner leaned in to hear what he was saying.

'Nearly there. Nearly there. Nearly there. Nearly there. Nearly there. Nearly there. Nearly there.'

Reiner put his hand on Oskar's shoulder and shook him. 'Come on, Oskar. We're going to see what's down the hall. Might be another way out, eh?'

Oskar pulled violently away. 'No! We must dig! We'll all die if we don't dig!' He began digging with renewed vigour, but no better results. The rock he was clawing at was stained a brownish-red from his blood.

Reiner sighed and turned. The others were frowning sleepily at him and Oskar. Reiner found Gustaf among them. 'Gustaf. Have you anything in your kit to quiet him?'

'Oh aye,' said the surgeon dryly. 'I've just the thing.'

Reiner caught his tone and shot him a hard look. 'If he dies of it, you'll follow him.'

Gustaf shrugged, and began unbuckling his kit.

'But, captain,' said Hals, 'why not just put him out of his misery? He has no mind no more, the poor fellow. He's no use to anybody, least of all himself.'

Reiner shook his head. 'With Erich deserting us, we need every man we have. Do you think we should leave Pavel behind just because he's having trouble keeping up?'

Hals stuck out his chin. 'No, sir. No, I wouldn't like that.'

'I'm feeling much better now, sir,' Pavel piped up anxiously.

Gustaf stepped forward and held out a small black bottle and a tin spoon. 'Here. A spoonful will calm him. Juice of the poppy. Nothing poisonous.'

Reiner took the bottle. 'Thank you. I'm familiar with it.'

Gustaf smiled slyly. 'I've no doubt.'

Reiner flushed. He pulled the cork and inhaled. The sweet, cloying scent teased his nose. He fought the urge to have a spoonful himself. It would be so nice to drift away from all this unpleasantness and get some real rest, but that was a bad idea. He had been down that road once before and nearly lost his way.

He filled the spoon and squatted beside Oskar. 'Here, lad. It'll give you strength for your digging.'

The gunner turned his head without stopping and opened his mouth. Reiner spooned some of the liquid into him. He felt like a nurse feeding an infant, which was near enough to the truth.

He stood and turned to the men. He sighed. It was time to face the music. 'Listen, you lot. I want to speak to you.' He paused, hesitant to go on, then cleared his throat and continued. 'It was I who got you into this mess. I led us up into these blasted mountains, I picked this path instead of the other one, and I threw poor

Oskar into those posts and brought the roof down on us. I'm about ready to stop playing at captain and let someone else take over. In fact, I'm a little surprised someone didn't murder me in my sleep just now and assume command.'

The others said nothing, only stared at him.

He swallowed. 'So, if anyone else wants the job, speak up. I'll step down, and happily.'

More silence, then finally Pavel coughed.

'Sorry, captain,' he said. 'We're only rankers. Peasants and merchants' sons and the like. Ye be gentry. Yer meant to lead. It's yer job.'

'But I'm making a mess of it! Look where we are! I did this! We are trapped in here because I lost my temper. You ought to be mutinying by now.'

'Naw, captain,' said Hals. 'We don't blame you for all that. You done your best, and none can ask more than that. It's when a captain starts to worry more about his own skin than the skins of his men. That's when… er, well, when things might happen.'

Reiner blushed, embarrassed. They thought so highly of him, and he was such a villain. His own skin was exactly what he was worried about. He'd taken the lead because he wanted the rest of the men around to protect him if things went wrong. It was only because he was endangering himself by doing so terrible a job that he wanted to pass the baton to someone more competent.

He sighed. 'Very well. If no one will take the burden.' He turned and began packing up his bedroll. 'Let's find a way out of this hole.'

By the time the others had collected their gear and choked down a dry breakfast, Oskar was slumped against the boulders with his eyes closed.

'Well done, Gustaf,' said Reiner. 'Now dress his wounds and tend to him. He's your patient now. Keep him moving.'

'A pleasure, sir,' said Gustaf. But he didn't mean it.

Gustaf bound Oskar's fingertips and got him on his feet while Hals lit two of their precious torches and Veirt's slotted lantern. Then they all shouldered their packs and they started into the darkness. Giano took point, creeping down the tunnel twenty paces ahead holding the lantern close-shuttered. Reiner and Franz led the rest. Ulf walked behind them, then came Pavel leaning on Hals, and Oskar leaning on Gustaf. They walked into a steady breeze, which gave Reiner hope. Moving air meant some passage to the outside. What was curious was that the breeze was sometimes cold and sometimes warm.

The tunnel joined another almost immediately, this one with two iron rails running down the centre fixed to wooden ties. Some of the rail was missing, and the ties rotten.

'Which way?' asked Giano, turning back to them.

'Let the wind be your guide,' said Reiner. 'Take whichever passage it blows from.'

Giano turned into the wind and they followed the glow of his lantern further into the mine. The tunnel dipped and turned eccentrically as it followed a seam of ore through the earth, and the longer they paced it the more cross tunnels and branching ways they passed. Sometimes it opened it out into wide columned areas where a particularly rich deposit had been found, only to narrow down again.

After a quarter of an hour Giano came hurrying back flapping his free hand. 'Douse torches!' he hissed. 'Douse torches.'

Reiner and Hals stabbed their torches into the dirt of the tunnel floor as Giano closed the lantern's slot. They were surprised to find that they were not in total darkness. A faint flickering glow reached them from around a bend in the passage, and the tramp of heavy feet echoed in the distance.

'Kurgan,' whispered Giano.

Reiner and the others drew their weapons and held their breath as the light grew brighter and the footsteps got louder. They began to hear gruff voices mumbling in a barbaric tongue. Reiner found himself gripping his sabre so hard that his knuckles ached, but after a long moment when it sounded as if the Kurgan were standing beside them, talking in their ears, the voices and the light faded again, and then disappeared altogether.

The party breathed a collective sigh of relief.

'Well,' said Reiner, trying for jocularity. 'I'm fairly sure there's another way out now.'

'Aye,' said Hals. 'Through them.'

They relit the torches, then rounded the bend and entered an intersection. The wind blew from the direction the Kurgan had taken. The rails went that way too. They took it.

'Just don't catch up with them,' Reiner said to Giano.

The Tilean grinned and returned to point position.

Soon they began to hear great clankings and groanings, and the susurrus of hundreds of voices shouting and talking. Harsh cries rose above the murmur, and crackings and clashings. A steady red glow filtered down the tunnel, and the wind gusted hot and cold. It began to smell of sweat and smoke and death.

As Reiner passed a right-hand tunnel he was buffeted by a blast of oven-hot air. He stopped. A spur of the rails branched into the tunnel. Red light shone on the rocky walls at the far end and the clanking and roaring was louder here.

'Giano,' he called softly. 'Back here.'

Reiner led his companions into the cross tunnel, edging cautiously toward the red light. Thirty paces in, the tunnel came to an abrupt end at a rough arch. Through it they could see underlit clouds of smoke rising from below. There was no floor beyond the arch, just two short lengths of twisted rail and the splintered remains of a wooden trestle jutting out over a precipitous drop.

Reiner slid forward and peered down into an enormous cave, the floor of which was a good forty feet below them.

The others crowded in behind him, craning their necks. A hellish panorama spread out before them. Directly below the opening was the source of the smoke – two giant, pyramid-shaped stone furnaces, each as big as an Altdorf row house. The smoke belched from square openings at their apexes. Into these holes two endless lines of slaves were dumping buckets of red-streaked black rocks. The slaves crawled up the sides of the pyramids like ants, dropped their burdens into the smoking chimneys, then filed away again to the far side of the cave to great mountains of the reddish stuff, where they filled their buckets again and repeated the journey, over and over again.

'So much ore,' said Ulf, awestruck. 'This rivals the ironworks of Nuln.'

To the right of the furnaces the cave narrowed down to a yawning black hole into which vanished more iron rails. A long train of slaves was shuffling into the hole, six abreast. They were shackled at the ankles and carried pickaxes over their shoulders. Huge Kurgan overseers herded them forward, bellowing and cracking whips over their heads. At their sides were huge, leashed hounds that lunged and barked at the slaves.

More slaves pushed large wooden carts out of the hole on the iron rails, then pulled them up long ramps supported by a wooden scaffolding that rose over the mounds of ore. They tipped the contents of the carts onto the heaps, then lowered them back down the ramp and into the hole again.

The slaves were men, women and children, but so gaunt and starved, so careworn and covered in filth that it was difficult to determine their sex or age. They all looked like stooped old men, hair lank and patchy, faces lined and slack. Their eyes were as dull as dry clay. Many were horribly maimed, missing fingers or hands or arms or eyes. Some limped around on poorly-fashioned wooden legs. Whip marks criss-crossed their naked backs, and shiny patches of scar tissue from countless burns covered their arms and legs. Their overseers took no pity on them, however, kicking and whipping those who lagged or paused in their labours, and beating mercilessly any that showed even the slightest glimmer of fight.

Franz clenched his fists. 'The animals! I'll kill them all!'

At the backs of the furnaces more slaves fed split logs into roaring fireboxes, while others worked great bellows, as big as rich men's beds. At the front, slaves in heavy aprons and thick gloves dragged stone moulds shaped like keg-sized loaves of bread under endless streams of white-hot molten iron. As each mould was filled, it was dragged aside and replaced by another. Off to one side, iron loaves that had cooled were knocked out of the moulds with wooden mauls and loaded onto carts.

Reiner watched a cart as it rolled into a further chamber. It was hard to see through the smoke, but he thought he could make out the fires of forges and the glistening bodies of smiths making armour and weapons with terrifying industry and piling them into great heaps. And beyond that... He squinted and shielded his eyes from a harsh white light. What fresh horror was this? It looked almost like... His heart lurched as he realised that he was looking outside, and that it was daylight. He hadn't realised how much he'd longed for it. But as his eyes adjusted to the brightness he saw buildings and stables and Chaos troops milling about, and most discouraging of all, the great stone battlements they had seen when they first entered the valley the night before.

Hals sighed. 'We've to get through all that?'

'We'll find a way, lad,' said Reiner. 'Don't worry.' But he wished someone would tell him how. He was about to ask for suggestions, when something else caught his eye. A wide column of Kurgan warriors was marching into the caves from outside. They looked to be the same fellows who had chased them here in the first place, but instead of the ragged leathers and bits and pieces of plundered armour they had worn before, now they wore matching suits of shining armour that encased breast, back, shoulders and arms. Close fitting helms hid their shaggy heads and long skirts of chainmail covered their legs. All was brand new, undented and flawless, and the spears and axes and swords they rested on their shoulders were freshly made as well, the honed edges flashing red in the furnace glow.

The column snaked out of the cave and back through the enclosure beyond with no end in sight. It looked like an army on the march, but where could they be marching to? There wasn't enough room for them all in the furnace cavern. Were they coming to slaughter all the slaves? That made no sense. Were there barracks further into the caves?

The head of the column wound between the furnaces and the mountains of ore, scattering slaves left and right, then marched straight into the minehead tunnel.

'Where are they going?' he muttered.

'Maybe there's been an insurrection in the mines,' said Franz hopefully.

Reiner shook his head. 'Look at those poor fellows. You think they have the energy to revolt? Let alone the will?'

'Captain,' said Pavel. 'Look!'

Reiner looked back toward the cave entrance. The end of the column of troops was at last in sight, and there was a sting in its tail. A phalanx of slaves was pulling a huge cannon on a massive gun carriage.

Ulf sucked in a horrified breath. 'Cannon!' he whispered. 'They have a cannon.'

'Impossible,' said Hals, pushing forward. 'Chaos troops don't have guns. They haven't the know-how.'

'Then someone has given it to them,' said Reiner.

# CHAPTER ELEVEN
## THE END OF THE EMPIRE

CAUTIOUSLY, SO AS not to draw attention to their hiding place, Reiner studied the massive cannon the slaves pulled. It was the biggest field piece he had ever seen, twice as long as the Empire's great cannon, with a muzzle as wide as a keg of Marienburg ale. Its mouth was decorated to resemble a screaming daemonic maw, ringed with fangs. The barrel was detailed in silver dragon scales and barbaric designs. The carriage that it rested upon was made in the shape of two crouching legs, also scaled, that gripped the axle in two immense bronze claws. Its wooden wheels were each as tall as a man.

Reiner shivered. 'A few of those would turn the tide of a battle, eh?'

Franz looked around at him, eyes wide. 'Sigmar! Pray there isn't more than one!'

'But where did they get the knowledge?' asked Ulf. 'The secrets of gunnery are the Empire's most closely guarded.'

His question was answered as they saw the figures that followed the gun, berating the slaves who pulled it. They were half the height of the smallest slave, but bulging with muscles, and wore beards braided to their knees.

'Dwarfs!' said Franz, gaping.

'Those are dwarfs?' asked Pavel, uncertainly.

Reiner looked closer. He hadn't seen many dwarfs in his lifetime – they didn't come much to Altdorf – but these fellows looked like no dwarf he'd ever encountered. They seemed almost deformed by their muscles: stumping around on twisted but powerful legs. Their heads were distorted by ridges of bone, and their hands crowded with extra fingers.

'Bent on the forge of Chaos,' said Gustaf under his breath.

Reiner shivered.

'The forces of Chaos with artillery,' groaned Ulf. 'This could mean the end of the Empire. They must be stopped. We must tell someone.'

'Certainly,' said Pavel sourly. 'Right after we get out of here.'

Reiner shook his head as the warriors continued to file into the tunnel. 'I don't understand it. They can't be going to make war underground. No one in their right mind, not even a Chaos-crazed berzerker, fires a cannon in a mine. What do they mean to do?'

'They go south to fight a battle,' said Gustaf. 'There are old tunnels beneath the mine that run the length of the range.'

Everyone turned to stare at him.

'How do you know this?' asked Reiner.

'I overheard the patrol who passed us speaking of it.'

Reiner raised an eyebrow. 'You understand their jabber?'

'Course he does,' said Hals, spitting. 'A servant always learns his master's tongue. I knew there was something wrong about you, y'daemon worshipping filth.'

'If I serve the dark ones, then why am I not betraying you now?'

'And how *do* you come to speak their language?' asked Reiner.

Gustaf looked for a moment as if he wasn't going to speak, then he sighed. 'I don't, but it is similar to the tongue of the Kossars. The company of lancers I served with in Kislev had a detachment of Kossar horse. I learned their speech – particularly their curses – when I treated their wounds.'

The others eyed him cooly, weighing this. They didn't look as if they believed him.

'What else did they say?' asked Reiner. 'Did they give any details?'

Gustaf shrugged. 'As I said, I only speak a few words. They said the word south, and tunnel, and castle. I got the idea that they were going to fight at the castle, though whether they were fighting to take it or defend it, I don't know. They said the name. Norse something? North, perhaps?'

Reiner's heart thudded in his chest. 'Nordbergbruche!'

'It might have been.'

'Ain't that Lord Manfred's castle?' asked Pavel. 'What Captain Veirt was going on about? Didn't he say the northers had taken it?'

'Aye,' said Reiner. He turned on Gustaf. 'Why didn't you tell us this earlier?'

'You didn't ask.'

Reiner curled his lip and turned back to the cave in time to see the cannon vanish into the tunnel. He thought furiously. It would be a terrible blow to the Empire if that cannon was loosed upon it. But did he care? The Empire had jailed and branded him unjustly. He owed it no favours. At the same time, it might be in his best interests to help his homeland. If Manfred could be convinced to reward them for warning him of his brother's treachery, how much bigger might the reward be if Reiner informed him of the coming of the cannon as well?

He gnawed a knuckle. Which was the least dangerous path? Which was the most profitable? How did he decide?

At last he turned. 'Well lads, I've a plan. I doubt any of you will like it much. But I think it's our best chance, so we'll put it to a vote, eh?'

The men waited patiently. Gustaf folded his arms.

Reiner swallowed. 'It's my guess that Count Manfred is waiting for Albrecht to join him before the two of them storm Nordbergbruche together. And as soon as he gets Lady Magda's banner Albrecht will be on his way, but not to help his brother. I think he's marching to fight him, army against army, and with that unholy thing on his side, Albrecht may well win.' Reiner coughed uneasily. 'If we somehow found a way out of here and made it down to the flatlands without running into more northers, it would take us weeks, maybe a month, to circle the mountains and make it to Nordbergbruche – if we're lucky and aren't eaten by Sigmar-knows-what along the way. By that time the battle might already have occurred. Albrecht may have won, and we would be too late to warn Manfred and collect our reward.' He pointed down toward the minehead. 'These fellows have found a short cut, a direct line from here to there. I... I say we take it.'

There were grunts of shock and dismay.

'I know it's a rotten idea,' said Reiner. 'But I think it's the only way we can make it in time. What do you say?'

There was a long silence. Finally Hals chuckled.

'Laddie,' he said. 'That speech you made, back there at the cave-in, about leading us wrong at every turn. Well, most of it was true, I suppose. But y'still have more ideas than the rest of us, and one's bound to come right one of these days, so... I'm with you.'

'And I,' said Pavel.

'And I,' said Franz.

'The Empire must be told of these cannon as soon as possible,' said Ulf. 'Count me in.'

Giano spread his hands. 'One way is as bad as the other, hey?'

'Go into the mine?' asked Oskar numbly.

Gustaf shrugged. 'I wouldn't make it on my own, would I?'

'You might not make it *with* us, daemon worshipper,' snarled Hals.

Gustaf curled his lip. 'That's as may be, but you certainly won't make it without me.'

'And what's the meaning of that?' asked Reiner, looking up.

Gustaf smirked. 'The Kurgan spoke of an obstacle, a choke point near the end of the tunnels, that we will have difficulty circumventing. But there is a way.'

'What is it?' asked Reiner. 'How do we get around it?'

Gustaf shook his head. 'Do you think me a fool? I know what you think of me. I know you'd stick a knife in my guts if you thought I was no longer useful to you. Consider this extra protection against... accidents.'

Reiner and the others glared at him.

'You really are a loathsome little worm,' said Reiner at last. He turned away before Gustaf had a chance to retort, and clapped his hands. 'Right then,' he said. 'It's decided. Now the trick is getting to the minehead undetected.'

'Go into the mines?' asked Oskar again, mournfully.

'Sorry, old man,' said Reiner. 'But Gustaf will take care of you.' He shot the surgeon a look. 'Won't you, Gustaf?'

They returned to the main passage. After fifty paces, the rails sloped down a ramp to the level of the cave floor as the noises of hammering and the roar of fire grew louder and louder. At its base, the ramp bent right into a short corridor. A narrow passage intersected it, and ten paces beyond that, it opened into the giant cavern. Reiner could see ranks of smiths at their anvils, hammering out swords and pieces of armour as slaves scurried around them, holding the work steady, feeding the fires, squeezing the bellows. The cross corridor looked more promising. It was small and dark and smelled of death, decay, and cooking meat.

'Smells like pork,' said Pavel hungrily.

Gustaf snorted. 'Two legged pork.'

'Shut your mouth, y'filthy dog,' snarled Hals.

'Quiet,' said Reiner. 'Now douse torches. Weapons out.'

The men drew their swords and daggers, then slipped around the corner into the dark passage. The stench was almost overwhelming and it only got worse as they continued – as did the noise. Twenty paces along they saw ahead of them on the left wall a tiny, leather-curtained doorway, through which came a ground-shaking hammering and flashes of blinding green light, and under the deafening banging, a chorus of guttural voices chanting in unison. A moment later the curtain flipped open and two slaves pushed through it, dragging a third, who was obviously dead.

Reiner and the others halted and held their breath, but the slaves looked neither left or right, only hauled their burden listlessly down the hall, oblivious. Reiner crept to the curtain and peeked through, then drew back reflexively at the sight that met his eyes. After waiting a moment to quiet his heart, he looked again. The others peered over his shoulders.

Through the tiny door was a pillared, seven-sided room that had been hacked crudely out of the living rock. Towering representations of blood-red daemons were painted on each of the seven walls, though whether they were seven different entities or seven aspects of the same god, Reiner didn't know. Seven pillars surrounded a raised dais. On his first glance Reiner had thought that the pillars were decorated with carvings of skulls, but a second look showed that the skulls were real – with chipped teeth and crushed crowns – and covered every inch of the pillars from floor to ceiling. There were thousands of them.

But what had made Reiner draw back in fear were the occupants of the room. A ring of armoured Kurgan stood along the walls, chanting unceasingly. They were bareheaded, and Reiner could see that their eyes were rolled back in their heads. Lines and sigils had been smeared on their cheeks with blood. The focus of their attention was the dais in the centre of the room. Here, where one would have expected some heathen altar, there stood instead a huge iron anvil, with a glowing furnace beside it, and a wide, shallow basin before it, filled with a red liquid that could only be blood. Behind the altar a hulking, barely-human smith worked a set of enormous bellows. He stood seven feet tall if he was an inch, and his massive, muscled arms each looked as big around as Reiner's ribcage. He was stripped to the waist and covered in a pattern of scars and burns that looked more decorative than accidental. Lank black hair hung over his face, hiding it, but Reiner could see the flash of white tusks jutting up from the corners of his mouth and two blunt horns pushing through the skin of his brow.

A wild-eyed shaman with a dreadlocked beard and hairy robes that seemed to have been stitched from scalps stood at his side, leading the chanting in a hoarse voice. Two Kurgan warriors stood at the edge of the dais holding a sagging slave between them. More slaves stood behind the first.

As Reiner and the others watched, the giant smith pulled a glowing blade from the furnace by the naked tang and set it on the anvil. He raised a mighty hammer over his head and began beating the edge of the blade with it. Though the blade glowed orange-white, the sparks that flew at each hammer-fall were an eerie green that burned Reiner's eyes as if he was looking directly into the sun. The host of Kurgan grunted in unison with each hammer fall.

With a final blow, the smith finished shaping the blade and held it flat on the anvil. As the chanting rose to a fever pitch, the shaman stepped forward, wielding a smaller hammer and an iron implement that looked something like a wine bottle. He set the base of the iron bottle on the blade, just above the tang, and smote it with the hammer as the warriors barked a two syllable word. More green sparks splashed and the smith raised the blade. It had been imprinted with a crude runic symbol that Reiner's eyes shied uneasily away from.

At a signal from the shaman, the Kurgan guards shoved a slave forward. In unison, the smith, the shaman and the assembled Kurgan shouted a short, guttural incantation, then the smith ran the slave through with the still glowing blade. It hissed. The slave screamed and doubled up. The smith, with inhuman strength, lifted the slave off the ground on the point and held him aloft until the blood from his wound ran, spitting and boiling, down the fuller to fill the pattern of the stamped rune.

Reiner flinched back involuntarily again, for as the blood touched the rune, the sword suddenly seemed to have a presence. It felt as if some malevolent entity had entered the temple. The warriors fell to their knees and raised their arms in adulation.

Reiner and the others cringed back from the curtain, grimacing, as the smith gave the blade to the shaman, who held it over his head and showed it to the ring of warriors. They roared their approval.

'Are we tainted just for seeing that?' asked Franz.

'It pains a son of Sigmar,' said Hals, 'to see a hammer used for so evil a purpose.'

Ulf raised a hand. 'The slaves return.'

The company backed into the shadows as the two slaves – a man and a woman, they could now see, both skeleton thin – padded back to the curtained door and passed through it. After a moment, they reappeared, dragging the body of the impaled slave behind them and disappeared once again down the dark hallway.

After waiting a moment, Reiner motioned them forward.

Franz shivered. 'I dread to see what lies at the end of this.'

Reiner patted the boy's shoulder. 'What in death could be worse than the life these poor souls have suffered in bondage?'

As they continued down the hall, the reek of death increased. There was more light ahead as well. Faint torch-glow shone from two curtained doorways, one on either side of the hall. They reached the left-hand one first and Reiner cautiously peeked in.

It was an enormous room: not deep, but so long that the two ends were hidden in darkness. A wide doorway on the opposite wall opened directly into the cavern that housed the furnaces, and through it Reiner could see the lines of bucket-toting slaves making their endless rounds. The room itself was filled with rank after rank of poorly-made plank beds, stacked six high and none as wide as Ulf's shoulders.

The beds to the left side of the door were empty. Those to the right were full of bony, huddled forms, their elbows, knees and hips raw and bruised from lying on the naked wood. They moaned and coughed and twitched in their fitful slumbers, or worse, moved not at all.

As Reiner watched, a curious procession came into view between two rows of beds. A Kurgan guard swaggered along, followed by four slaves pushing a flat cart piled with bodies. The Kurgan had a sharp stick, and with it, he prodded the sleeping slaves one by one. Most flinched and cried out. Those that didn't, the Kurgan jabbed again, harder this time. If a slave still failed to respond, the Kurgan dragged him off his plank and threw him on the cart, then moved on.

At the end of the row the cart was full and the Kurgan barked an order. Reiner ducked back as the slaves turned the cart toward him, and waved the others back down the hall into the shadows.

The Kurgan led the slaves out of the barracks and into the door on the opposite side of the hall. After a pause Reiner edged to it, at once compelled by curiosity and terrified at what he might see. The others followed. Reiner looked in, hoping against hope that what he would see would be some kind of embalming chamber or garbage pit. It was not. It was what his nose told him it would be: a kitchen. He pulled back, disgusted, and pushed Franz past the door. 'Don't look, lad. Keep moving.'

Franz made to protest, but Reiner shoved him roughly down the hall. He and the others slipped past in ones and twos as it was safe, and continued down the hall, shuddering with revulsion at the sights within the kitchen. Reiner wished he could get the smell of meat out of his nose.

A little further on, Ulf stopped at another open door. 'Wait,' he whispered. 'In here.'

He entered the room. The others looked in. Ulf was picking though piles of poorly made picks and shovels that were heaped against the walls along with stacks of pitch-smeared torches, coils of rope, wooden buckets, lengths of chain, sections of iron rail, iron wheels, leather aprons and gloves. All were of poorest quality – made by slaves, for slaves.

'If we are to travel long underground,' said Ulf as the others entered, 'we will want torches and rope, and possibly picks and shovels as well. Everyone should take what they can.'

'We're not all built like pack horses, engineer,' said Hals.

Ulf slung a coil of rope over his shoulder. 'We've encountered one cave-in already. We may have to dig our way out of another. Then there are the dangers of pitfalls, uncrossable chasms, unscalable cliffs. We may need to widen a passage to get through. Or block a passage to prevent pursuit. And...'

'All right, Urquart,' said Reiner quickly. 'You've made your point. We don't want to give Oskar the fibertygibbits again. Everyone take torches and rope. For the rest you may do as you please.'

Everyone did as he asked. Hals, though he had complained the loudest, took a pick and gave a shovel to Pavel. When all had been packed away, they moved on.

The passage ended fifty paces later in a doorway through which shone the red glow of the main cavern. Reiner and the others eased forward to peer through. The doorway came out just behind the two massive furnaces. The slaves that fed the fires and their overseers were less than three long strides from the door. Reiner could have spat on them. Instead, he looked toward the minehead, just beyond the furnaces to the right. It was close. A short sprint and they would be within its shadow and away, but that sprint was fraught with dangers.

At least a dozen Kurgan guards stood between them and the mine head, and there were a hundred within easy call. Reiner frowned. If only there was some way to distract them, to draw the attention of the entire room for the few seconds they needed to dart through unnoticed.

And just as he thought it, a great, almost musical, crash sounded through the cavern. Every head looked up, Kurgan and slave alike. The crash came again. Reiner craned his neck and saw to the left, a Kurgan beating a cracked gong, hung from a rope, as out of the wide door that led from the sleeping quarters came a procession of slaves staggering under the weight of huge steaming cauldrons they carried on long poles.

The overseers barked orders to their work parties and motioned them toward the centre of the cavern where the kitchen slaves were setting the cauldrons. There was no need for orders. The slaves downed tools and flocked toward the stew pots like wolves running down a deer, licking their lips and fighting each other to be first in line.

Pavel turned away, shuddering.

'Don't blame them, lad,' said Reiner. 'Blame the fiends who drove them to it. Now pull yourselves together. We daren't miss this chance.'

The furnaces were deserted. Reiner and the rest darted around the right hand one, taking cover behind its great bulk. They were instantly drenched in sweat from the heat that radiated from it. To their left the cave wall narrowed to the blackness of the minehead. They crept along it, crouching low.

Halfway to the hole they ran out of cover. They would have to make the last thirty feet out in the open. Reiner stood on his toes to see where the Kurgan were. All of them seemed fully occupied at the stew pots, the overseers reaching in and stealing the choicer bits of flesh from the slaves. He turned to the men.

'Ready, lads?'

Everyone except Oskar nodded.

'Keep him pointed in the right direction.' Reiner said to Gustaf, then took one last look toward the centre of the cave. 'Right,' he said. 'Run.'

The men ran fast and low, Gustaf holding Oskar down by the scruff of the neck. The run lasted only a few seconds, but it seemed an eternity to Reiner, who swore he could feel the eyes of every Kurgan in the cave turning towards him. But as they sprinted into the black mouth of the mine no shouts echoed down the cave, no gongs crashed, no arrows rattled off the rocks around them. They reined to a stop twenty paces into the shadow and looked back. No one was coming after them.

'We make it, hey?' said Giano, smiling.

'Aye,' said Pavel dryly. 'The first step in a thousand-league journey.'

'Less of that, pikeman!' growled Reiner, unconsciously mimicking Veirt. 'Now come on. I want to be well away from here.'

'As do I,' said Hals.

They started down the long dark passage, not yet sure enough of their surroundings to light torches. Behind him, Reiner could hear Oskar whimper as the blackness closed in completely around them.

# CHAPTER TWELVE
# THERE IS NO GOOD DECISION HERE

AFTER A HALF hour of utter darkness and silence it seemed safe to light torches, and all breathed sighs of relief. All except Oskar. The soothing effects of Gustaf's draught were wearing off and he began to look around uneasily and mutter about, 'The weight. The stone. There is no air.'

'Why ever did you decide to become a soldier, gunner?' grumbled Hals. 'Is there nothing you ain't afraid of?'

'I never meant to be a soldier,' murmured Oskar, slurring a little. 'I was m'lord Gottenstet's secretary. I wrote his correspondence for him. Read it too. Illiterate, the old fool. But one day...' he sighed and stopped.

The others waited for him to continue, but he seemed to have forgotten he was talking.

'One day, what?' asked Pavel, annoyed.

'Eh?' said Oskar. 'Oh... yes. Well, one day I was with m'lord as he was surveying some land he owned. He wanted to build a, a hunting lodge I think it was. And while the surveyor was using his plumb line and his measuring sticks to calculate distances and heights, I was guessing, and coming right almost to the foot. I picked out far away things that the surveyor needed his spyglass to make out. "Sigmar's lightning, lad," says Gottenstet. "Y've the making of a fine mortar man." And nothing would do but he must send me to the Artillery School at Nuln. Me! A scholar! I tried to tell him that though my eyes might be strong, my insides were weak, but he would have none of it.' He shrugged. 'Of course I didn't help matters by coming out top of my class. I liked the work: making the sightings, calling out the degrees, but on the field...' He shivered and hugged his shoulders. 'Did you ever see the fire from the sky? The thing with the mouths.' He looked around him suddenly as if waking up, his eyes widening as he took in the close stone walls, the low ceiling. 'The weight,' he murmured. 'Sigmar, save us, the weight. Can't breathe.'

Reiner grimaced, uncomfortable. 'Gustaf, give him another sip, will you?'

THE CORRIDOR SANK deeper and deeper into the mountains. Occasionally corridors branched off to the left and right, iron rails gleaming away into the shadows. Some were barricaded off and the party could see evidence of cave-ins behind them, but there was no confusion on which way to go. The deep tracks of the cannon's wheels always pointed the way.

A while later the iron rails began to sing, and soon after came a metallic rumbling. The company doused their torches and ducked into a side tunnel. After a moment a train of carts rolled by, full of ore, each pushed by a team of shackled slaves, their eyes dull. A Kurgan overseer reclined in the first cart, a lantern at his side.

Franz cursed under his breath once they'd passed. 'So many of them, and one of him. Couldn't they strangle him? Dump him down a shaft?'

'And then?' asked Reiner.

The boy grunted with frustration, but couldn't answer.

As the train's rumble faded, it revealed nearer sounds: the thud and chunk of picks biting into rock, the crack of whips, the barking of hounds. They stepped back into the main corridor and looked forward. A faint light picked out distant sections of wall, the glint of rails.

Reiner looked at the cannon's wheel tracks, running straight ahead and sighed. 'It looks as if the warband marched beyond the work party. We will have to take side corridors around them and hope we can find the tracks on the other side. Keep the torches dark. We'll travel by the lantern only.'

They continued forward in the main tunnel until the reflected light became bright enough for them to be able to see each other's faces, then began hunting for cross corridors. The sounds of mining came mostly from the left of the main tunnel, so they edged right, taking thinner tunnels and winding crawlways.

After a time they found a promising corridor that paralleled the main corridor. It was nearly as wide and had rails running down the centre. These seemed both newer and cruder than the rails they had followed from the ironworks. The sounds of mining reached them only as echoes here, and came more from their left than from in front of them. Reiner began to feel almost hopeful. As long as they could find a way back to the main tunnel from here, there was a good chance they would pass the work party without incident.

But just as he thought it, the rails began to ring and rattle. There were carts coming. Reiner groaned. 'Speak of evil...'

There was a small side tunnel up ahead. Reiner pointed to it. 'In there. It has no rails.' They hurried into it. It ended after thirty paces in a round, dug-out area with no other exit – a dead end.

'Right,' said Reiner. 'We'll wait here until they pass.'

The echoing rumble of wheels grew suddenly louder, and the torch glow much brighter, as if the approaching carts had turned a corner. The men faced back to the wide corridor, hands on their weapons. Giano shuttered his lantern and hid it behind him. As they watched, a procession of four heavily loaded carts passed by their hiding place. A Kurgan guard followed the carts, torch in one hand and a huge hound on a leash snuffling along at his side.

The Kurgan walked on, kicking pebbles, but the hound stopped, sniffing at the mouth of the tunnel. The Kurgan tugged on his leash, but the hound refused to move.

Reiner's shoulders tensed. 'Go,' he whispered under his breath. 'Go. Go!'

The Kurgan stopped and cursed the hound, jerking its leash. The hound snarled at him, then began barking down the corridor.

'Sigmar curse you, heathen,' muttered Hals. 'Beat that cur. Make him heel.'

But the Kurgan had decided that the hound was on to something and came forward warily, the hound still barking and straining at his leash.

Reiner and the rest backed out of sight into the round chamber. 'Better kill 'em quick,' whispered Reiner, drawing his sword. 'But no guns, or they'll all be down on us.'

The others armed themselves.

'We should draw 'em in,' said Hals. 'Get 'em from all sides.'

'Good idea,' said Reiner. 'Franz, you're the bait.'

'What?' said Franz, confused.

Reiner shoved the boy hard between the shoulder blades. He stumbled out of cover and froze like a rabbit, staring up the tunnel at the advancing Kurgan in wide-eyed terror. The Kurgan roared a challenge and ran forward, dropping the hound's leash and drawing a hand axe.

The hound bounded forward, baying savagely. Franz scurried for the back wall. 'You bastard!' he shrieked at Reiner. 'You dirty bastard!'

Pavel stuck his spear out across the opening at ankle height as the Kurgan and the hound charged in. The beast leapt it easily, but the norther fell flat on his face and Hals, Giano and Reiner stuck him with their spears and swords. Ulf swung his maul at the hound and knocked it sideways as it lunged at Franz.

The monster landed, snarling, and spun to meet this new threat. Ulf raised his hammer as it leapt, and jammed the haft between its gaping jaws, stopping its fangs from reaching his neck, but the beast was so massive it knocked the big man flat and began raking at him with its claws.

The Kurgan surged up, screaming fury and bleeding from three grievous wounds. Reiner was afraid they had another iron-skinned berserker on their hands, but fortunately, though as big as a bull, the guard was no chosen champion, only a ranker, stuck in the mines guarding slaves while others won glory on the fields of honour. Reiner chopped halfway through his windpipe and he died on his knees, breathing his last through his neck.

The hound was another matter. Franz and Oskar were slashing at it with their swords, but their blows couldn't penetrate the beast's matted coat. Ulf, on his back under the monster, was forcing its head back with the haft of his maul, but his straining arms were being shredded by its claws.

Reiner ran forward with Hals and Pavel. Giano dropped his sword and unslung his crossbow, drawing a bolt from his quiver. Gustaf kept out of the way, as usual.

Reiner slashed at the hound's back legs, severing its left hamstring. It howled and turned, but fell as it put weight on its dead leg. Pavel and Hals gored it in the side with their spears. Still it fought, twisting so savagely that Pavel's spear was wrenched out of his fever-weakened hands and cracked Hals in the forehead. The hound lunged for the dazed pikeman, but Ulf, freed of its weight, clubbed it with all his might, square on its spinal ridge. It dropped flat, its legs splayed. Giano stepped forward and fired his crossbow point blank. The bolt pinned the monster's head to the ground. It died in a spreading pool of blood.

'Nice work, lads,' said Reiner. 'Ulf, are you badly hurt? Hals?'

'Just a little swimmy, captain,' said Hals. 'It'll pass.'

'I've had worse,' said Ulf, grimacing as he examined his lacerated biceps. 'But not by much.'

'Just coming,' said Gustaf. He began opening his kit.

Reiner looked toward the corridor, listening for reinforcements, and froze, heart thudding, as he saw half a dozen faces looking back at him. The slaves were peering anxiously down the tunnel at them. Reiner had forgotten all about them.

'What do we do about that lot?' asked Hals, joining him.

Pavel looked up. 'Poor devils.'

'We must free them!' said Franz. 'Bring them with us.'

'You crazy, boy,' said Giano. 'They slow us down. We no make it.'

'But we can't leave 'em here,' said Pavel. 'The Kurgan'd kill 'em sure.'

Ulf grunted as Gustaf cleaned his wounds. 'The Kurgan will kill them regardless, whether now or later.'

'It's your decision, captain,' said Hals.

Reiner cursed under his breath. 'This is exactly why I don't want to lead. There is no good decision here.'

He chewed his lip, thinking, but whichever way he turned it, it was bad.

'Your best course is to put them out of their misery,' said Gustaf. 'They are no longer men.'

'What does a monster know of men?' spit Hals.

Reiner wanted to punch Gustaf, not for being wrong, but for being right. The surgeon always took the bleakest view of every situation, had the most cynical view of human nature, and so often turned out to be one Reiner should have listened to. Killing them *would* be best. The slaves were too weak to keep up, and would stretch their food supply much too thin, but Reiner could feel Franz's eyes hot upon him, and Pavel's one-eyed gaze as well, and couldn't give the order.

'We... we'll free them, and... and offer them the choice to follow us or not.' He flushed as he said it, for it was a horrible equivocation, a mere sop to common sense. What other choice did the slaves have? He was dooming the men who depended on him because he hadn't the heart to kill men who were virtually dead already.

Franz and Pavel nodded, satisfied, but Gustaf made a disgusted sound and Giano groaned. The rest looked non-committal. Reiner fished the keys from the dead Kurgan's belt and started down the tunnel to the larger corridor.

Franz fell in beside him. 'That was a rotten trick just then, pushing me into danger.'

Reiner's teeth clenched. He was tired of feeling guilty. 'I had faith in you.'

'But I've lost a little in you,' the boy countered, then shrugged. 'Though you do a brave thing here.'

'I do a foolish thing here.'

The slaves edged warily back as Reiner and his men came out of the tunnel. There were sixteen of them, four teams to push the four carts, which were filled with waste rock. Each starveling quartet was shackled together at the ankles.

Reiner held up the keys. 'Don't be afraid. We're going to free you.'

The slaves stared, uncomprehending, and flinched back again as he approached them.

'Hold still.'

The slaves did as they were told. Commands seemed the only speech they understood. Reiner squatted and unlocked the four locks in turn. Franz and Pavel followed behind him, pulling the chain that linked them out through the slaves' shackles until all were free.

Reiner faced them. 'There you are. You are slaves no more. We welcome you to follow us to freedom, or... or to take what path you think best.'

The slaves blinked at him, eyes blank. Reiner coughed. What was wrong with them? Were they deaf? 'Do you understand? You're free. You can travel with us if you wish.'

One of the slaves, a woman with no hair, began to weep, a dry, scratchy sound.

'It's a trick,' said another. 'They mean to trap us again.'

'Stop torturing us!' cried a third.

'It isn't a trick,' said Franz, as the slaves whispered among themselves. 'You are truly free.'

'Don't listen to them!' said the slave who had first spoken. 'They only mean to catch us out. Go back to the work face! Warn the masters!'

He backed away from Reiner and began running back down the corridor. The others ran with him, like sheep running because other sheep were running.

'Curse it!' growled Reiner. 'Stop!' He grabbed at a fleeing slave, but the skeletal man squirmed out of his fingers. 'Stop them!' he called to the others.

'What are they doing?' asked Franz, confounded, as the others tried to corral the slaves. 'Why are they running?'

'They are lost, as I told you,' said Gustaf, sneering.

Pavel, Hals, Oskar and Giano grabbed a handful of the slaves and pushed them to the floor, but more were disappearing into darkness.

'Never mind why,' said Reiner, running down the hall. 'We have to shut them up before they bring their overseers down on us. Giano, bring the lantern!'

Reiner and Franz chased the slaves with Giano, Ulf and Hals running behind them, Giano's slotted lantern throwing dancing bars of light on the uneven walls. Reiner was surprised at how fast the slaves moved. He thought they would be weak from starvation, but it seemed that their constant labour had given them a wiry strength, and Reiner and the others had difficulty keeping up, let alone catching up, for the slaves seemed to know every inch of the tunnels in the dark.

'Come back, curse you!' he called after them, but this order they did not follow.

The slaves reached the main corridor and turned right. As he angled in behind them, Reiner could see the glow of torches up ahead. He put on a burst of speed and caught the last slave around the neck, bringing him down.

The slave cried out. The others leapt ahead, wailing, and scattered. Some continued down the main corridor. Some swerved into side corridors. All started shouting as loud as their rusty voices would allow.

'Masters! Masters! Help!'

'Interlopers, masters! Protect us!'

'They have killed our overseer!'

Franz darted into the first side corridor after two slaves, but Reiner collared him and pulled him back.

'Don't be a fool! We must stick together.'

'Too late anyway,' sighed Giano, as hounds began to bay and harsh Kurgan orders echoed through the tunnels. The thud of heavy boots began to converge on them.

Reiner groaned. 'Back to the others, quick.'

He turned and started running back down the corridor, Franz, Giano, Oskar and Hals following in his wake.

Franz seemed almost on the point of tears. 'Why did they do it? We only wanted to help them.'

'Been underground so long,' said Hals, 'they believe no more in the sun.'

'I don't understand,' Franz wailed.

'I'll explain it to you if we live,' said Reiner. 'Now run.'

They sprinted back toward where they had left the others. The Kurgan were too big to move quickly, and did not gain on them, but the hounds were faster than horses. Reiner could hear their baying coming closer and closer. At last he rounded a bend in the corridor and saw Pavel, Oskar, and Gustaf by the mine carts, standing guard over the slaves they had caught.

'Run!' called Reiner.

'Up, you lot,' growled Pavel to the slaves, prodding them with his spear. 'Get moving.'

But when he and Oskar let them up the slaves ran toward Reiner and his companions. Reiner tried to stop one as she ran by, as did Franz, but the slaves dodged away from them and ran on, toward the hounds.

'The fools,' sobbed Franz.

The company squeezed past the mine carts. Screams of agony and animal snarls echoed from behind. Reiner felt a stab of self-loathing as he found himself hoping that the hounds would stop to eat the slaves that he had gone to such pains to free only moments earlier. This did not appear to be the case, for the baying and shouting continued to grow louder.

They rounded another bend and Giano fell sprawling over some loose rock. The lantern bounced out of his hand and smashed on the rail. The flame went out. Total darkness closed over them. They jumbled to a stop.

'Myrmidia curse me!' cried Giano.

'No one move,' said Reiner as the baying and running boots echoed ever closer. 'All hold hands. If you are not holding a hand, speak up.'

He stretched out and took a rough hand. He had no idea who it was.

'I stand alone,' said Gustaf.

'You certainly do, mate,' said Hals.

Reiner reached toward Gustaf's voice. 'Take my hand.'

Gustaf's soft fleshy hand batted at his, then caught it.

'Hurry!' wailed Oskar. 'They're coming!'

Reiner looked back. Far down the corridor, huge hound shadows bounded and swooped along the walls. Then the hounds themselves came into view, massive black silhouettes running ahead of the Chaos troops' torches.

Reiner turned and ran, forgetting to give an order. There was no need. The rest ran with him, blind as bats, whimpering in their throats. They all knew it was useless to run, but it was impossible not to. Fear drove their legs, not thought – the primal instinct for flight in the face of certain death.

Reiner tripped over the rails, caught himself, and crowded against the wall to avoid the ties. He could hear Gustaf wheezing and stumbling behind him, and not twenty paces behind him, the panting and snarling of the hounds.

So this was it, Reiner thought. He was going to die, lost to all he loved and all who loved him, in a black tunnel under the Middle Mountains, eaten by monstrous hounds. The things he had yet to do crowded into his head, all the money he hadn't yet won or spent, all the women he had yet to bed, books unread, the loves unloved. He found himself weeping with regret. It had all been so damned useless, the whole horrible journey – his whole life.

Franz shrieked from the back of the line. Ulf roared something incoherent and Reiner heard an impact and an animal yelp. He looked back, but there was little to see except leaping shadows and bobbing torches in the distance.

'Franz?'

The boy's answer was lost as, at the head of the line, Giano screamed. His scream was repeated by Pavel and Hals. And there was a sound of rattling pebbles and strange echoes. Reiner tried to halt before he ran into the hidden danger, but Gustaf, Ulf and Franz piled into him from behind, sending him flying forward again.

'Wait!' he cried. 'Something…'

His left foot came down on empty air. He yelled in surprise and threw his hands out, expecting to hit the tunnel floor face first. His hands touched nothing. There was nothing below him.

He was falling into a bottomless void.

# CHAPTER THIRTEEN
# ALL IS NOT ENTIRELY LOST

THE FALL WAS just long enough to allow Reiner to wonder how far down the bottom was, and too tense for the inevitable fatal bone-shattering, organ-exploding impact. But when it came at last it was less of a slam than a slide.

Not that it wasn't painful.

Reiner's first thought was that he was scraping against the cliff he was falling past, but the surface that was abrading his clothes was loose and crumbly and slid with him. It quickly turned into an almost perpendicular slope, made up of gravel, dirt and large rocks. Reiner caught one of these amidships and curled up in blinding pain. He began rolling and bouncing down the slope at breakneck speed, scraping and bashing his elbows and knees and shoulders. His brain bounced around in his head until he had no idea which way was up, if he was alive or dead, broken or whole. Only half conscious, he buried his head in his arms as the angle of the slope began to grow less acute and the speed of his fall to lessen.

He was just slowing to a stop, sliding down the mound, half buried in an avalanche of gravel, and thinking that he might possibly have survived, when a body dropped on his chest, crushing his ribs, and bounced away again, grunting. Reiner gasped, but couldn't draw a breath. It felt as if his lungs were locked in a vice.

A second body, lighter, but bonier, landed on his face. A knee cracked him in the nose and blood flooded his mouth. He slid at last to a stop, sucking air and spitting blood. All around him weak voices moaned and cried in pain. There were lights dancing in the centre of his vision. At first he thought they were after effects of the fall, but then he realised that they were torches, about as far above him as the top of a castle wall. He would have sworn he had fallen much farther than that. The Kurgan were looking down into the void to see what had become of them. He thought he heard them laughing. He doubted they could see anything.

'N...' He tried to speak and failed. He hadn't enough breath. After a moment he tried again. 'No one... strike... a light. Wait.'

He heard a hacking chuckle from nearby. 'No fear of that, captain,' said Hals. 'Dead men got no use for torches.'

After a moment the torches disappeared and they were left in total darkness.

'Unfortunately,' said Reiner at last, 'we appear to still live. If you've your flint handy, Hals?'

'Aye, captain.'

Reiner heard him shift around, then hiss in sudden pain. 'Ah, Sigmar's blood! I think I've bust my leg.'

'Any more hurt?' asked Reiner, though he was afraid to ask. 'Pavel?'

There was a muffled reply, then a curse. 'I've lost a bloody tooth.'

'Oskar?'

'I... I know not. I don't feel much of anything.'

'Franz? Did that monster get you?'

'I... I'm fine.'

'Ulf?'

There was no reply.

'Ulf?'

Silence.

'Just a moment, sir,' said Hals. 'Light's on its way.'

Reiner resumed the roll call. 'Gustaf?'

'I've lost some skin, that's all.'

'That's a relief. I hope you haven't lost your kit.'

'I have it.'

'Giano?'

'A rock, she cut me. I bleed a lot, I think.'

Light flashed as Hals struck sparks off his flint, followed by a steady glow as his tinder started. He touched it to a taper.

Reiner raised his head. His face felt twice as big as it ought to be, and twice as heavy. He looked around, squinting in the yellow light. The men were strewn like broken dolls at the base of a huge scree of gravel and loose rock that rose up into the darkness above them. This was obviously where the slaves dumped the waste rock they chipped away as they mined the ore. He looked at the men one by one.

Pavel was sitting up, holding his mouth, his fingers dripping blood. Hals was near him, holding aloft the candle. One of his legs was bent at an angle. Franz lay further down the slope, curled up and clutching his side. Reiner couldn't see the boy's face, but he seemed to be trembling. Oskar lay flat on his back staring straight up. He held one of his arms against his chest. Gustaf was hunched over his pack, sorting out his supplies. His canvas jacket was ripped to shreds on his left side, as was the skin under it. He bled from a hundred minor lacerations. Giano sat, naked to the waist, pressing a cut in his thigh with his shirt. His arms, shoulders and chest were mottled with blossoming bruises.

Reiner was certain that all of them looked just the same under their clothes. Ulf he found at last, at the edge of the candle light, a motionless mass lying on his side at the base of the mound.

'Gustaf,' said Reiner, lowering his head again. 'Could you see if Master Urquart still lives.'

'Aye.'

Gustaf made his way cautiously down the slope, slipping and sinking into the loose gravel. He bent over Ulf, touching his neck and chest, and peeling back his eyelids. 'He lives,' he said. 'But he has struck his head. I don't know when he will wake. It is possible he won't.'

Reiner groaned. Just what they needed.

"Tis a miracle,' said Pavel unclearly, as Gustaf climbed the slope again to Giano, who was bleeding the most. 'All of us alive. Sigmar must be watching over us.'

'If Sigmar was watching over us,' said Hals dryly as he lit a torch from the taper, 'he wouldn't have let us fall off the cursed cliff in the first place.'

'If your hammer god care one bit of damn for us,' spat Giano, 'he not let us take this fooling mission.'

'I can't work here,' said Gustaf. He had tied off Giano's gash, but his kit was sliding away down the slope, and he was sunk in almost to his knees. 'We must find somewhere flat.'

With a groan Reiner sat up and looked around as Hals's torch flared to life and the others began slowly and painfully to stand. The hole they had fallen into was a natural crevasse, deep and wide, that wandered off into darkness to their left and right. The hill of gravel they lay on spread out in a semi-circle across an uneven mud floor that made Reiner think water ran through the chasm occasionally. He was wondering if one direction was better than the other when he noticed that there was a circular opening in the opposite wall of the crevasse. More decisions. Which way was best?

Then he remembered that he had Veirt's compass, taken from his dead body, in his belt pouch. He took it out and frowned at it. South pointed almost directly at the circular opening. 'Try in there,' he said, pointing to it.

Pavel began helping Hals down the slope, arms over each other's shoulder, both of them hissing and grunting in pain. Reiner felt as bad as they sounded. His ribs ached with every breath, and every joint seemed to have its own separate and particular pain. He and Giano opened a blanket and rolled Ulf's supine body onto it, then, with Gustaf's help, they pulled the blanket and Ulf down to the floor.

Oskar and Franz brought up the rear, Oskar holding his left arm with his right, Franz clutching his ribs and crabbing along, almost bent double. His jacket was torn at the back, and his breeks, below it, were turning black with blood.

'Lad,' said Reiner. 'Are you certain you're well?'

'It's nothing,' the boy grunted between clenched teeth. 'Nothing.'

Dragging Ulf across the dried mud floor took quite an effort and Reiner's ribs and muscles complained mightily, but it got easier once they entered the tunnel. Though crudely worked, it was almost perfectly circular, and the floor was worn smooth from what must have been centuries of traffic. Adding to the slickness was a hard, oily coating that covered everything like a glaze. It was as if the whole tunnel had been varnished. Reiner was repulsed by the feel of it, yet it made pulling Ulf almost effortless.

Giano sniffed suspiciously. 'Smell of rat-men.'

Reiner chuckled. 'Don't be a fool, man. Rat-men are a myth.'

'Is not true. They live.'

Pavel smirked back over his shoulder. 'Giant rats that talk? Come on, Tilean. What do y'take us for?'

Giano pulled himself up, insulted. 'They live, I tell you. My whole village they kill. My mama and papa. Come out of ground and kill everybodies. I have swear vengeance upon them.'

'Bit difficult, seeing as they don't exist.'

Giano sniffed. 'Men of Empire think they know everythings.'

'Captain,' called Hals. 'Found a room of sorts. Might do for a surgery.'

He was sticking his torch into a round opening in the tunnel wall. Letting go of Ulf's makeshift stretcher, Reiner joined him and looked in. The hole opened into a round, curve-walled chamber with eight smaller chambers branching off it like the fingers of a glove. Reiner took the torch from Hals and stepped in. A chill ran up his spine. At some time in the past the chamber had been occupied, though by who or what he couldn't say. The walls were carved with jagged, geometric reliefs that Reiner could make neither head nor tail of. A few warped wooden shelves leaned against them, with a scattering of cracked clay jugs and bowls upon them. Reiner poked the torch into each of the eight chambers. They were small and nearly circular, the floors calf deep in scraps of cloth and straw. Reiner wrinkled his nose. They smelled of dust and animal musk. The whole place gave him an uneasy feeling, but it was dry and flat and there appeared to be no danger.

'Excellent,' he said with more enthusiasm than he felt. He waved the others forward. 'Come on, in we go.'

Pavel and Hals limped in first, followed by Gustaf and Giano, dragging Ulf. Giano grimaced. 'You see. Rat-men. We find nest.'

'You don't know that,' said Reiner. 'Anybody could have made these holes.'

'Looks more like orc work,' said Ulf, toeing aside a broken jug. 'Crude stuff.'

Pavel and Hals exchanged a nervous look.

'Only orcs?' said Hals dryly. 'That's a relief.'

'Can you no see?' asked Giano, pointing at the walls. 'Look. Rat faces. Rat bodies.'

Reiner looked at the reliefs again as Franz and Oskar entered. The designs might have been rat heads with wide-set eyes and sharp fangs, but they were so abstract and poorly carved that they might have been anything.

He waved a dismissive hand. 'Orcs or rat-men, whoever lived here is long gone.' He stuck his torch upright in the mouth of an unbroken urn and turned to Gustaf. 'Surgeon, what do you need of us?' He was trying his best to be bright and efficient like a good captain should, but his head ached abominably and his stomach was churning from all the blood that ran from his nose down the back of his throat.

Gustaf left Ulf on his blanket in the centre of the floor and opened his kit. 'Decide who is most injured. I will work from worst to least. If someone can break down these shelves for splints it would be a help. And if someone can sacrifice a shirt, I am running short of bandages.'

'I think Franz must be seen to first,' said Reiner. 'He is losing blood.'

'No!' said the boy, white-lipped. 'I am fine. I can attend to myself.' He limped hurriedly to one of the little chambers and disappeared inside.

'Come back here, you little brat,' barked Reiner. 'You are in no way fine.' With a grunt of annoyance he followed the boy into the room.

Franz was bracing himself against the wall with one trembling arm, his head bowed to his chest. His breath came in ragged gasps, and he pressed his left elbow against his side. The cloth of his shirt made a wet, squelching sound. 'Get out!' he gasped. 'Leave me be.'

Reiner glared at him. 'Don't be a fool, lad. You're grievously injured. You must let Gustaf have a look at you.'

'No,' whimpered Franz. 'He... he mustn't. No one...'

'But lad, you...'

The boy's knees gave way and he slid down the wall to sprawl on the floor.

'Curse it,' said Reiner. He returned to the main chamber. 'Surgeon, the boy's collapsed.'

Gustaf rose from examining Oskar's wrist. 'I'll see to him.' As he passed Reiner, he raised an eyebrow. 'Your nose is on sideways, captain. I believe you've broken it.'

Reiner raised his hand to his face. 'Ah. That would explain why my head feels as big as a melon.'

'I'll set it momentarily,' said the surgeon. 'In the meantime, if you could rip your shirt into strips.' He ducked into the small chamber with his kit.

Reiner joined the others on the floor and took off his jerkin and shirt. The air in the chamber was stuffy, but much warmer than that in the mine. It was almost comfortable. Hals was sawing at his spear with his dagger, trying to fashion it into a crutch. Giano was breaking the shelves into usable lengths. Oskar rocked back and forth, holding his arm. Pavel was pressing a rag of shirt against his mouth. His upper lip was split to his nose and bleeding freely.

He grinned at Reiner, showing red teeth. 'And I didn't think I could get any uglier.'

'Maybe y'll lose the other eye,' said Hals. 'So y'won't have to look at yerself.'

Pavel chuckled. 'I can only hope.'

After a short time Gustaf returned. Reiner thought there was something odd about his expression, a suppressed smirk possibly, but the surgeon always looked like he was stifling an evil thought, so he couldn't be sure.

'How's the boy,' Reiner asked.

Gustaf's smirk broadened for a moment, then disappeared. 'He sleeps. I gave him a draught. He was clawed along the ribs by the hound, then a sharp stone became lodged in the wound during the fall. Very painful. I removed the stone and bound the wound. He will be weak for a while, but he will live.' He snorted. 'If any of us do.'

'Brave little fool,' said Reiner with grudging respect. 'He tries too hard to be hard.'

'Yes,' said Gustaf, then crossed to Pavel and took out a needle and thread.

Just as he crouched down, Ulf suddenly jack-knifed into a sitting position, flailing and roaring. 'The beasts! The beasts!' He clubbed Gustaf and Oskar with his wild swings. The others edged away from him.

Reiner stood. 'Ulf! Urquart! Calm yourself. The hounds are gone.'

Ulf's fists slowed and he blinked around him. 'What…?'

'We fell. You don't remember?'

'I… I thought… '

'You've hit your head,' said Gustaf, as he recovered himself. 'How do you feel?'

Ulf rubbed his eyes. He swayed where he sat, as if drunk. 'My head hurts. Eyes blurry. We fell?'

'Down a tailings pit,' said Reiner. 'We're all hurt.'

'But at least we escaped the hounds!' laughed Hals.

Gustaf looked in Ulf's eyes. 'You are concussed. Let me know if your vision fails to improve.' He returned to stitching up Pavel's lip.

'But where are we?' asked Ulf, suddenly anxious. 'Where is the Kurgan warband? Have we lost them? Can we get back to where we were? Are we lost in here?'

'Shut up, fool!' shouted Reiner. 'I don't need two Oskars on my hands. Gustaf will run out of elixir.'

He groaned. The engineer had said too much. He could see anxiety spreading from face to face.

'Calm yourselves,' he said. 'All of you. Yes we're in a tight spot, but as Hals just said, we have escaped the hounds, so we're better off than we were, right? Now, I don't know where the warband is from here, or where here is for that matter, but someone made these tunnels. They must lead somewhere.' he fished out Veirt's compass again. 'And for the moment they lead south, which is the way we want to go, so all is not entirely lost.'

He closed his eyes for a second and almost forgot to open them again, he was so weary. 'I say we rest here,' he said at last. 'There are rooms for all of us. When our surgeon has finished doctoring us we will turn in, and decide a course of action when we wake and can think straight, fair enough?'

He sighed with relief as he saw the men nodding and calming themselves. 'Good. We'll set two watches. I'll take the second if someone feels up to taking the first.'

'I will,' said Gustaf quickly. 'I am the least wounded of all of us.'

Reiner nodded his thanks, though he was slightly puzzled. The surgeon had never volunteered for watch before.

They made a curious discovery after Gustaf had bound and set all their wounds and breaks and they had settled into the eight little rooms. The darkness was no longer absolute. They had expected to be plunged into blackness once Gustaf stationed himself in the main room and snuffed the torch, but a faint light, so dim they were at first not sure it was there, illuminated the chambers. The greenish luminescence seemed to come from the walls, or more accurately, from the slick glaze that covered the walls.

'That's a small blessing,' said Pavel from his and Hals's chamber.

Yes, thought Reiner, as he lowered his head carefully into his nest of smelly rags. At least we will be able to see whatever cyclopean horror slithers out of the tunnels and kills us.

AN AGONISED SCREAM jerked Reiner from a dream of dicing with a mysterious opponent. He knew the fellow was using loaded dice, and yet he kept playing, kept betting, though he lost every time.

He blinked around in the green murk, for a moment at a loss as to where he was. The scream came again. He recognised it as Gustaf's voice this time. Gustaf! Gustaf was on watch. They were under attack! He jumped up and grabbed his sword, and almost fell again, his body ached so much in so many places. It felt like he was bound in iron ropes that tightened with each movement.

He forced himself to move through the pain and stumbled out into the main chamber. The others were peeking out of their rooms as well, weapons in hand. Oskar wasn't there.

Reiner limped to the tunnel, but a horrible rattling groan echoing from Franz's chamber stopped him. Reiner turned, and he and the others crowded into it, ready to fight.

A confusing tableau met their eyes. Franz was pressed against the wall, eyes wild, one hand holding his jerkin closed, the other gripping a bloody dagger. Gustaf lay at his feet in a pool of red, clutching at a wound in his throat that would never close. As Reiner watched, his arms relaxed and flopped loosely to the ground. The room filled with the smell of urine.

'Sigmar's holy hammer, boy!' said Reiner, aghast. 'What have you done?'

'He…' said Franz. He seemed not quite awake.

'He's killed our only hope of getting out of here, is what he's done,' growled Hals angrily. 'Stupid little fool! I ought to ring your neck!'

Franz hugged himself. 'He tried to… to put his hands on me.'

'That again?' said Hals. 'Well it won't fly, lad. You were with us when Gustaf went after that poor girl. He don't care for boys, no matter how unmanly they are.'

'Who care what the fellow do!' cried Giano. 'If he want to eat you, you give him you arm. We need him. How we be now if he not fix us up, eh?' He spat on Franz's boots.

'Gustaf knew the way out,' said a voice behind them. It was Oskar, clinging to the wall, looking too alert for his own good. 'You remember. There was some obstacle further on. He wouldn't tell us.'

'He wouldn't tell us, so we wouldn't kill him,' said Hals. 'And now this fool has gone and killed him!' He balled his fists. 'I think it's time we show this mewling baby what it means to be a man. I say we give him a few hard lessons, hey?'

'No!' said Reiner. 'We're all hurt enough as it is. It's a bad thing he's done, I admit. But we need all the hands we have, and...'

'Shhhh!' said Ulf, from the door. 'Do you hear something?'

They all fell silent and listened. There was something, more a vibration in the rock than a heard sound.

'Into the tunnel,' said Reiner.

They tiptoed into the hall, leaving Franz with Gustaf's corpse, and stood, ears cocked.

The sound was louder here, a rumbling murmur. The vibrations seemed to be coming from above them and far forward. There was a song over the murmur, a harsh, angry chant.

'The warband!' said Oskar. 'It must be!'

Pavel grinned. 'Never thought I'd be glad to hear Kurgan marching.'

Reiner smiled. 'Right then, get your gear together. We leave immediately.'

They re-entered the round room. 'Go when you're packed,' said Reiner, stepping to Franz's chamber. 'I'll be along shortly. I want a word alone with young Master Shoentag.'

'Aye, captain,' said Hals.

Reiner entered the chamber as the others began collecting their things. The boy was inching painfully into his leather doublet, teeth clenched, his feet pulled fastidiously back from the puddle of blood spreading from beneath Gustaf's corpse.

Reiner folded his arms and leaned against the wall. 'All right, laddie. Let's have it.'

Franz glanced up at him, then away. 'I don't know what you mean.'

'Don't play the fool with me, boy. I know there's more to this than there appears. Hals was right. Gustaf fancied girls, not boys, so your excuse won't work this time. What did he want from you? Was he blackmailing you?'

'No,' Franz said, surly. 'Why… why would he?'

'That's for you to tell me. My guess is he found out something about you while he was doctoring you. Some secret you want hidden.'

The boy, clutched his knees and stared at the floor. He didn't answer.

'Come now, lad,' said Reiner kindly, 'I'm no raving Sigmarite. I'll not turn you over to the witch hunters, but if I'm to lead you well, I need to know who I'm leading: your strengths, your weaknesses, the little things from your past that might trip us up in the future?'

Franz just sniffed miserably.

'So what is it?' Reiner asked. 'Do you bear the brand of some heathen god upon you? Are you warp-touched? Have you a second pair of arms? Or a mouth in your belly? Are you a lover of men?'

'I can't tell you,' said Franz. 'I can't.'

'Oh come, it can't be worse than what I've just said. Just tell me and be done with it.'

Franz's shoulders slumped. His head touched his knees. Then, with a sigh, he climbed painfully to his feet. He looked to the door. The others were filing into the tunnel. When they were gone he turned to Reiner. 'Do you promise to tell no one.'

'I make no promises, boy, so I never have to break any. But I can keep a secret, if there's a reason to.'

Franz frowned at this, then sighed again. With reluctant hands he undid the ties that held his shirt together and pulled it open. His chest was bandaged from his armpits to his belly.

Reiner grimaced. 'Were you wounded so badly?'

'The wound is bad,' said Franz, 'but the bandages are only partly for the wound.' And with eyes lowered he tugged the tight bindings down to his ribs.

Reiner gaped. The boy *was* deformed! Two plump pink protuberances rose from his chest. By the gods, Reiner thought, the poor lad truly was warp-touched. It almost looked as if he had…

'Sigmar's balls! You're a girl!'

# CHAPTER FOURTEEN
## COME TASTE IMPERIAL STEEL

'Shhh!' whispered the girl harshly as she tugged her bandages back into place. 'Please don't betray me! I beg you!'

'Betray you?' said Reiner. 'I ought to thrash you!' Reiner was deeply chagrined. How could he, a connoisseur of womanhood in all its forms, have been fooled this way? How could he not have known? Now that the truth was revealed it was so obvious as to be painful. The beardless jaw, the slight frame, the full lips, the large, dark eyes. Why, he had seen girls disguised as boys in plays who were more convincing. It must have been, he decided, the audacity of the thing that had made it possible. A man simply could not accept that a woman would disguise herself as a soldier, or could live a soldier's life, so any faults in the charade, any uncertainties about her sex, were dismissed before they could be considered, because one would never even think to contemplate that a soldier could be a woman.

He shook his head. 'What do you mean by this foolishness, you lunatic child? What possessed you to engage in this pitiful charade?'

The girl raised her chin. 'I do my duty. I protect my homeland.'

'Your duty as a woman is to give birth to more soldiers, not to take up arms yourself.'

The girl sneered. 'Really? And do the harlots you consort with in the brothels of Altdorf perform such a duty?'

The question caught Reiner off guard. He expected the girl to cower before him, not counter his arguments. 'Er, some do, I suppose. I'm certain they do. But that's beside the point. What you have done is a perversion. An outrage!'

'You sound like a fanatical priest. I thought you were a man of the world. A sophisticate.'

Reiner flushed. She was right. In the theatres and brothels he had frequented before being called up he had known women who dressed like men and men who dressed like women and had thought little of it. He was more outraged at being tricked than by what she had done. But he was still troubled. 'But women aren't cut out to be soldiers! They are too weak. They can't do the work required. They haven't the stomach for killing.'

The girl drew herself up. 'Have you found my soldiering lacking? Did I lag behind on the trail? Did I shirk my duties? Did I flinch from danger? I admit I am not strong, and I am nothing with a sword, but what bowman is? Was I less of a soldier for that?'

'You were,' said Reiner, feeling at last on solid ground. 'For look at the trouble you've caused. The nonsense about not sharing a tent, Not allowing a surgeon to heal you. And you have killed fellow soldiers twice to keep them from revealing your secret – the poor fellow you were jailed for murdering, and now Gustaf.'

'I did not kill them to keep my secret,' said the girl sharply. 'I would have been angry at them had they betrayed me, but I wouldn't have killed them.' She looked Reiner in the eye. 'I told the truth in our prison. When my tentmate learned my sex, he attempted to force himself upon me, thinking I would do his will in order to keep him quiet.' She shivered. 'Gustaf tried the same, only worse. He said he would give me another reason for my bandages. He tried to cut me, with his scalpel, as he had that poor girl.'

Reiner winced. 'The monster.' He looked up at the girl. 'But, you realise, if you had been a man, neither of them would have tried anything. The temptation would not have been there.'

The girl clenched her fists. 'No. They would have only assaulted peasant girls and harlots instead, and no one would have stopped them!' She calmed herself and hung her head. 'Forgive me. I forget myself. I know I don't belong in the army – that my presence is a disruption, a crime.' She looked up at Reiner pleadingly. 'But are we all not criminals? Are we not a band of outlaws? Must you cast me out for it? In all other things I am a good soldier. I beg you, don't tell the others. I couldn't bear it if they turned on me, or worse, treated me like a porcelain doll. Let me serve out at least this mission. When we return to the Empire, you may do as you wish. I will make no complaint.'

Reiner stared at the girl for a long time. Revealing the girl's secret would be more of a disruption than keeping it, and yet it went against every instinct he had as a gentleman and a lover of women to allow a girl to fight and come into harm's way. He ground his teeth. He must think as a captain and do the thing that was best for the group, not the individual. It was better for the group to have more fighters and to work smoothly as a unit.

'What's your name, girl?'

'Franka. Franka Mueller.'

Reiner sighed and pinched the bridge of his nose. 'That was foolish of me. It would have been much smarter not to know you by any other name than Franz. That way it would be impossible to make a mistake.' He shrugged. 'Ah well, can't be helped. Get your kit together, the rest are getting far ahead.'

Franka looked at him uncertainly. 'So you won't betray me?'

'No, confound you, I won't. I need you. But I make no promises for when we return to civilisation, I hope that's understood.'

Franka saluted smartly, her lips twitching a smile. 'Perfectly, captain. And my thanks.'

Reiner grunted and began gathering up Gustaf's kit, trying to get the image of Franka's naked breasts out of his head. It was going to be difficult thinking of the girl as a lad again.

THEY CAUGHT UP to the others a short while later.

Hals shot Franka a dirty look. 'I'm surprised he didn't murder you too, captain. You being alone with him and all.'

'Less of it, pikeman,' said Reiner. 'I've listened to the las... to the lad's story and I believe it. He showed me cuts on his chest like those Gustaf carved into that girl. It seems our surgeon had more wide-ranging tastes than we suspected.'

'That's as may be,' said Pavel. 'But don't expect me to bunk with him.'

The men continued following the distant sounds of marching. There were no stairs in the strange round tunnels, just sharply sloping ramps that connected one level to the other. The ramps were cut with toe holds that seemed to have been placed for beasts with four legs, not two, which set Giano raving about rat-men again. The marching continued to echo down from above them, and they climbed through five levels before the sound began coming from ahead of them.

'Let's increase our pace until we find the cannon tracks,' said Reiner. 'I don't want to miss our way.'

They walked faster, though all were exhausted from their interrupted sleep. Hals hopped gamely on his makeshift crutch, while Giano kept a hand on Ulf's elbow, for the big man hadn't fully recovered his balance after his blow to the head. Oskar shuffled somnambulantly in the middle of the pack, at peace now that Reiner had given him another sip from Gustaf's bottle. The journey was made somewhat easier because they no longer needed torches. The pale green glow of the walls was just enough to see by, though it gave them all a sickly cast that was unpleasant to look at.

A few hours into their march Hals found a broken cleaver discarded in a shallow alcove. It was enormous, the handle so big even Ulf had a hard time closing his fingers around it. There was dried blood caked on its snapped blade.

'Orcs,' said Pavel. 'Right enough.'

Hals poked at the crusted blood. It flaked away. 'No way to tell if this was dropped last week or last century.'

Reiner swallowed unhappily. 'Well, we can't be more alert than we already are, can we? Carry on.'

They resumed their march and despite Reiner's words, the men were indeed more alert, looking nervously over their shoulders at every turn and jumping at shadows.

Reiner let the others get a little ahead and walked with Franka. 'I still don't understand how you became a soldier,' he said. 'What possessed you to take up this life?'

Franka sighed. 'Love.'

'Love?'

'I am the daughter of a miller in a town called Hovern. Do you know it?'

'I think so. Just south of Nuln, yes?'

'Aye. My father arranged a marriage for me to the son of a Nuln wheat merchant. He hoped to win a better wholesale price from the boy's father. I, unfortunately, was in love with the son of a farmer who came often to our mill with his wheat – Yarl. I didn't like the merchant's son. He was an ass. But my father didn't listen to my wishes.'

'As fathers so often fail to do,' said Reiner wryly, thinking of his own less than understanding father.

'The merchant's son and I were to be married last spring, and I thought I could bear it if I could slip away and see Yarl now and then, but then the hordes began their advance and Yarl was called by Lord von Goss to string his bow in defence of the Empire.' She chuckled bitterly. 'The merchant's son got a dispensation because he and his father were provisioning the army. It came to me suddenly that I would be alone with that puny braggart while Yarl was away fighting, and that… and that Yarl might not come back.'

'Such is the lot of women since the beginning of time,' said Reiner.

'Chaos take the "lot of women",' sneered Franka. 'On the eve of my wedding I could stand it no longer. I cut my hair, stole my father's bow, and ran off to Gossheim where Lord von Goss's army was mustering for the march north. I enlisted as Yarl's younger brother Franz and took his last name. It was…' She blushed. 'It was the best six months of my life. We ate together, tented together. Every happiness I dreamed marriage would bring, we had.'

It was Reiner's turn to blush. 'But how did you pass? How did you learn the bow? The ways of the soldier? A life of embroidery and dresses…'

Franka laughed. 'Do you think me a noblewoman? I was a miller's daughter, and not a rich one. My mother had no sons. I milled. I lifted sacks of grain. I haggled and joked with the farmers and the draysmen.'

'But the bow?'

Franka smiled. 'Yarl taught me. He was my playmate from childhood. We ran in the fields. Hunted squirrels on his father's farm. Played at prince and princess. I wanted to do everything he did, so I learned the bow at his side. When he vouched for me at von Goss's camp no one gave me a second look.'

'So how did you come to kill the fellow who...'

Franka hung her head. 'Yarl died. At Vodny Field. Killed by a diseased arrow. I could have run away then, I suppose. Many did. But the idea of returning to the merchant's son and his big house with the big bed and the cowering servants...' she shivered. 'I couldn't face it. And I had come to like the army. Yarl and I had made good friends there. We were a band of brothers...'

'And one sister,' quipped Reiner.

'A band of brothers,' continued Franka, ignoring him. 'United against a great enemy. I felt I had a purpose in life. And with Yarl gone, I needed something to make me want to keep living.' She shook her head. 'I was a fool. I thought I could keep my secret, but of course my captain assigned me a new tent-mate, and it wasn't long before the dog caught me out and... well, you know the rest.'

They walked in silence for a moment.

'You are a singular woman,' Reiner said at last.

Franka snorted. 'Aye, that's a word for it.' She stopped and turned suddenly, ear cocked. 'Do you hear...'

Reiner listened behind them and heard it as well. What he had thought of as a faint echo of the Kurgan marching, was growing louder. 'Curse it,' he growled. 'Have we got ahead of them? Or is it a second force on the heels of the first? Are we trapped again?'

They ran to catch up with the others.

'Marchers coming up behind us,' Reiner announced. 'Are you positive the warband is still before us?'

'Can't you hear 'em singing, captain?' asked Hals.

Reiner listened. The dull, two-toned chant was clear. 'Then who in Sigmar's name is behind us?'

'I'll go back, captain,' said Franka.

'No,' said Reiner. 'I forbid it. You aren't...'

'Captain!' Franka interrupted quickly. 'I am recovered from Gustaf's assault. There is no need to treat me with kid gloves.'

'No,' said Reiner, cursing her inwardly. The foolish girl was deliberately trying to force him to put her into danger. 'But you lost more blood than any of us. You are still weak. Giano will scout back. We will continue forward at march pace and leave way marks at any turnings we make.'

Franka stuck her lip out. Giano sighed. 'The thanking I get for be quick on my foots.'

He hurried back down the tunnel as Reiner and the rest continued forward. Franka glared straight ahead as they marched and said not a word. Reiner sighed.

After another quarter hour, they began closing on the Chaos column. The different sounds were becoming distinct from one another. The creak and groan of the cannon's wheels, the monotonous chant of the soldiers, the ragged rumble of hundreds of marching feet. They entered a larger but still perfectly cylindrical tunnel with many branching side tunnels, and found at last the tracks of the great gun carriage, so heavy that it cracked the floor's greenish glaze and turned it to a resinous powder. Reiner used his dagger to scrape an arrow in the tunnel wall to indicate to Giano the direction they were taking and they continued on.

'Cautiously now, men,' he said. 'They're just a few bends ahead.' He shot a look at Franka. 'Er, I'll take the lead. Give me thirty paces.'

Franka sniffed as he crept ahead. They proceeded forward in that fashion until at last Reiner could see the tail of the Kurgan train ahead of him – shambling horned silhouettes against the yellow glow of torches in the distance. He stopped and raised a hand to the others, at once fearful and relieved. It was like following a bear through the woods to find a stream. He didn't want to lose the bear, but letting it know of his presence was suicide.

The others caught up with him.

'Move at this pace,' he said, 'and we should just keep them in...'

Running footsteps interrupted him. The men turned, weapons at the ready. Giano came out of the darkness, wheezing and wild-eyed.

'Greenskins!' he said between gasps. 'Half league back. Almost they see me.'

'Quiet!' whispered Reiner, pointing down the tunnel. 'The Kurgan are just there.'

'They coming fast,' Giano continued more quietly. 'Hunting. Little bands, spreading out, every way?'

'Hunting for us?' asked Reiner.

'Does it matter?' asked Franka.

Hals groaned. 'Trapped again. Sigmar curse this whole enterprise!'

'He has, mate,' said Pavel. 'Trust me.'

'Not trapped yet,' said Reiner. 'We've more tunnels to manoeuvre in here. If we can...'

A rumbling voice called a challenge from down the tunnel.

Reiner jumped. He and the rest turned toward the enemy troops' line of march in time to see Kurgan-shaped shadows step out of a side tunnel fifty paces away. It was hard to tell in the murky green light, but they seemed to be looking their way. Reiner groaned. 'Right. Now we're trapped. Back away, and if they start toward us, run.'

The party backed down the corridor as more Kurgan came out of the side tunnel.

The challenge came again.

'What's the point, captain?' asked Hals. 'We can't outrun 'em, banged up like this. We might as well die gloriously.'

'I'd rather live ingloriously,' said Reiner. 'If it's all the same to you. Come now, speed it up. I have a plan.'

Hals muttered something Reiner couldn't quite hear about 'too many cursed plans' but he hobbled along gamely with the rest of them as they hurried further down the hall.

Their challenge unanswered, the Kurgan came forward cautiously, unslinging axes that glinted green in the eerie glow of the walls. One of them went trotting down the tunnel toward the main force. It seemed to Reiner that the axe-men were being more circumspect than Kurgan had a reputation for, and he wondered if they too knew that there were orcs in the area. He cursed himself for not expecting the Kurgan to have outriders patrolling the line of march. It was something a real captain would have known instinctively.

The men had just reached the side tunnel they'd originally entered from, when a lone Kurgan poked his head out of another tunnel directly behind them. He laughed and called back to the squad derisively. Reiner couldn't understand the words, but the meaning was clear – 'It's only men.'

An answering laugh echoed from the axe squad and Reiner heard them start forward at a trot.

'Run!' cried Reiner, motioning them into the side tunnel. Oskar, Franka and Ulf ran in first, followed by Giano, still winded from his reconnaissance. Pavel and Hals came last, Hals skipping with his crutch and wincing at each step. It was clear to Reiner that Hals would soon fall behind, and that Pavel wouldn't leave his side.

'Ulf! Carry Hals! Pavel, keep Ulf steady!'

'No sir,' protested Hals. 'No man carries me.'

'I have him, sir,' said Pavel. 'We'll keep up.'

'Damn your pride, the both of you,' said Reiner. 'I'll not have you die of it. Ulf!'

The engineer fell back and hoisted Hals onto his back and they ran on, Pavel keeping a hand on the concussed engineer's arm to guide him.

Reiner could hear the axe men turning into the tunnel behind them. They were already gaining. 'Shout, lads!' he bellowed. 'Shout as loud as you can!'

'Hey?' cried Giano, confused. 'You want they find us?'

'Not just them,' said Reiner, then raised his voice to a piercing cry. 'Hoy! Greenies! Fresh meat here! Come and get us!'

'Ah,' said Franka, grinning in spite of herself. 'I see.' She too raised her voice. 'Coo-ee! Pig snouts! Where are you? Come taste Imperial steel!'

Bouncing on Ulf's back, Hals laughed. 'You *are* mad, captain! But 'tis my kind of madness.' He began to roar. 'Come on, y'green bastards! Show us what y've got! I'll paint the walls with yer green blood, y'great lumbering cowards!'

Reiner heard an angry roar behind him and the Kurgans' loping gait quickened to a run. It seemed they had guessed Reiner's strategy as well, and were less than happy about it. They were getting closer by the second.

But an answering roar came from before them, and the floor shook with heavy footsteps.

Reiner sent up a silent thanks to Sigmar. 'Eyes out for a side tunnel, lads. We don't want to be pinched between when the hammer hits the anvil.'

'This way, greenskins!' shouted Franka. 'Dinner's on the table!'

'Aie!' cried Giano suddenly. 'They come! Hide!'

Reiner got a quick flash of huge, blurred forms holding enormous black-iron cleavers, before he and the rest ducked into a side corridor.

The Kurgan behind them cried out, but their voices were drowned out almost instantly by a roar of hideous animal triumph from the other direction. Voices that were more like the squealing of angry boars than anything human rose in fury as the orcs charged forward.

The impact as the orcs and the Chaos marauders came together sounded like two iron wagons full of meat slamming into each other at unimaginable speed. It was followed instantly by the clash of cleavers and axes and screams of frenzy and agony. Reiner couldn't resist a look back. All he could see in the uncertain green light were giant, indistinct shapes in violent movement and the slashing gleam of cutting edges rising and falling.

'On, boys, on!' he called. 'Look for a way back to the main…'

But Giano was suddenly skidding to a stop. Ulf crashed into him.

'What's the matter?' asked Reiner.

'Yer plan worked too well, laddie,' said Hals, from Ulf's shoulders. 'There's another lot coming.'

Reiner cursed as he saw more lumbering shadows approaching in the distance. Fortunately the area was honeycombed with tunnels and they were able to slip down another passage before the orcs saw them. But now the sound of heavy feet echoed from every direction. There seemed no way to go that wasn't clogged with orcs.

'My genius continues to astound me,' said Reiner through clenched teeth, as they edged down a curving tunnel.

'Oh, you do all right,' said Pavel. 'You always get us out of our tight spots.'

'And into tighter ones,' muttered Hals.

At last they wormed their way through the maze, dodging hurrying squads of orcs and Kurgan as they went, and reached the main tunnel safely. They started after the Kurgan column again, but hadn't taken twenty steps before they saw a detachment of fifty or so Kurgan marauders running toward them, torches bobbing. They were led by a giant in black chainmail skirts, an axeman trotting beside him, pointing out the way. But before the northers could turn into the side tunnel, orcs burst from other tunnels all along their flanks, roaring and squealing, and tore into them, cleavers swinging.

Reiner and the others took refuge in a side corridor and watched awestruck the murderous melee that unfolded before them. It was a swirling chaos of flailing limbs, slashing blades, and flying bodies. The orcs attacked with animal fury, making up for an utter lack of discipline by the brute mass of their charge. The Kurgan, by human standards almost impossibly muscular, were puny in comparison to the orcs, whose mere skeletons probably weighed more than most men. They knocked the Kurgan flat from both sides, and chopped those who fell to pieces with cleavers the size of shields.

The Chaos marauders were marginally more disciplined. After the initial shock of the orc ambush, their captains roared rallying cries and the marauders crowded around them, facing out to make primitive squares. In this posture of defence they formed a whirling wall of steel, huge axes slashing in figure-eights, and severing the hands and arms of any orc who tried to pierce it.

Stymied by this simple manoeuvre, the orcs began hurling things at the Kurgan from a distance. There were very few rocks in the smooth tunnels, so they threw severed heads and limbs and entire bodies, both marauder and orc, then followed up this bombardment with charges. But though flying orc carcasses flattened more than a few Kurgan, the northers were prepared for the charges now, and their skill and the reach of their axes began to turn the tide.

A few more squads of orcs spilled out of the side tunnels and joined the fray, but the Kurgan held their own until a further detachment of marauders came howling down the tunnel. They plowed into the fray like a battering ram, and the orcs quickly lost any stomach for the fight. They scattered into side tunnels like rats fleeing a terrier, leaving their wounded to the tender mercies of the marauders.

Reiner and his men shrunk back, prepared to flee if any of the orcs came their way. None did. Nor did the Kurgan, who didn't bother to pursue their attackers. Instead, they slaughtered the wounded orcs, stripped the bodies of weapons and armour, and marched back toward the main column.

'Men,' said Reiner, letting out a long held breath, 'I think we're back on track.'

The men started forward at an easy pace, following the sounds of the receding Kurgan.

They tailed the warband at a cautious distance until they stopped to make camp. Reiner backed up the tunnel for more than half a league before he felt it safe enough to bed down. He wanted to be well clear of any pickets the marauders might set around their perimeter. The night – if it was night, for there was no telling in the sunless tunnels – passed without incident, and when they woke to the sound of the Kurgan preparing to march again, they did the same, more refreshed than they had been since they entered the endless underworld.

Reiner spooned another dose of poppy into Oskar as they got under way. He hoped that they were nearing the end of the tunnels, for the supply was running low.

As they travelled, side tunnels and doors began to become more numerous, until the underworld felt less like a system of tunnels and more like the halls and rooms of a castle, or the streets and avenues of a city, the chambers between them houses and tenements. More frequent, as well, were the steep ramps that led to higher levels.

'Whoever built these tunnels,' said Reiner, as they looked around them in wonder, 'this was their Altdorf.'

'Maybe this *is* Altdorf,' said Oskar dreamily. 'Maybe we are under Karl Franz Strasse and nearly home.'

Hals snorted. 'Don't be daft, lad. We haven't travelled near that far.'

'It feels like we've half crossed the world,' said Franka with feeling.

'Shhhh, all you,' said Giano, flapping a hand. 'I think they stopping again.'

The company stopped and listened, trying to determine by sound alone what was happening. At this distance it was difficult. They could hear orders being shouted and the sound of great bustle and activity, but a new sound, a deep booming howl that sounded like wind in a canyon, drowned out all the details.

'We'll have to reconnoitre,' said Reiner. 'Maybe we can use the upper levels to spy down on them. Giano, come with me..' Franka gave him another dirty look, but there was nothing she could say.

Reiner and Giano climbed a nearby ramp and began to weave their way through a warren of tunnels, galleries and chambers. They passed rooms, and suites of rooms, that had at one time had low wooden doors, but these had long ago been smashed in, and the contents, whatever they might have been, stolen away. At each turning they listened to be sure that the sound of the Kurgan was coming from ahead of them, then crept on.

At last, after climbing to a third level, they turned a corner and torchlight and noise welled out of a round opening before them. Giano motioned for Reiner to drop to his hands and knees and they crawled to the entrance. It opened out onto a wide tier that ringed an enormous circular chamber. There were tiers above and below them, set back like seats in an amphitheatre, with the same steep ramps connecting them at regular intervals. The walls of the tiers were riddled with round holes, most of which led into small rooms, though whether they had been storerooms or dwellings Reiner could not begin to guess.

The floor of the chamber was entirely filled by the Chaos warband, who were crowded together so tightly they hardly had room to turn around. Most were sitting on their packs, or eating quick meals. The cannon squatted in the middle of them like some bird of prey surrounded by her brood. Reiner edged to the lip of the tier and looked right and left. To the right was the entrance to the chamber, a large black arch into which the tail of the Kurgan column disappeared. These men too sat where they had stopped, waiting with the resignation of soldiers everywhere. To the left was the reason for the wait and the source of the booming sound Reiner and his companions had been hearing since the halt.

It was a wide, swift river, its channel slicing through the left wall of the huge chamber at a shallow angle like a sword cutting through the top of a skull. The rushing current roared like a dragon, crashing against the broken piers of a ruined stone bridge with such force that permanent bow waves rose up around them in great white ruffles. A heavy but clumsily built wooden bridge had been constructed upon these ruins, and it was this that had brought the march to a halt. It was only wide enough to allow three men to march abreast.

A massively armoured warrior was calling the various captains and chieftains forward to lead their squads over the bridge one at a time, while bawling overseers directed slaves as they began pushing and turning the cannon in order to bring it into line.

Reiner groaned as he eyed the narrow crossing. He could see no other way across the river. 'I believe we have at last found Gustaf's "obstacle".'

# CHAPTER FIFTEEN
## BREASTPLATES WON'T BE ENOUGH TO SAVE US

'WE HAVE TWO options, as I see it,' said Reiner when he and Giano returned to the others and gave them the news. 'We can look for other ways to cross the river, or we can wait at the back of the queue and follow the Kurgan over once they've gone.'

'I ain't keen on waiting,' said Hals. 'What's to stop another column coming up behind us and catching us in the middle again?'

'We mustn't wait,' said Ulf. 'If we are to reach Count Manfred in time to warm him of the Kurgans' coming, we must get out before they do.'

'I don't know if that's entirely possible,' said Reiner. 'Seeing as they are crossing already, but the sooner the better, as you say.'

'Did not Gustaf say he knew a way around?' asked Oskar, worriedly.

'Aye,' said Hals, giving Franka a significant look. 'But Gustaf is dead.'

'We can only hope we come across it as we search,' said Reiner hurriedly. 'We'll split into two squads and search east and west of the bridge for another way across, then meet back here when we're done. Giano, take Pavel and Oskar west. I'll take Franz and Ulf. Hals, you stay here. If any more Chaos troops come through move one level up. We'll find you there.'

'Aye, captain,' said Hals.

The others split off into left and right passages, leaving him alone.

REINER, FRANKA AND Ulf gave the river chamber a wide berth, travelling east as far as the warren of tunnels would allow, then moving south to find the river. It was easy to find. Its roaring filled the tunnels, and they used the noise and the wet wind that accompanied it as a compass. After a short while they found a tunnel that seemed to parallel it. They could feel the current vibrating the left wall. The tunnel began to descend gradually and soon they were splashing through shallow water.

About thirty paces ahead a hole had been worn through the wall by the constant abrasion of the water. Reiner could see the river through it, and a brackish backwater filled the tunnel to knee height just inside it. More water lapped in and out constantly with each cresting swell.

Reiner and the others waded down to the hole and looked through. Reiner winced as the fiercely cold water topped his boots and trickled down his calves. There was little to see. The river rushed out of darkness on the left and into darkness on the right. There was no sign of a bridge.

They moved on, winding though tunnels and galleries, tall chambers, and passages through which they had to crawl on hands and knees. There were many openings to the river, some intentional, some, like the first they had encountered, mere erosion, but no bridge. They found once the remains of one – a spur of rock that jutted out only a few steps over the river. There was another spur on the opposite side, and a tunnel mouth, beckoning invitingly.

'Can we bridge it?' Reiner asked Ulf. 'If we found some timber?'

Ulf shook his head. 'No, captain. The river is too wide and too fast. We would need two tall trees and a pier in the centre to span it.'

'All right. Let's try further on.'

But there was nothing. Closer to the main chamber, they found the first of a series of narrow landings – built out into the water at the bottom of stone ramps – but these didn't reach far enough to be of any use. There were a few on the opposite side as well. Some of them had stone pilings that jutted up like crocodile teeth along the water's edge.

At last they could go no further. The last landing they discovered was so close to the main chamber that they could see part of the bridge from it, and hear the bellowing of the Kurgan over the rush of the water.

Ulf squinted at the rebuilt bridge with a critical eye. 'Orc work,' he said with a sniff. 'Shoddy construction. The biggest bits of timber they can find, and string to hold it together. Surprised it's still standing.'

Reiner shrugged. 'Maybe they'll all fall in.' He turned back the way they had come. 'Let's get back and see if the others have found anything.'

Ulf followed, but Franka continued to stare at the bridge. 'I don't suppose we could float down to it from here, then cross underneath it through all those beams.'

'What?' said Reiner, turning back. He smirked. 'Well, you could, I suppose, if you didn't get swept away by the current, but then where would you be? Trapped under the bridge on the far side with the Kurgan marching over your head. And soaking wet to boot.'

'Aye,' agreed Franka. 'But what if there was another landing on the other side, downstream from the bridge?'

'You would still be swept away,' said Reiner.

'Not if you used ropes,' said Ulf, rubbing his chin thoughtfully. 'Yes. If we did it in stages, it might work.'

Reiner scowled, thinking of the cold water in his boots and imagining immersing himself entirely in it. He sighed. 'Let's see if the others have found a more civilized crossing.'

THEY HADN'T. ALL paths stopped at the river.

'But,' said Pavel, when Franka had mentioned her floating-down-the-river plan, 'there was a landing on the far side of the river, now that you mention it. About thirty paces below it.'

'Fifty-five feet,' said Oskar sleepily. 'Give or take a foot.'

Everybody turned to stare at him.

'Can you truly be so precise?' asked Reiner.

Oskar shrugged. 'It is my curse.'

'The landing above the bridge is roughly the same distance,' said Ulf. 'Perhaps a little closer.'

They moved away from the main tunnel into the crisscross of side passages and measured out all the rope they had. Some of them had lost theirs in all the running and falling and hiding, but among them they had more than a hundred and fifty feet.

Ulf nodded, satisfied. 'This may work.'

Reiner though it was the first time he had seen the big man happy.

Once they had worked out who would do what and how, they made their way through the twists and turns of the city of tunnels until they reached the river again.

Reiner and the others eyed the water with trepidation. Talking about jumping into it was one thing, the reality was quite another. It was terrifyingly swift and sure to be colder than glacier ice. Visions of smashing into the granite piers at full speed filled Reiner's head, and from the shivers and swallows of the others they were having similar thoughts.

'I can't swim,' said Hals, anxiously.

'Nor can I,' said Pavel.

'There will be no swimming involved,' said Ulf, tying the longest length of rope around a stone piling. 'The current will carry you faster than you could swim anyway.'

'What you must do,' said Reiner, dreading it himself even as he did his best to make it sound easy, 'is hold your breath and try to stay underwater until you are beneath the bridge. We don't want some dirt-eater looking over and seeing us floundering about.'

'We shall have to leave our breastplates behind,' said Ulf, 'or we will sink like stones.'

'Leave our breastplates!' cried Hals. 'Are you mad? What if we have to fight the Kurgan?'

'If we find ourselves fighting the Kurgan,' said Reiner, 'breastplates won't be enough to save us.'

Ulf looked toward the bridge again, paying out rope, then turned to Oskar. 'Gunner, how far to the bridge?'

Oskar was examining a hole in his jerkin with an all-consuming interest.

'Oskar,' said Reiner. 'Oskar, wake up, lad. How far is it to the bridge?'

Oskar looked up, blinking, then squinted at the bridge. 'Forty-seven feet. I'd like another sip from the bottle, please.'

'When we reach the far shore,' said Reiner.

Ulf paid out forty-seven feet of rope, using his enormous boot as a measure. 'Too little and we won't reach the bridge,' he said. 'Too much and we'll bash our heads in.'

Reiner swallowed thickly, 'Then I better go first, as I have the thickest head.' He wanted to go last, but it was expected of the leader that he lead.

Ulf tied the rope around Reiner's waist. 'Don't gasp as you come up,' he said. 'They may hear.'

'Why not tie a stone to my feet and knock me senseless,' snarled Reiner. 'They'd never see me then.'

Ulf looked as if he was considering it.

Reiner turned and sat on the edge of the stone pier. He took a deep breath, and then another. He realised that no amount of deep breaths was going to prepare him, so with a sigh he began to lower himself into the river.

The shock of the cold water almost made him scream, and the strength of the current pulled at his legs so fiercely that what he had meant to be a silent graceful slide became a clumsy plop as he was yanked away from the landing by the rushing water. There was no difficulty in staying underwater. The river pulled him down like a lover. He could see nothing – feel nothing but cold and the pummelling power of the current. But almost as soon as the journey had begun it was over. He jolted to a stop, face down, the rope pulling tight around his waist, and the river knocking him back and forth like a kite in a high wind. He stretched out his arms, feeling for the pier.

It was almost impossible to push against the current, to hold his arm out to his side. If he relaxed at all his arms snapped above his head. His lungs were burning, exploding, desperate to take a breath. At last his left hand touched stone and he pulled himself toward the pier.

His head broke water and he remembered at the last moment not to gasp, inhaling slowly instead, though he longed to suck in air in great gulps. The granite pier rose only a few feet out of the water. He climbed onto its crumbling top and clung, shivering and weak, to the wooden understructure of the orc bridge. He looked up, listening for some sign that he had been spotted, but heard nothing except the endless tread of Kurgan boots passing overhead. He was so cold he could barely feel his fingers. When he had recovered himself somewhat he untied the rope, gave it a sharp tug, and let it slip back into the water. He watched it slither away into the shadows like a snake on the rolling surface of the water.

After what seemed to him to be an endless wait, in which he became convinced that the rest of the party had been discovered and slaughtered and that he was stuck on this pier alone, surrounded by Kurgan in an endless underworld, Oskar broke the water an arm's length from the pier. He was remarkably calm, and Reiner pulled him in with no trouble.

'All right, Oskar?' he whispered.

'Oh yes,' said Oskar, wiping water from his eyes. 'I have no fear of water. I was raised near a lake. It is remarkably cold, though. I might just have a little sip, to keep the chill away.'

'This is not yet the other side.'

They sent the rope back and were joined in turn by Franka, Pavel, Hals and Giano and lastly Ulf. Everyone made their landing quietly except Hals, who cried out in pain because the rope had twisted around his broken leg and wrenched it when he stopped short. Pavel clapped a hand over his friend's mouth until he had recovered himself and everyone looked up, waiting for a horned helmet to peer down at them. Fortunately the roar of the rushing water was loud enough to cover incidental noises.

When at last Ulf arrived and had untied himself, he pried a piece of crumbling rock from the pier and fixed it to the end of the rope so that it would sink and not betray their presence by floating on the surface.

'First part accomplished,' said Reiner, relieved. 'Now for the far wall.'

In a drier environment, those of the party who had a full complement of working limbs would have had little trouble navigating the understructure of the bridge, for the logs were wide and numerous. Unfortunately, the wood had not been seasoned or treated in any way – and was in fact just fresh-cut trees, with sap still oozing from the cut ends – and was slimy with moss and algae, so each step had to be carefully made. In places the logs were so poorly joined – tied together with rope rather than pinned with nails or dowels – that they shifted when weight was put on them. It reminded Reiner of a time when he had been fooling about in the apple trees of his father's orchard after a spring rain and sprained his wrist when he lost his footing. For Hals, with his broken leg, and Oskar with his broken arm, the journey was impossible unassisted. They had to be helped every step of the way. Pavel looked after Hals as usual, and Reiner stayed at Oskar's side, bracing him and taking his hand when he needed it. There were a few near disastrous slips, but at last they all reached the far wall and sat or leaned on the slick logs, catching their breath.

Ulf was shaking his head in dismay. 'Shocking. A child could have built a sturdier bridge. Look.' He poked a thick finger at the ropes that held the logs together. 'They have used the poorest quality rope. It has loosened and rotted in the damp. Why a few strokes with a knife here and there and the whole structure would…' He trailed off, his eyes glazing over.

'Not on your life, you madman,' said Reiner, catching on.

'But we must!' whispered Ulf, suddenly alive with urgency. 'We must! We can stop them in their tracks. More than half of their force would be trapped behind the river. The cannon as well. It would take them days, maybe weeks to rebuild it.'

'What's this now?' asked Hals. 'What does he mean to do?'

'He wants to knock down the bridge,' said Reiner. 'With us on it.' He shook his head at Ulf. 'You'll kill us all.'

'I won't!' said Ulf. There was a catch of desperate hope in his voice. 'If I loosen it just enough, I can tie a rope to a key support and pull it out once we are all clear.'

'And if you loosen it too much, it all falls on our heads before you get a chance,' countered Reiner.

Ulf clenched his fists, controlling his temper. 'Captain, I am an engineer. This is what I know. Will you not trust me in my field as I have trusted you in yours?'

'I do trust you, as an engineer. My fear is that you are allowing your eagerness to stop the Kurgan to drown your engineering knowledge in wishful dreams.'

They all looked up as they became aware that there was silence above them. No troops were crossing the bridge.

'Have they all gone?' asked Franka.

'They can't have,' said Hals.

The silence ended with a fresh roaring and cracking of whips, followed after a long moment by a creaking of wood, a groaning of slaves, and a grinding of iron on stone.

'The cannon,' said Pavel. 'They're moving the cannon.'

Ulf turned to Reiner, eyes pleading. 'Captain, this is an opportunity not to be missed. If we can drop the cannon in the river, we will not only slow them, we will... *castrate* them! They will be half the threat they are now. They may even give up and go home.'

Reiner bit his lip. They didn't have long to act. 'All right,' he said at last. 'What do we need to do?'

Ulf grinned, and began tying what was left of their rope to the support closest to the wall. 'Hals and Oskar. You will tie yourselves to this rope and wait here. The rest of us will spread out along this side of the bridge and cut the ropes that join the supports together. Once you unwind the rope, bring it here and tie one end to this pillar, the other around your waist. We do not want to leap into the river untethered, but if the bridge begins to go, jump, tethered or not. You understand me?'

'I understand yer a madman, and yer going to kill us all,' said Hals, but began to tie the rope around his waist.

Reiner, Ulf, Franka, Pavel and Giano started working their way quickly back through the timbers. The cannon was rolling closer. There wasn't much time. Reiner braced himself in a V and began sawing at a knotted mass of rope that lashed two logs together. For all of Ulf's talk of rotten rope, the fibres were tough and fought his blade. He longed to chop at them, but didn't want to risk the noise. To his left Franka was cutting feverishly. Giano was on his right, cursing under his breath as he worked and looking up constantly.

The cannon was picking up speed, and despite being wet and half frozen, Reiner started to sweat. There was a good chance the great gun would bring the bridge down without their help. Visions of being pinned to the river bottom flashed before his eyes.

Shouts of alarm came from above and the bridge shook with a jarring impact. Reiner clung to the supports as they shivered and swayed. He held his breath. Amazingly, the bridge remained intact. He exhaled. He could hear the Kurgan screaming and a fresh flurry of whip cracking. It sounded as if the slaves had steered the cannon into one of the railings.

A reprieve. Reiner began cutting again as the slaves moaned out a weary chant and began pulling the cannon back for another try. At last he parted the heavy hemp and started unwinding it, reaching around the trunk again and again like a tailor measuring the waist of a fat priest.

He had the binding unwound and had sawn halfway through the fixed end when the cannon rumbled forward again, and this time the slaves' aim was true. The heavy, iron-shod wheels boomed onto the wooden planks and the entire bridge groaned in pain. Reiner could feel the timbers compressing and shifting around him.

When the bridge didn't collapse immediately, he returned to cutting. Franka spidered past him, a coil of rope over one shoulder. Giano was nearly finished as well. They'd done it!

A sudden cry and a splash from the far end of the bridge snapped Reiner's head around. Pavel was clinging to a support beam, his legs dangling over the water. A length of tree trunk was bobbing away down the river, followed by a tangle of rope.

'Sigmar's balls!' cursed Reiner, glancing up fearfully. Had the Chaos troops heard? He chopped through the last few strands of his rope, slung it over his shoulder, and monkeyed toward Pavel as fast as he could. The pikeman's hands were slipping as he tried to get purchase on the slimy log.

A harsh voice barked down from above. Reiner looked up, and locked eyes with a Kurgan overseer, his helmet glinting in the torchlight. For a moment, both of them froze, then the overseer disappeared and Reiner heard him shouting a warning. The cannon stopped.

'Ulf!' Reiner cried as he reached Pavel. 'We have been discovered! Rope off and into the water.'

'But I must still remove the centre joist!' came Ulf's reply.

'It's too late!' Reiner braced himself, grabbed Pavel's arm and pulled.

'Shouldn't we just drop in?' the pikeman asked as he struggled to get on top of the log.

'Without tying off?' asked Reiner. 'We'd never stop.'

Pavel was fortunately wiry and light. With Reiner's help he got a fresh grip on the log and swung his legs up to brace against another. 'Sorry, captain,' he said as he scrambled to his feet. 'It fell away as I stepped on it.'

'Forget it. Just move. We need to tie off by the wall or we'll miss the landing.'

But as they turned toward the south bank, Kurgan began climbing over the side of the bridge.

'Hurry!' said Reiner, drawing his sword.

As he and Pavel clambered through the beams, the cannon began moving again, but this time it was moving back toward the north side of the bridge. The slaves were pulling it back, out of danger.

'No!' wailed Ulf. He started forward, maul in hand, ducking recklessly though the supports. 'The cannon must fall!'

'Urquart! Fall back!' Reiner bellowed. 'I order you...!'

A Kurgan dropped on the beam before him, roaring and swinging his axe – and immediately slipped and fell into the rushing water. He disappeared instantly. Reiner laughed, but a second, a hulking heathen with a flaming red beard, was more cautious, bracing with one hand while menacing Reiner with his sword. More were climbing down behind him.

'We'll never get through that lot,' said Pavel.

Reiner pulled the coiled rope off his shoulder and handed it back to the pikeman, his eyes never leaving the advancing Kurgan. 'Tie off. We'll go together.'

Pavel hesitated. 'But did you not say…'

'We'll have to risk it. It may be death, but it's not certain death.'

The redbearded Kurgan lashed out. Reiner ducked and the heavy sword bit into a support trunk. Reiner had a clear shot. He thrust at the man's chest, but his sword glanced off the norther's mail shirt.

Reiner retreated back behind the pillar as red beard's blade splintered it again. Behind the giant another Kurgan screamed and tumbled into the water. The others turned. Ulf was behind them, wading into them, maul swinging. Reiner gasped, amazed at the big man's agility on the treacherous framework. He seemed more at home there than on solid ground. All those years clambering up and down scaffolding, building fortifications, Reiner decided.

For a foolish moment, as another Kurgan fell victim to Ulf's maul, Reiner thought the engineer might win, but more and more Kurgan were climbing over the rail. There was an endless supply of them. The battle could not be won.

'Tied off, captain,' said Pavel, behind him.

'Tie my waist.' Reiner dodged another cautious blow from red beard and backed up. He felt Pavel's hands go around his waist. 'Ulf!' he bellowed. 'Fall back! Abandon the bridge!'

'No!' shouted the engineer. 'I must strike just one blow!' He dodged back from two Kurgan, then slipped around the far side of a pillar, ending up behind them. 'Jump!' he called. 'Everyone jump! I will join you.'

Red-beard leapt forward and lunged at Reiner. Reiner jumped back desperately and evaded the blade by a finger's-width, but lost his balance. His feet flew out from under him and he fell backward. He had a brief flash of Pavel flailing, and then icy black water closed over him. The current yanked him down river like a giant hand.

The answer to whether Pavel had finished tying him off came almost immediately. He jerked to a brutal stop, the thin rope biting painfully into his waist. Something slammed into his left side. Pavel. The current stretched them out in the water like men side by side on a rack. The cold was unbearable. Reiner fought to bring his arms down and grab the rope. He tried to raise his head out of the river. The water split at his chin like the prow of a ship. It filled his mouth.

Reiner at last caught the rope. He pulled, and rose a little from the water. He sucked air. Pavel was struggling to do the same at his side. Reiner let go with one hand and grabbed him behind the neck. He nearly fell back again for this kindness, but Pavel at last found the rope and they both got their shoulders above the waves, though the strain was considerable.

To his right, Reiner could see that Oskar, Franka, Hals and Giano were in the water as well, all together in a knot at the end of their ropes. They were tantalisingly close to the landing and were straining to reach it. A Kurgan splashed by between them, trying to swim, and Reiner looked back at the bridge.

The cannon had nearly reached the north bank again, with slaves pushing and pulling at it fore and aft. Below them, Ulf was swinging at a support post in the centre of the bridge as Kurgan climbed toward him from all directions.

He struck a mighty blow that Reiner heard above even the noise of the water, but the post remained in place. He swung again, but a Kurgan leapt at him and spoiled his aim. Then they were all around him, slashing and thrusting. Ulf took a cut in the shoulder, another in the leg. He roared and swung in a circle, knocking three Kurgan into the drink. Five took their place.

Pavel began pulling at the rope, trying to climb toward the bridge, against the current. 'Curse the lummox!' he cried. 'Pull, captain! We have to help him!'

'Ulf!' screamed Reiner. 'Jump, you fool.'

Ulf laid about him like Sigmar-in-the-pass and amazingly, for a moment, the Kurgan fell back before him, uncertain on the precarious struts. With a desperate, all or nothing swing, Ulf bashed the post again, a terrific smash that jarred it loose at last. It spun out of place and bounced down through the joists and beams to splash into the water.

The Kurgan under the bridge froze, looking around uneasily. At first it seemed that nothing would happen, then the bridge groaned like a dyspeptic giant. Another post fell out of place and dropped into the river, then another.

With a roar of rage, one of the Kurgan leapt at Ulf, bringing his sword down like a headsman's axe. Reiner watched in horror as the stroke chopped down through the engineer's collarbone all the way to his heart, causing an eruption of blood.

Ulf was dead, but it seemed that, by slaying him, the Kurgan had slain the bridge as well, for as Ulf fell, so did the span, twisting and collapsing with a slow grace.

'The damned fool,' said Reiner, swallowing hard. 'I told him…'

The bridge sagged first in the centre, and then disintegrated all along its length. On the north side the overseers were screeching at the cannon slaves to pull faster, but the great gun was still on the planks, and began rolling back down the swiftly steepening incline, dragging slaves and Chaos marauders with it, until at last its weight proved too much for the remaining supports, and it crashed through into the drooping understructure. The cannon crushed Ulf and the Kurgan warriors and took them and the bridge with it as it plunged into the river with an enormous splash.

A huge swell of water rose and began rolling down the river as the cannon's daemon mouth sank below the waves like some sea monster in its death throes. Reiner felt the tension on the rope around his waist slacken as the bridge became free-floating debris, all of which was heading their way.

'Brace yourself!' Reiner cried to Pavel, and risked a glance toward Hals, Franka, Oskar and Giano. They were just pulling themselves onto the landing. Franka lay gasping on the flagstones. Giano was trying desperately to get a leg up. Then the wave hit, covering the landing in a waist deep blanket of water. As he was lifted and tossed about on the swell, Reiner saw Franka and Giano swept off the landing and back into the river with Oskar and Hals as if by a broom.

Their only piece of fortune – if it could be called that – was that the wave pushed the four toward Reiner and Pavel; almost drove them into them in fact. Reiner had to raise his hands to fend off Oskar's knees as he whirled past him.

'Catch them!' Reiner called to Pavel. 'Hold 'em fast!'

He and Pavel grabbed at the spinning mass of limbs and torsos. Through the splash and foam, Reiner locked eyes with Franka. He grabbed her arm and pulled her close. Pavel had Hals by the collar.

'At least,' choked Giano, spitting water, 'we all die together, eh?'

'Watch out!' shouted Franka.

Reiner looked back, and almost had his head caved in by a huge log rising and turning on the swell. He kicked it away and another struck him in the back. The remains of the bridge were bounding past them, tumbling and knocking together with great hollow thuds, ropes like spiderwebs tangling them together.

A rope caught Oskar across the chest, jerking him forward, which in turn dragged his companions. Hals pulled the rope up and over Oskar's head. The artilleryman was barely conscious. Hals and Pavel tried to hold him out of the water, but they were sinking as well.

Reiner caught a rope-draped log and clung to it. 'Climb on! All of you.'

The light, which had been dimming quickly as they sped away from the Kurgan's torches, went out entirely as the river took them around a bend. Reiner pulled Franka to the log by feel and she threw an arm over it. Reiner heard the others doing the same as the current swept them further into the darkness at a terrifying speed.

# CHAPTER SIXTEEN
## FELLOWS OF THE BRAND

THEY CLUNG SILENTLY to the log as it hurtled through the deafening black, the sound of their gasping breaths lost in the rushing roar of the river. All of them were too cold, too battered and too frightened to speak. There was no room in Reiner's head for wondering what might happen next, for making plans. He was a rat, clutching at flotsam, trying to keep his head above water, fighting for one more breath, all higher thoughts gone, surrendered to the unconquerable animal instinct to hold on to life while there was yet strength in his limbs.

Other pieces of debris glanced off them, causing fresh cries of pain and fear, and they careered bruisingly into the walls as the river whipped them around corners, each time making Reiner think that they had crashed into the invisible obstacle that would at last break their bodies and crack their skulls.

His brain was so numb that he failed to wonder what the steadily growing roaring in his ears might mean until he and the log and his companions flew helter skelter down smooth, stairstepped rapids and plunged into a roiling boil of leaping water.

After a frightening liquid battering, the log resurfaced and Reiner found that they were floating in relatively calm water. When he had caught his breath, he raised his voice. 'Are we all here?'

'Aye, captain,' said Pavel.

'Here,' said Franka.

'And where might here be?' grumbled Hals.

'We are swallowed by the dragon,' said Oskar. 'He will use us as fuel for his fire.'

'Shut you mouth, crazy man,' said Giano angrily.

From the echoes they seemed to be in a large cavern. There was still a current, pulling them insistently along, but there were no waves. A hollow knocking – almost musical – came from their left. It sounded to Reiner like enormous wooden wind chimes banging together.

Reiner had been in the cold water for so long he hardly felt it anymore, but he had a dangerous urge to sleep, to let go of the log and drift away. He shook himself.

'I don't suppose anyone's tinder is dry enough to...' He paused as the roar of the rapids, which had been growing gradually quieter, got louder once again. 'Are we coming to a second set of rapids?' he asked.

'I don't believe so,' said Franka, her teeth chattering. 'For the other sound is still to our left.'

The rapids roared in their ears and they were splashed with spray, then after a moment the rumble once again diminished, while the wood-on-wood sound remained a constant.

'We are travelling in a circle,' said Reiner, his stomach sinking. 'We are caught in a vortex, a whirlpool.'

There was a short silence as this sunk in, then Pavel spoke.

'So what's to be done? What d'we do?'

'Do?' Reiner laughed mirthlessly. 'My dear pikeman, we are doing it.'

'But captain,' said Hals uneasily. 'You must have a plan. Y'haven't failed us yet.'

Reiner cursed inwardly. Damn them and their confidence in him. In his mind he had failed them at every turn. Why couldn't they see it? 'I'm sorry, lad. I'm fresh out.'

The sound of the rapids came and went again, but this time not so loudly, while the hollow wooden knocking grew slowly but steadily louder. The current was getting stronger as well, pulling them around the vortex more and more quickly, while at the same time tugging them down as well. Their tired arms were finding it harder and harder to hold onto the log.

'Is no shore to swim?' asked Giano querulously.

'I know not,' said Reiner. 'But feel free to explore.'

The Tilean didn't seem so inclined.

As they passed the sound of the rapids for the sixth or seventh time Reiner noted a strange phenomenon. The surface of the water was not level. It sloped away on their left like the side of a soup bowl, and now the wooden knocking was drowning out everything else.

'The bridge,' said Reiner, understanding at last. 'All the timbers have gathered here, but wood doesn't sink.'

'Oh!' Franka cried. 'It's pulling me down!'

'By Sigmar,' said Hals. 'It has me too!'

'Hold fast!' Reiner cried, though he knew now it was hopeless.

The current pulled almost straight down now. Their log slid down the side of the soup bowl and smashed end-on into the others as they spun in a violent circle, held forever in agitated equilibrium in the centre of the vortex by the current that pulled them down and their buoyancy that forced them up. The impact jarred Reiner so hard his teeth snapped. He lost his grip and was instantly sucked down the whirlpool's maw. The swirling logs bludgeoned him as he sank, but he was soon below them, pulled inexorably down, as if some sea-serpent had him by the legs and dragged him to its underwater lair.

Once again animal instinct overcame him, and though he knew that struggle was useless, he clawed at the water, trying desperately to swim to the surface, to reach air again, while his lungs screamed in fiery agony.

The current angled suddenly sideways and his shoulder struck a rocky surface hard enough that he almost gasped. He was dragged into an airless tunnel, scraping along the rough roof at a furious pace. He could feel his clothes, and then his skin shredding. All became a jumble of pain and speed and disorientation. He knew not if he was alive or dead, cold or hot, in pain or unable to feel anything at all. Red lines wormed across the blackness of his vision. A rapid thumping pounded in his ears. His chest felt as if it were being crushed in a vice.

And then, suddenly, there was air.

And he was falling.

Into water.

Again.

THE FIRST THING Reiner thought when he broke the surface was, 'What is that Sigmar-cursed light?' For a unbearable brightness seared through his eyelids. Then he began coughing violently, retching out great quantities of water as he paddled his arms to stay afloat. He could hear others around him doing the same. His eyes watered. His nose ran. His throat felt like he had swallowed broken glass, but at last he cleared his lungs and looked around.

He and his companions were bobbing in a small mountain lake, surrounded by tall pines. A high waterfall dropped to the lake from a cleft in a crag. A pair of ducks skimmed into a landing on the water. He was outside. The bright light was the sun, setting over a carpet of evergreens. They were out of the tunnels at last!

Pavel gurgled beside him. 'Captain, I... Hals is... I can't...'

Reiner looked at him. The pikeman was thrashing around, trying unsuccessfully to keep his head above water. Hals floated face down beside him, not moving. Beyond them, Oskar was calmly paddling one-handed for the shore, while Franka and Giano recovered themselves.

'Giano, Franz,' called Reiner. 'Can you swim?'

'Aye,' they said in unison.

'Then help Pavel to shore.'

Reiner caught Hals around the shoulders and turned him face up, then swam him to the nearest landfall, a muddy bank, thick with rushes.

As they reached the shallows Pavel crawled out under his own power and Franka and Giano helped Reiner drag Hals out and lay him on his side. Reiner pounded him on the back.

For a moment Hals didn't move, and Pavel sat watching anxiously. But at last, with a violent convulsion, the pikeman began coughing and spewed an alarming amount of water out onto the mud. Reiner held his head until he was through.

'All right, pikeman?' asked Reiner.

Hals looked at him with bloodshot eyes. 'I'm... never bathing... again.'

Pavel grinned with relief. 'And why should ye start now anyway, y'old goat?'

Reiner patted Hals's shoulder and stood, looking at them all. He shook his head. 'A sorrier lot of wretches I have never seen.'

Hals laughed. 'Yer no beauty yerself, captain.' He sneezed and shivered.

They were all shivering. Franka's teeth were chattering uncontrollably and Reiner realised that his were doing the same. Tremors racked his body. His fingers were blue. Though there were buds sprouting on the nearby dogwoods it was only early spring yet, and they were still high in the mountains. 'Any missing fingers? Any bones broken?'

They all shook their heads, but it was clear that they had all been badly battered by the river and the vortex. Hals has lost his crutch. Pavel's eye-patch was missing and his eye socket gaped like a red cave. Oskar had a fresh wound on his brow. Giano's forearm was badly scraped and Franka's shirt was newly red, as if the gashes she had received from the warhound had reopened.

Reiner squinted at the nearby mountain tops, looking for familiar landmarks. 'Have we any idea where we are?' he asked.

Hals sat up and looked around. 'It don't look familiar,' he said. 'But by the sun we must be on the southern face of the Middle Mountains.'

Reiner nodded. 'Wherever we are, we must find shelter. We need to dry off in front of a fire before we all catch our deaths.'

'There's chimney smoke down the hill, captain,' said Oskar. 'And do you still have the bottle?'

Reiner was loath to give Oskar any more of the juice. It already seemed to have him in its clutches, but he'd been most helpful of late. He put his hand in his jerkin. The vial was gone. 'Sorry, old son. I've lost the bottle.'

Oskar swallowed, and nodded. 'I see. Very well.' He hugged his arms and shivered.

Reiner coughed and sniffed. 'Right. Come on, you lot. Let us go take advantage of their hospitality, whoever they are.'

The party got to their feet and began limping and staggering down the piney slope.

Reiner looked back at the waterfall. It was as high as three houses. He shook his head. It seemed incredible they had survived.

'Water is a softer landing than rock,' said Franka, reading his thoughts.

Reiner grimaced. 'Not by much.' They started after the others.

Reiner stole a sidelong look at the girl, who walked contentedly beside him. Curse her for being so companionable, he thought. It was unnerving for a woman to be so easy to get along with, so much like a friend, and yet so…

He shook his head, trying to dislodge the image of her standing before him, naked to the waist.

It was only a short walk to the village – a good thing, for none of them were capable of a long walk, and they were ill-equipped to face any danger they might come across. In addition to being lame and sore, they were almost entirely unarmed. Though Reiner had his pistols – but no powder or shot – and he and Giano still had swords, the river had taken almost everything they hadn't lost earlier. Giano's crossbow was gone. Oskar's long gun, Franka's bow, Pavel's spear, Hals's crutch-that-was-once-a-spear, all lost in the darkness of the underworld, leaving them with only their daggers.

They reached the village just as the sun disappeared behind the mountains and the landscape shaded to purple. At first, as they came upon it through the trees, it seemed a quaint place, strangely untouched by the war – a few small stone and shingle cottages tucked in a fold of hills by the stream that wound away from the lake. Smoke rose from a few chimneys.

Reiner heard Franka choke back a sob beside him.

'It's so much like home,' she said, recovering herself.

Reiner knew just how she felt. After so long in such an alien place, these little huts, which he wouldn't have given a second look a fortnight ago, looked more welcoming to him now than the finest inn in Altdorf.

But as they got closer, the hair began to rise on Reiner's neck. Though he couldn't put a finger on it, something didn't feel quite right. Despite the smoke coming from the chimneys, the place had a neglected, deserted air. Weeds grew unrestrained around the houses and windows gaped open, their shutters hanging off their hinges. There was a disconcerting look of vacancy about the whole place.

The companions walked warily up the muddy street to the well at the centre. Not a sound of human occupation did they hear: not a voice or movement, not the crying of a child or the hammering of a smith. They looked around them, hands on the pommels of their swords and daggers. The empty windows stared back at them.

'Ahoy, the village!' called Reiner.

His voice echoed between the houses and away into the woods.

'Where are they?' asked Franka in a hushed voice. 'Where have they gone?'

'And whose smoke is that coming from the chimneys?' grunted Hals.

'Maybe they went for a walk,' said Oskar.

'And maybe you'll die finding out,' said a rough voice behind them.

The companions whipped around. A gaunt man with lank hair that hung over his forehead stood at the corner of a house. He was dressed in patched and filthy clothes and carried a bow, an arrow nocked and ready. He raised a hand and more ragged men stepped out behind him, and from behind every house that faced the square. All levelled bows at Reiner's men. They were surrounded.

The gaunt man stepped into the square with two lieutenants, a short, pug-nosed fellow with a tuft of sandy beard on his chin, and a grim, powerfully built warrior with long braids that hung to his chest. They gave the companions a once over. The leader grinned, revealing teeth like a horse's.

'Yer a sorry lot,' he said. 'What chewed you up?'

'Almost not worth jumping,' said pug-nose with a sneer.

Braids pointed at the Reiner's leather jerkin, then Hals's and Pavel's. 'Their kit's regulation, what's left of it. They're soldiers.'

The smirk died on horse-face's lips. His eyes turned cold. 'You hunting us?' he asked Reiner. 'You scouts?'

'Best to kill 'em, Horst,' said pug-nose. 'Just t'be safe.'

'Aye,' said horse-face, pushing his hair aside to rub his brow. 'Aye, I suppose we must.' As his hair fell back, Reiner thought he saw a familiar scar on his forehead. The bandit signalled his men and Reiner heard the creak of two-dozen bowstrings being pulled back.

'Wait!' cried Pavel.

'What we do?' gabbled Giano, anxiously. 'What we do?'

'Take off your gloves, quick!' said Reiner.

'Take off…?' echoed Giano, puzzled.

Reiner yanked off his still-damp glove with his teeth and held up his hand, showing the scar on the back. 'Brothers!' he shouted, smiling as wide as he could. 'How glad we are to see fellows of the brand.'

The men paused. Horse-face and his lieutenants squinted at his hand in the dying twilight as Reiner's companions tore off their gloves and showed their brands as well. The ring of archers relaxed their strings, but did not yet lower their bows.

'We… we are recently escaped from a convict column,' said Reiner, making it up as he said it. 'On the way to Middenheim to slave in the rebuilding of the walls. We were closely hounded by wolf swords, and nearly…'

Braids stepped forward, menacing. 'You have brought Knights of Ulric into our hills?'

'No, no,' said Reiner quickly, holding up his hands. 'No, no. We lost them a day ago, but then, alas, became lost ourselves. And many a misadventure have we had since. There was the bear…'

'And the waterfall,' added Franka, picking it up.

Reiner nodded. 'And the tumble down the cliff.'

Braids grabbed Reiner's hand in an iron grip and examined the brand closely. He rubbed it with his thumb, as if he expected it to smear. When it didn't, he grunted and turned away.

Horse-face grinned. 'You really are a sad bunch, ain't you? Tenderfoot flatlanders stumbling about in the hills like little lost babes.'

Reiner drew himself up. 'We are not yet hard-bitten brigands like yourselves. Our brands are still fresh. But we have all our lives to learn.'

Horse-face and pug-nose laughed and their men joined in.

'Well then, my young sprouts,' said horse-face. 'Let us start you off on the right foot. Let us show you the joys of the life of the outlaw.' He bowed. 'Welcome to our humble home.'

And as he said it, a few gaunt women and dirty children stepped out of hiding and peered from the windows and doors of the rundown huts to stare at the newcomers.

Reiner frowned, confused, as Horse-face led him and the others to the largest house. It was fully dark now. '*Are* you bandits? Or is this your village?'

Horse-face grimaced. 'Well, both, really. A lot of us lived here before the war. Or here abouts. But then we went off to fight for Karl Franz – and much thanks we got for it I can tell ye. Cut down in our thousands while the knights made fine speeches.' He waved a hand. 'But y'know all about that, yes? At any rate, when we returned, they're all dead, our mothers and fathers, sisters and sons…' He sighed and looked around. 'We'd love to live here again, but with them northern devils nesting up in the hills, we've to be on our guard. Can't set up anything permanent.'

'You do a good job of disappearing,' said Reiner.

'Aye,' said Horse-face. 'Plenty of practice.' He shrugged. 'If we could ask m'lord Hulshelft for protection he'd root the heathen out and make this land safe again, but, well, we're marked men, most of us, like you. He'd string us up sooner than help us.'

They entered the house. Reiner's visions of venison and boar roasting on spits and wine flowing from casks of stolen monastery wine were dashed as Horse-face offered him and his companions a place at the small fireplace and called for food. There was no furniture. They sat on the floor. The wind whistled through the missing windows and leaves and dirt gathered in drifts in the corners. The fire was barely large enough to warm Reiner's hands, let alone dry his clothes.

Though they had little, the bandits weren't stingy. They filled bowls and cups for them and refilled them when they were empty. There was no venison. No boar. Only stringy rabbits and squirrels crisping on sticks, and a thin gruel of oats and wild carrots that was mostly water. At least it filled their bellies and warmed their bones.

As he gnawed the last bits from the bones of a rabbit, Hals leaned in and murmured in Reiner's ear. 'Why don't we throw in our lot with these lads?' said the pikeman. 'They seem a likely bunch.'

Reiner made a face. In the light of the fire it was easy to see how malnourished the bandits were, their faces hollow and sickly. These were not merry outlaws living a life free from care. They were wanted men, hard hunted and longing to return to their former lives – a dream as impossible for them as flying to Mannslieb on the back of a griffin.

'Why not?' Reiner asked. 'Because I'd be at home here as you would be in the court of the king of Bretonnia.'

'Ah,' said Hals. '"Tain't so bad.'

'You think not? Look at them. They're starving.'

'That's winter,' said Pavel, joining in. 'Things get a touch lean in the winter, certain. But it's spring now. There'll be food aplenty soon.'

'And another winter next year.'

Hals shrugged.

Reiner lowered his voice and hunched closer to them. He didn't want the bandits to hear. 'You're more than welcome to stay. I'll not stop you.' He held up his scarred hand. 'But there's a chance at the end of this journey to erase this mark and return to a normal life – for me to go back to my card rooms and taverns, for you to go back to your farms. That sounds better to me than mucking about in the woods eating coneys for the rest of our lives.'

Hals and Pavel frowned and sat back to whisper between themselves. After a moment Hals leaned forward again, looking sheepish. 'We're with ye, captain.' He shrugged. 'We... well, sometimes it's a mite hard to believe in going home, after everything what's happened.'

'Aye,' said Reiner. 'I know.'

A hand slapped his back and Horse-face sat down next to him with Pug-nose and Braids at his sides. 'Well, how do you like our homely fare?' he asked with a grin.

'The best we've had in days,' said Reiner truthfully. 'And we thank you for your hospitality.'

The bandit waved a dismissive hand. '"Tisn't hospitality. Y'll pay for it, one way or the other. If you stay with us y'll pull yer weight. If you leave us, yer purses will be lighter.' He grinned. 'Have y'decided which it's to be?'

Reiner sighed. He had expected something like this. The men were bandits after all. 'I believe we will be moving on. You have been more than generous, but I can see that you have little to share. You have no need of six more mouths to feed.'

'Where will you go?' asked braids.

Reiner frowned and rubbed his hand. 'The man who gave us these brands rides with Count Manfred, who means to win back Nordbergbruche from the northers. We have unfinished business with that man, if we can find Nordbergbruche.' He grinned wryly. 'We're sorely lost.'

Pug-nose made a face. 'You would run back to the arms of your executioners? Are you mad?'

'We are willing to die, so long as our nemesis does as well.'

'They go to betray us,' said Braids. 'They hope to win clemency by turning us in.'

Reiner glared at him. 'Do you think I am such a fool, sir? I know the Empire's justice as well as any. There is no clemency for one who wears the hammer brand. They may spare me the axe, but only to give me a pick and shovel. I will die in chains one way or the other.'

Braids snorted, but Horse-face waved an annoyed hand at him. 'Leave off, Gherholt. You would suspect Sigmar himself.' He smiled at Reiner. 'You've picked a busy destination. We spied Manfred marching toward Nordbergbruche this morning, and Chaos troops have been coming down out of the crags to defend it. We mean to go there after the battle, to pick the bones of the dead.'

A thrill of fear ran up Reiner's spine. 'Do you think battle has already been joined, then? Did you see the troops of the count's brother, Baron Albrecht?'

'Afraid your nemesis might die without your help?' asked Pug-nose.

'Precisely. I don't want some filthy norther cheating me of my vengeance.'

Horse-face shook his head. 'Manfred wouldn't have reached Nordbergbruche before dark. They won't form up until daybreak. We didn't see his brother.'

Reiner made a noise halfway between a sigh of relief and a moan. He was relieved that they hadn't come too late, but almost undone by the realisation of what they must now do. 'And how far is Nordbergbruche from here? Can we reach it by morning?'

Pug-nose laughed. 'In your condition? I doubt you'll make it at all.'

'Ye'll walk all night,' said Horse-face. 'But you'll be there before dawn.'

Reiner's companions groaned.

'Can y'tell us the way?' asked Hals.

'Aye, we can,' said Pug-nose.

They waited for him to continue, but he didn't.

'*Will* y'tell us the way?' asked Pavel.

Horse-face shrugged. 'Well, friends, that depends on the contents of your purses.'

Reiner smirked. He had known it would eventually come to this. Fortunately, unlike the cut and thrust of duelling, hard bargaining was a kind of melee he was comfortable engaging in. Here he could lead with confidence.

'Well, we don't have much to barter with, do we? For if you don't like our offer you can just kill us and take what you want. Therefore I must call upon your honour as brothers of the brand to deal squarely with us, and to remind you that cornered rats bite. You will get a fair price for your help if we make a bargain. You will get more than you bargained for if you fight us.'

Horse-face exchanged a look with his companions, then nodded. 'Fair enough. Tell us what you want, and make your offer.'

IN THE END, they got away with their lives, but it cost Reiner all Veirt's gold crowns, one of his pistols, and the sword his father had given him to do it. He hadn't minded giving away the gold. Gold always came and went. That was its purpose. And if Count Manfred rewarded them as he hoped, they would all soon be knee-deep in gold. The sword however was a painful parting. Certainly he could buy a better sword with Manfred's gold, but it wouldn't be *his* sword, would it?

In addition to not killing them, the bandits had patched their wounds – though not as expertly as Gustaf would have – given them directions and provided them all with weapons: a lesser sword for Reiner, spears for Pavel and Hals – as well as a crutch – bows for Franka and Giano, and an enormous old blunderbuss for

Oskar, but only enough powder or shot for a handful of charges.

As per the bandits' directions, they followed the stream down the mountain until it reached a rutted track, took that east until it crossed a main road, and then travelled north and east as fast as their bruised, exhausted bodies would carry them.

Franka grinned as she walked beside Reiner. 'Never have I heard someone lie like that. So fluently, so credibly. Hurrying to kill the man who branded us. Ha!'

'Well, isn't it the truth?' asked Reiner. 'We may not have the pleasure of killing Albrecht with our own swords, but if we succeed, we will certainly cause his downfall.'

'But that is not what you implied. You made us out to be the most bloodthirsty of villains, out for terrible vengeance. Never have I known such a master of deceit.'

Reiner smirked. 'Have you glanced in a looking glass lately?'

Franka punched him and looked around anxiously to see if anyone else had heard.

They followed the road all night, shambling like sleepwalkers for mile upon endless mile. Soon all conversations ceased. All pretences of vigilance fell by the wayside. Reiner felt in a dream. Sometimes it seemed he walked in place and the world rolled beneath him. Sometimes he seemed to float above himself, watching from the clouds the line of ragged, limping figures as they wound through the dark woods and moonlit wastelands. It grew colder as they marched into the early morning and the warmth of the fire became a distant memory. They huddled in their torn and threadbare jerkins, longing for the heavy cloaks they had been issued at the beginning of this mad journey.

Long after the moons had set, they reached the turning the bandits had mentioned and began to climb back into the hills. Their pace became even slower. More than once Reiner caught himself just before his knees buckled. He wanted more than anything in the world to curl up and sleep, right in the middle of the road, if need be. His chin sank to his chest at regular intervals, and there were a few times when he opened his eyes and couldn't be sure when he had closed them.

At last, just as a faint pink light was touching the snowy peaks of the mountains, they crested a pass and saw in the distance a massive stone castle looming like a vulture over a shadowed valley. The valley opened before Reiner and his companions like a Y, with the castle perched on a high crag at the intersection of the two arms. At the base of the Y, just below where they stood, was a village. No lights shone there, but further up the valley, a cautious distance from the castle, the morning campfires of a great army shone in the darkness.

'Come on, lads,' said Reiner. 'Journey's end.'

'One way or the other,' grumbled Hals, but he was too tired to put much feeling into it.

They marched wearily down the hill to the valley floor. As they reached the village they saw that it had been destroyed. Not a building had its roof, or all four of its walls. Most had been burned to the ground. The yawning holes of the burned-out windows stared at them reproachfully, like betrayed comrades come back from the dead. The silence was utter. Though dawn was breaking, not a bird sang. No wind stirred the blackened, leafless trees. It felt as if the world had died, had uttered its last breath, and lay cold and motionless at their feet.

As they trudged up the dirt road that ran up the middle of the valley, the camp began to appear over the intervening trees and hedgerows – the white tents in their ordered ranks, the banners of the knights or companies housed within hanging limp above them, Manfred's banner of a lion in white and gold rising over them all, and to Reiner's relief, no sign what so ever of the manticore banner.

Noise returned to the world as they got closer – pots and pans clanked, ropes and harnesses creaked, hooves thudded, grindstones whirred, sleepy soldiers coughed and grumbled. Smells followed the sounds: porridge and bacon, horse, man, leather and canvas, wood smoke and gunpowder. Reiner and his companions inhaled deeply. Though Reiner had enlisted with reluctance, and would have sworn that he'd hated every minute of his time in the army, the sounds and smells of the camp filled him with such homesick joy that there were tears in his eyes.

He had to swallow a few times before he could speak. 'Cover your brands. We don't want to be thrown in the brig *before* we see Manfred.'

At the perimeter of the camp a picket stopped them. 'Who goes there!' cried a sentry.

'Couriers, with news for Count Manfred,' said Reiner, with as much military brusqueness as he could muster.

The picket stepped out of the shadows, eight men led by a sergeant – a square-shouldered, square-jawed swordsman. He wrinkled his nose and gave Reiner's company a suspicious once over. 'You look more like tinkers. Where is your seal?'

'We have been set upon, as you can see,' said Reiner. 'And have lost almost everything, but we have urgent news of Baron Albrecht's advance that the count must hear.'

'I'll decide that. What's the news?'

'It isn't for your ears, damn your eyes!' said Reiner drawing himself up. 'Do you think I'd tell a mere sergeant what torture couldn't get out of me? My name is Captain Reiner Hetzau and I demand to see Count Manfred!'

The sergeant gave Reiner a dirty look for pulling rank, and turned to one of his men. 'Hergig. Take his lordship and his men to see Captain Shaffer. I've had enough of him.'

This comedy was repeated four times in front of various captains, lieutenants and knights – before Reiner and his companions were at last led to the majestic white tent with the gold and white pennons in the centre of the camp.

'Your men will wait out here,' said the captain of the count's guard. 'And you will hand over your sword and daggers.'

Reiner did as he was told and the knight ushered him through the canvas flap.

In the tent, Count Manfred Valdenheim was at his breakfast. He sat at big table, wolfing down ham and eggs and ale while his generals stood around him, splendid in their brightly polished armour and colourful capes, debating positions and strategies on the map spread out under the count's plates and cups. Manfred was still in his small clothes and shirt, his hair rumpled from sleep. A soldier's camp bed heaped with furs sat unmade in one corner, the count's suit of gold-chased steel armour standing like a sentinel on a rack at its foot.

The count was much like his younger brother in size and build, a large, barrel-chested man with the general aspect of an all-in wrestler, but where Albrecht's face had a cruel, shrewd cast, Manfred, with silver touching his temples and streaking his beard, had a kindly, bemused look. He seemed, in fact, almost too gentle to be the leader of a great army. But when the captain who had ushered Reiner into the tent whispered in his ear and he looked up, the ice blue gaze he turned on Reiner showed the steel beneath his fatherly exterior. He wasn't a wolf in sheep's clothing, thought Reiner, for he sensed that the count's easy nature was not a pretence, but rather a sheep who ate wolves for dinner – a man to be wary of, a man it would not be wise to lie to.

'What news, courier?' he asked briskly.

Reiner dropped to one knee, as much from exhaustion as deference. 'My lord, I have news of your brother which I am afraid you will not want to hear or wish to believe.'

The generals paused in their muttering and looked up at him.

Manfred lowered his knife and fork. 'Go on, my son.'

Reiner swallowed. Now that it came time to speak, he was afraid to tell his tale. It seemed so damned implausible. 'My lord, a fortnight ago, I and my companions were ordered by your brother to escort the Lady Magda Bandauer, an abbess of Shallya, to a Shallyan convent in the foothills of the Middle Mountains, where she was to open a sealed vault and retrieve from it a battle standard of great power.'

'Valnir's Bane,' said Manfred. 'I know of it, though the nuns always denied they had it.'

'And well they might, my lord,' said Reiner. 'For it is no longer the mighty weapon for good it once was. The blood of Valnir has soaked into the very fibre of the banner and corrupted it, making it into a thing of great evil. But when we discovered this, Lady Magda was not dissuaded from taking it. Instead she attacked us with its malevolent power and escaped, killing our captain and leaving us to die.'

Manfred raised an eyebrow.

Reiner hurried on. 'My lord, at the beginning of the journey we were led to believe that your brother hoped to use the banner to aid you in retaking Nordbergbruche, but I believe now that this is not the case.'

The generals muttered in consternation. Manfred waved them silent.

'I do not wish to speak ill of your brother,' continued Reiner. 'But Lady Magda is an ambitious woman who longs for power, and I believe that under her influence, Albrecht has come to share her ambitions. It is my fear that he marches south under Valnir's Bane not to help you win back Nordbergbruche, but to take it for his own.'

'Lies!' cried a voice as the generals erupted in angry babbling. 'It's all lies!'

Reiner turned with the others.

Standing in the tent's opening were Lady Magda, once again the stiff, stern sister of Shallya, and Erich von

Eisenberg, resplendent in beautiful blued steel armour, a plumed helmet tucked under his arm. It was he who had spoken.

# CHAPTER SEVENTEEN
## THE BANNER HAS ENSLAVED THEM

'This man is a traitor and a murderer,' said Lady Magda, pointing at Reiner. 'Arrest him immediately.'

'It is he, not the reverend abbess,' chimed in Erich, 'who tried to take the banner for his own. It is he who murdered the valiant Captain Veirt and nearly slew me when I came to Lady Magda's aid.'

'My lord,' said Reiner, turning to Manfred. 'I beseech you. Do not believe them. They mean you ill…'

'Enough!' cried Manfred. 'All of you.' He turned on Erich and Lady Magda. 'What is this intrusion? What is your business here?'

Erich saluted. 'My lord, we come from your brother. He bids you a good morning and wishes to inform you that he is an hour away with a force of two thousand men. They are well rested and will be at your disposal upon their arrival.'

The generals met these words with glad cries, but Manfred looked from Erich to Reiner and back with a scowl of uncertainty upon his brow. 'Until a moment ago I would have welcomed this news, for two thousand men will almost double our army, but now…'

'My lord,' said Erich, 'you mustn't believe him. This man is a traitor, a convicted sorcerer, charged with a hundred murders by witchcraft.'

'That isn't true, my lord,' countered Reiner. 'Your brother himself acknowledged that the charges against me were false.'

'If that is so,' said Erich, 'then ask him to remove his left glove and explain the brand he wears there.'

'You wear the hammer brand?' asked Manfred.

Reiner pulled off his glove and raised his hand for Manfred to see. 'We all do,' he said. 'Baron Albrecht chose all the men for the mission in secret from the brig at Smallhof – more proof that his intentions were less than above board. He branded us all to make it more difficult for us to desert. Master von Eisenberg wears it as well.'

Erich smiled. 'He convicts himself out of his own mouth, my lord.' He drew off his mailed gauntlet and held up his hand. 'I have no brand, as you can see.'

Reiner stared. The back of Erich's hand was smooth and unblemished. The scar was gone. Reiner thought he saw a cruel smirk flash across Lady Magda's haughty face.

'My lord,' Reiner cried. 'It was part of the bargain! Baron Albrecht promised us that he would have a sage of the Order of Light remove the brands when we returned with Lady Magda and the banner! Von Eisenberg is as much a criminal as any of us. He was to be hanged for murdering a child.'

'He piles lie upon lie, my lord,' said Erich. 'He knows not when to stop.'

'Nor do you, sir,' said Manfred, hotly. 'Now be silent both of you and let me think.'

Reiner closed his mouth on further protests and watched as Manfred eyed them both appraisingly. Reiner groaned.

Though he hoped against hope, he knew he had lost. Erich's last thrust had struck home, and even if it hadn't, he looked the hero of the piece, with his shining armour and handsome face, his golden beard and noble bearing, he was every inch a champion of the Empire. While Reiner, though he was loath to admit it, looked like a villain, with his half-starved, unshaven face, his unwashed black hair and gambler's moustache, his filthy, shredded clothes, his ancient, rusty sword. Even freshly scrubbed and impeccably dressed he had always looked a bit of a rogue. In his present condition, he looked the worst sort of guttersnipe, an alley-basher and ne'er-do-well.

A knight burst through the tent flap. 'My lords! The Chaos troops are moving! They form up in front of the castle!'

'What?' cried a general. 'They leave the protection of the castle? Are they mad?'

'Mad indeed,' said Manfred, standing and wiping his mouth. 'They are warptouched. But there is method here.' He crossed to his armour, snapping his fingers for his valets to begin dressing him. 'If their look outs have told them of Albrecht's approach then they may mean to destroy us before we double our strength.' He looked at his generals. 'Call your men to arms. I will have all units in position within a half hour.'

The generals saluted and filed out of the tent.

The knight who had brought Reiner in stepped forward. 'My lord, what would you have me do with this one?'

Manfred glanced up at Reiner as if he had already forgotten who he was. He waved a hand. 'Hold him and his companions until the battle is over. I will decide what to do with them later.' He turned to Erich and Lady Magda. 'Return to my brother. Tell him to advance with all possible speed.'

Erich saluted. 'At once, my lord.'

As he and Lady Magda turned to leave, Erich caught Reiner's eye. He curled his lip in a triumphant sneer. Reiner tried to give him a rude gesture in response, but the knight grabbed his arm in a crushing grip and marched him out before he could get his fingers up.

There was no brig in the camp, so after they had been fed and their wounds seen to by a hurried field surgeon, they were placed under guard in a dry-goods tent behind the camp kitchen. They could see nothing but the sacks of flour they sat on and the jars of cooking oil and lard and the dried peas and lentils that were stacked around them, but through the thin canvas they could hear the cries and horn blasts of captains calling their companies to order, the thudding thunder of cavalry galloping by, the trot of infantry quick-marching into position to the sharp tattoo of regimental drums.

Pavel and Hals fidgeted at the sounds like the old warhorses they were, turning at every new sound, longing to be part of the action. Oskar sat huddled in a corner, shivering. He had asked Reiner twenty times for a sip from Gustaf's bottle, forgetting each time that Reiner had lost it in the tunnels. In another corner Giano cursed and muttered to himself in his native tongue.

Reiner was too angry to sit. He paced back and forth between the hessian sacks.

'Damn Manfred,' he growled. 'Damn Karl Franz. Damn the whole bloody Empire! Here we are, a bunch of villians and ne'er-do-wells, going against our nature and our self interest to do them a good turn, to save them from not one, but two grave dangers and do they thank us? Do they heap riches at our feet, feed us oranges and ambrosia? No! They ignore our warnings and fit us for the noose again.' He kicked a pickle barrel. 'Well, I for one have finished playing at heroes. Chaos can take Karl Franz, Count Manfred and all the other high-born fools. From now on I am no longer a citizen of the Empire. I will be free of its grim pieties and stifling stoicism. From now on, I will be a citizen of the world. Who needs Aldorf when I have Marienburg, Tilea, Estalia, Araby, even far Cathay and all the mysteries of the unknown east? I will drink deep of freedom and call for more.' He turned to his companions, fire in his eyes. 'Who's with me? Who wants to walk a free man in a place where the hammer brand means nothing?'

The others stared at him, blinking.

'That was quite a speech,' said Hals. 'Almost as good as the one y'gave us about being homesick if we left the Empire, when you wanted us to stay with you.'

'Which one's the truth?' asked Pavel.

Reiner frowned. He'd forgotten the other speech. 'Er, why, both. I don't say I won't be homesick. I will. Altdorf is where my heart is, but as the Empire has turned its back on us, I will turn my back on it. And I'll be damned if I'll be miserable doing it. I'll go laughing, and to the depths with them all.'

Hals grinned. 'I hope y'never try to sell me a cow. I bet I'd end up giving ye my farm to buy it.'

'He's right all the same,' said Pavel. 'The jaggers have done us down. We owe 'em no favours. I'm in.'

'Oh, aye,' said Hals. 'Me as well.'

'And me,' chimed in Franka.

'You come to Tilea?' Giano grinned. 'I bring you my home. Cook you Tilean feasting, hey?'

'I certainly don't want to stay here,' said Oskar. 'I think they mean to hang us.'

'Good lads,' said Reiner. 'So where shall it be first? We'll need to make some money before we travel too far.'

'I vote for Marienburg,' said Hals. 'They speak our language. They pay good gold for willing pikes, and...' he nodded knowingly at Reiner. 'I hear their card-rooms rival Altdorf's.'

Reiner smirked. 'Hardly. But it is a port city. From there we can go anywhere. Are we agreed?'

The others nodded.

'Excellent.' Reiner looked around. 'Then we should find a way out of this tent.' He crossed to the tent flap and peeked out. The two guards who were meant to be guarding them stood well away from the opening, craning their necks, trying to see over the intervening tents to the field of battle. The camp seemed otherwise deserted, doused campfires smouldering and pennants flapping limply in a fitful breeze.

Reiner turned to his companions. 'Well, I don't think we'll have much trouble…'

A hair-raising noise interrupted him. It was the sound of five thousand savage throats raised in unison, roaring a barbaric war cry. The ground shook beneath Reiner's feet, and the muffled reports of cannon buffeted the tent.

'They've charged us,' said Franka. 'It's begun.'

Pavel and Hals were rooted to the spot. Giano's eyes darted around, anxious. Oskar flinched.

A second roar answered the first and the ground shook again. The noise rose to a continuous low rumble, pierced with shouts and trumpet blasts.

Reiner peeked through the tent flap again. Their two guards had almost disappeared around the mess tent. Their whole posture said that they longed to be supporting their fellows, not stuck far behind the lines.

Reiner turned back. 'Under the back wall. Our jailers will pay us no mind.' He paused as he saw Pavel and Hals's faces. They were stricken and grim. 'Have you changed your mind so soon?'

The pikemen were tortured with indecision. It was obvious that the idea of leaving their countrymen to fight the Chaos troops alone was odious to them, but at the same time, their sense of honour and justice had been wounded.

At last Hals shrugged. 'After the way they treated us? Let Chaos take them. I care not.'

'Nor do I,' said Pavel, but Reiner could tell he felt uncomfortable saying it.

'Then now is the time,' Reiner crossed to the back wall of the tent and began shifting sacks of flour out of the way. The others joined in. There was little danger of discovery. The air was filled with the sound of cannon fire, screaming horses, and the clash of arms.

When the sacks were cleared they pulled up on the bottom of the canvas wall until they loosened a tent peg, then wormed through the gap. Reiner stood watch behind the tent as the others squirmed out behind him. They were close to the south edge of the camp, in the stem of the Y-shaped valley. The sounds of the battle came from the north.

'Now,' said Reiner. 'Back to the road we came in on and west to Marienburg.'

'Wait,' said Giano, dragging a flour sack out of the tent. 'Prepare this time.' The sack had been emptied of most of its flour and filled with various dry goods. He grinned at them as he slung it over his shoulder and gestured around at the nearby tents. 'Store is open.'

Reiner smirked. 'You haven't a clear idea of the difference 'twixt mine and thine, do you, Tilean?'

He shrugged. 'If they want, they would take with them.'

Hals and Pavel scowled at him, but they joined in the hunt for weapons, clothes, armour, packs and cooking utensils. There was almost no one in the camp, only a few camp-followers and cooks – easily avoided, and though the soldiers had taken their main weapons to the battle, they had left all manner of swords and daggers, bows and spears behind. Reiner found a brace of pistols with powder and shot in a knight's tent. Oskar found a caisson full of handguns and took one, though he found it difficult to load with his left arm in a sling. Within the space of half an hour they were almost as well kitted out as they had been when Albrecht first freed them.

They assembled at the edge of camp, dressed in the colours of half a dozen companies, weapons bristling from belts and scabbards, and bulging packs over their shoulders.

'Now are we ready?' asked Reiner.

His companions nodded, though Pavel, Hals and Franka looked a trifle uncomfortable to be wearing gear stolen from their fellow soldiers.

'Then we march.'

They followed the path that had led them to the camp not two hours before. They were still dead tired, but their confinement had allowed them something resembling rest, and they were at least alert.

They had almost reached the village at the south end of the valley when Oskar pointed over the burned out buildings. 'Look.'

Winding down the hill beyond the town was a column of marching men, spearpoints and helms aglitter in the morning sun. The head of the column was hidden within the town, but there was no question as to whose army they must be.

'Albrecht,' said Pavel.

'Aye,' said Reiner. 'Come, we'll take cover 'til they pass.'

They hurried to a blackened barn on the outskirts of the town and hid inside it. Almost instantly they heard the tramp of marching feet and the clop of hooves. They stepped to the walls and peered through the charred boards as the head of the column emerged from the town. First to appear were Albrecht, Erich and Lady Magda, leading a company of more than a hundred knights. Erich rode between the baron and the abbess on a white charger clad in shining barding, but though Albrecht was splendid in his dark blue armour and a scarlet-plumed helm, and the company of knights was a magnificent sight that should have filled the hearts of men of the Empire with pride, the sight of the blood-red banner that Erich held aloft, couched in his lance socket, killed all emotions except an all pervading dread.

It was awesome and awful to look upon, slapping thickly against its pike, less like heavy cloth than a square of flesh cut from some umber giant, and though Reiner couldn't take his eyes off it, it was at the same time hard to look upon directly, for it radiated gloom and dread like a black sun. He felt at once physically sick, and at the same time compelled to join the column of men that followed it. Its power was a hundredfold greater than it had been in the crypt. Held by a hero at the head of an army, it had acquired at last its full allure. It tugged at Reiner like a magnet, and as he tore his eyes from it and looked around at his companions he could see that it affected them the same way. Pavel and Hals white-knuckled their spears. Franka and Giano stared, grimacing. Oskar was standing, stepping out from cover.

'Get down, you fool,' hissed Reiner, pulling the artilleryman back by his jerkin. He was glad of the distraction. Anything to keep him from looking at the banner again.

'Myrmidia,' breathed Franka. 'Look at them. The poor damned souls.'

Reiner reluctantly peered again through the wall. The knights had emerged entirely from the town and now companies of pike, sword and gun were marching out after them. In a way it was the most ordinary sight in the world, soldiers of the Empire on the march – simple farmers, millers, blacksmiths and merchants taking up arms in a time of war as they had done for centuries. But there was something about them, something almost indefinable, that was repulsive. They marched well enough, almost perfectly in fact, all in step, ranks dressed neat enough to warm a sergeant major's heart, but there was something about their gait, something loose and boneless, that reminded of Reiner of sleepwalkers. They stared straight ahead, jaws slack, eyes glazed. Not one of them looked left or right, or squinted at the sun to judge the time, or talked to his companions, or scratched his backside. Their eyes seemed fixed on the banner before them. They hardly seemed to blink.

'Zombies,' said Giano, making a warding sign.

'The banner has enslaved them,' said Franka, shuddering.

Reiner nodded. 'There is no longer any doubt of Albrecht's intentions. He comes not as his brother's saviour, but as his slayer.' He whistled out a breath. 'I'm glad we will be nowhere near when Manfred gets pinched 'twixt that hammer and the Kurgan anvil.'

The last of the mindless troops trailed out of the town. Reiner shouldered his pack and stood, but the others hesitated, gazing after the receding column.

'Captain,' said Hals, uncertainly. 'We can't just...' He trailed off.

'What do you mean?' asked Reiner.

Hals scratched his neck and made a face. He shifted uncomfortably on his feet. 'Captain. I know what I said before. I care not a fig what happens to Manfred. I hope he and Albrecht tear each other to pieces, but those lads back there in the camp...'

'*And* the ones in the column...' said Franka.

'Aye,' continued Hals. 'Them too. Enslaved or not, they're our mates. It's them who'll be pinched 'twixt hammer and anvil. It's them what will die in their thousands.'

'It ain't right to see Empire men fighting one another,' added Pavel. 'Brother against brother. It's wrong.'

'This is no war to protect Empire lands,' said Franka. 'Those men go to die so that Lady Magda can be a countess. So that Albrecht can take from his brother what he was not given at birth.'

Reiner swallowed a curse. He didn't like where this was going. 'So, do you say that we go and die as well? What side do you suggest we fight on?'

'I say that we do what Captain Veirt was trying to do when he died,' said Franka. 'Destroy the banner.'

Pavel and Hals nodded emphatically.

'Maybe we get our rewards then, hey?' said Giano.

'But what about freedom?' asked Reiner. 'What about Marienburg and Tilea and all the rest? What about drinking the world dry?'

The others shrugged uncomfortably. Even Giano wouldn't meet his eye.

'Sorry, captain,' said Hals at last.

Reiner groaned and looked longingly toward the path that rose up out of the valley. On the far side of that hill was the road to freedom. He had only to climb it and Albrecht, Manfred and Lady Magda would be mere unpleasant memories. What did he care about the fates of a few thousand peasants? It wasn't he who was leading them to their doom. All he wanted was a quiet life, free from evil banners, power-hungry nuns and mad barons. All he wanted was to be back in Altdorf or, if he must, Marienburg or Tilea, parting fools from their money by day and dallying with delicious doxies by night.

And yet...

And yet, though he was reluctant to admit it, the banner and the mindless marchers who followed it had sickened him as well. He had always had a problem with authority. That, more than any faintness of heart was the reason he had done his best to avoid serving in the army. He valued his individuality too much to obey orders without questioning them. He knew too many noble idiots – his beloved father came to mind, not to mention Erich von Eisenberg – to think that a lord was always right just because he was a lord. The idea of some eldritch relic that could remove one's ability to question an order, that took away one's individuality entirely and made of one a mindless drone, enslaved to the will of one's leader, filled him with outrage.

The banner was an abomination. He could imagine the whole Empire falling under its sway. A whole nation blindly following the whims of its leader, taking over its neighbours until there were no more Marienburgs or Tileas to escape to, until at last Reiner too marched along with all the others, just one more sheep happily following the butcher to the slaughterhouse.

'Right,' he said suddenly. 'On your feet. We'll need to cut wide to avoid their line of march, then hurry back on the double to beat them there.'

Pavel and Hals let out great sighs of relief. Franka smiled. Giano nodded. Oskar looked upset, but fell in line with the others as they started across the muddy stubblefields north of the village.

# CHAPTER EIGHTEEN
## THE CLAWS OF THE MANTICORE

THE JOURNEY CROSS-COUNTRY was harder than they expected. Climbing fieldstone walls and hunting for openings in high hedges slowed them down, and they were still as sore as they had been the evening before. Hals winced with each step, not just from the pain of his broken leg, but from the raw skin under his arm from the rubbing of his makeshift crutch.

Reiner shook his head as he surveyed them. What chance had the likes of them to destroy the banner? They would most likely have to fight Albrecht to do it, not to mention Erich and a host of knights. It was ridiculous. They were like beggars planning to storm Middenheim.

They lost sight of Albrecht's column as they stole back through Manfred's deserted camp and came at last upon the battlefield. From their position far behind Manfred's lines it was difficult to see anything, just a confusion of men and horses and horned helmets appearing and disappearing through drifting streamers of smoke. Reiner couldn't tell which, if any, were Albrecht's men or if they had even arrived yet.

'We need a better view,' he said. The steep hills to the right of the camp seemed a good vantage point. 'Up there.'

Hals groaned, but with Pavel assisting him he gamely limped up the slope behind the others. After a while, they found a goat path that made the climb easier and led them along the side of the hill to a spot where the battle was laid out before them like a painting.

They stood facing west above the branching of the Y-shaped valley. Nordbergbruche castle was a little to their north, rising from the promontory between the angled arms of the Y. Manfred's camp was to the south, well within the stem of the Y. From the armies' current positions, it was easy for Reiner to picture how the battle had begun. The Chaos troops had spilled out of the castle's gate and formed a long line that spanned the valley just below the branching arms. Manfred had lined up to face them in the mouth of the stem. He was outnumbered two to one, and was downhill from the Kurgan force, but he had two minor advantages: the steep hills on either side of the valley made it difficult for the Kurgan to flank him, and a rocky hill with a small wooden shrine of Sigmar at its top jutted up out of a thicket of bare-branched trees just inside the mouth of the stem, further narrowing the front that the Kurgan could attack him on, as well as providing a perfect platform for his mortars and cannon. The hill was virtually a cliff at its northern end, but sloped away gently to the south, and Manfred's army was split, one half on either side of it.

Unsurprisingly, Manfred's army had been giving ground. The Chaos force were forcing them into the stem like a handgunner packing wadding into the barrel of his gun. They had not yet pushed Manfred so far south that he had lost the advantage of the rocky hill, though this looked likely on the east side of the hill, where Manfred's forces were stretched thinner and the Kurgan forces were heaviest. If this happened it would be disaster for Manfred, for the Kurgan would then be able to sweep around the little hill from the south and attack the forces on the west side of the hill from the rear.

Hals sucked air through his teeth. 'Looks grim.'

'Aye,' said Reiner. 'But imagine how much worse it would be if we hadn't tipped the northers' cannon into the river. If they were firing that monster from the castle ramparts it might be over by now.'

'Where's Albrecht?' asked Franka.

'There,' said Oskar.

Reiner and the others looked where he was pointing. Through the haze of smoke that wafted over the battlefield, Reiner could just see a troop of knights riding out of patchy woods on a hillside on the far side of the valley. Albrecht was at their head, a vexillary holding aloft his family banner beside him. Several companies of swordsmen and handgunners followed the knights, and four cannon crews began to wheel their pieces into position. Somehow the baron had found a path through the hills and had come out north of the battle line. A charge down the steep hillside and he could take the Chaos force in the rear.

'And there,' said Oskar again, pointing south.

Reiner looked left. Out of Manfred's camp came company after company of spearmen, all marching in the disturbing loose-limbed gait Reiner's companions had seen before. They formed a broad front two hundred paces behind Manfred's lines.

'Does he support Manfred after all?' asked Pavel, confused. 'Have we been wrong all along?'

A great cheer went up as Manfred's beleaguered army noticed Albrecht's forces, and they began to fight with renewed vigour. The Kurgan saw the fresh troops as well, and began frantically trying to manoeuvre men into position to meet Albrecht's knights. But the elation of the men and the terror of the Kurgan were both short-lived, for strangely, though they were in excellent positions to attack and support, Albrecht's troops, both on the hill and behind Manfred's lines, remained where they were, silent watchers to the bloody battle before them.

'What is he waiting for?' asked Hals angrily. 'He could have 'em on the run.'

'Where is the banner?' asked Reiner.

They looked for it, but couldn't see it.

Meanwhile, the few feet of ground Manfred's troops had won back when the Chaos force had become confused by the new threat were rapidly being lost again as the northers fought desperately to beat the foe they faced before the new foe attacked.

Beside Reiner, Franka choked. 'There it is! On the little hill.'

Reiner and the others followed her gaze. Riding up the rocky hill in the centre of Manfred's line was Erich, mounted on his white charger and holding the vile banner in his lance socket. Reiner could see Manfred's gun crews advancing toward the young knight, weapons drawn, but they didn't attack. Instead, the men fell to their knees before the banner and let him pass.

Erich reached the crest of the hill and raised the banner high over his head. It flapped thickly in the wind. Though there was no change in the weather, a pall seemed to fall across the whole valley, as if the banner sucked up light. Reiner felt a chill shiver through him. Franka moaned. The effect on the troops in the valley was even stronger. Manfred's men faltered and fell back all along his line, stunned into inaction by the banner's dread influence.

The Chaos troops hesitated as well, confused by this strange symbol, but they seemed not to fear it as the men of the Empire did, and took advantage of their foes' numb horror to press their attack. Manfred's army defended itself, but it was clear that their morale was at low ebb, and they fought as if distracted.

'We've got to reach that banner before it's too late,' said Franka.

'Is already too late,' said Giano. 'I want to help, but they dead men. We go, hey?'

Reiner shook his head. It was strange. He could hear the screams of the dying and the bellowing of captains and sergeants trying desperately to rally dispirited troops. He knew the situation was hopeless. He knew riding into that mess was suicide. If he did what was in his best interest, he would be slinking over the hill with his tail between his legs, but he couldn't do it. He couldn't let that stiff-necked clot Erich win the day. He couldn't let Lady Magda and that overstuffed sausage Albrecht have their way either. 'No. We stay. Come on. Straight for the hill.'

He started down the steep hill with his companions limping and grunting behind him. They reached the valley flood just south of Manfred's line, where field surgeons and camp followers were dragging the dead and the wounded away from the fighting and broken men moaned on the ground. A hundred paces to their left, standing in eerie silence, was Albrecht's infantry: rank after rank of spearmen and archers gazing blankly forward like flesh statues. Reiner's companions began picking their way across the body-littered field. Dressed as they were in Empire colours, none of Manfred's troops paid them any mind.

Halfway across, a movement out of the corner of his eye made Reiner look up. On top of the rocky hill, Erich was standing in his stirrups and waving the evil banner in a circle over his head.

'Sigmar's hammer!' grunted Hals. 'Here they come.'

Reiner looked to his left. Albrecht's infantry were advancing in perfect unison, spears lowered, eyes dead. Behind them, the archers aimed at the sky and loosed their arrows.

'Run!' Reiner cried. 'Run for the hill!'

The company ran as fast as they could, hobbling and stumbling and cursing as a cloud of arrows arched overhead, momentarily blocking out the sun, then fell to earth like black rain. Fortunately, the archers' target was Manfred's line, and only a few that fell short landed near them. It wasn't so fortunate for Manfred's men, who screamed in surprise and terror as the arrows cut them down.

'The traitor!' cried Franka.

Over the shoulder of the rocky hill, Reiner could see that Albrecht and his knights had answered Erich's signal as well. They were charging down into the valley, lances levelled. From Reiner's vantage, it was impossible to see who they were attacking, but the barbaric howl of rage that echoed across the valley gave the answer. Albrecht had lowered the boom on the Kurgan at last.

'He attacks both sides!' barked Hals as he limped on. 'What is the mad fool about.'

'Mad?' gasped Reiner. 'He has more genius than I credited him with. He wants the castle for himself, so he waits until each side has weakened the other, then attacks both.'

They reached the thin woods that surrounded the rocky hill just as Albrecht's spears overran their latitude. Manfred's battle line, already much depleted, had divided into two back-to-back fronts, one line continuing to face the Kurgan, the other turning to face their ensorcelled brothers, who at the last twenty paces broke into a charge.

It was a disturbing sight, for Albrecht's troops showed no emotion as they rushed forward. They raised no battle cry, snarled no challenge, only stared dead ahead as they drove their spears into Manfred's ragged line in perfect unison. And yet for all their lack of emotion, they were savagely bloodthirsty, slashing and hacking like butchers, biting and clawing and gouging eyes as they came to grips with their foes, and all the while gazing blankly into the middle distance.

Adding to the slaughter was the fact that Manfred's troops were hesitant to attack the spearmen. Cries of

'Erhardt, what ails you? Do you not know me?' and 'Beren, brother, I beg you, stop!' rose over the melee, only to end in gurgling screams. Reiner heard a sob beside him and saw that Hals was weeping. The only factor even slightly in Manfred's troops' favour was that Albrecht's spears, though unimaginably fierce and brutal, were also clumsy and awkward – puppets manipulated by a poor master.

'Up the hill,' said Reiner, turning Hals away from the battle and pushing him into the bare woods. 'Hurry.'

But before they got far, they saw that the base of the slope was guarded by a unit of swordsmen, all with the glazed look of the slaves of the banner.

'This way,' said Reiner, and quietly led the others north along the side of the rising hill until the swordsmen were out of sight behind them. The hill angled up like a board pried out of a plank floor and the sides were steep. Reiner pushed through brambles and brush until he reached it.

'Oskar, take my arm.'

He helped the artilleryman mount the slanting strata while Pavel did the same for Hals. Franka and Giano spidered up around them. They pulled themselves over the edge a third of the way up the slope and crouched in a clump of bushes, looking down to see if the swords had noticed them. The men continued to stare blankly into the woods. Further up the hill Manfred's gun crews were back at work at their cannons, and it was with a sick lurch of the heart that Reiner realised that they were firing on their own troops. The banner had turned them against their own. Beyond the gun crews, at the crest of the hill, Erich stood, facing out over the battle field, banner held high. His back was protected by six more swordsmen. Lady Magda stood beside him, watching the battle intensely.

A grunt came from the nearest cannon. One of the crew was shambling toward them, eyes dull, his ram-rod raised like a weapon. Reiner looked down the hill. The swords hadn't yet noticed him.

'Shoot him,' he whispered.

Franka hesitated. 'He isn't our enemy. He is one of Manfred's men.'

The man's grunts were getting louder as he tried to warn his fellows. He waved the ram-rod around his head.

'No longer. Shoot him.'

'But his mind is not his own.'

A dull thwack sounded beside them and the crewman dropped with a crossbow bolt in his chest.

Giano shrugged and reloaded. 'Any man try to kill me is enemy.'

But he had silenced the man too late. The swordsmen had heard him, and were lumbering up the hill, while more cannoneers were turning their way.

'That's torn it,' said Reiner. 'We'll be surrounded in a minute.'

'Just a moment,' said Oskar suddenly. 'I have an idea.' He hurried toward the approaching cannon crew.

'Oskar!' Reiner groaned, then started after him. 'Come on you lot,' he said over his shoulder. 'It's now or never.'

'Since when does that one have ideas?' growled Hals, as he and the others followed.

Oskar dodged around the gunners' clumsy swings and ran for their gun. Pavel clubbed one of the gunners aside with the haft of his spear and Reiner kicked the other to the ground, reluctant despite his orders to Franka to kill the befuddled soldiers.

At the cannon, Oskar uncorked a keg of black powder, stuffed a length of lit match-cord in the hole, and kicked it down the hill. It rolled and bounced down the slope toward the advancing swords, fuse fizzing, as he primed a second keg.

Reiner grinned. It *was* a good idea. He hadn't thought the gunner had it in him.

As Oskar started the second keg rolling, the first hit one of the advancing swordsmen in the chest, knocking him flat. The others turned somnambulantly to look at him –

and paid the price. The keg exploded amidst them, blowing them all to red ruin.

Oskar gaped. 'They... they didn't run.'

Reiner grimaced. 'You haven't been paying attention.'

The second keg bounded past the troops' maimed bodies and exploded in the woods at the base of the hill. A dozen trees caught fire, and the flames began to spread.

'That'll keep reinforcements at bay,' said Pavel.

'They won't need reinforcements,' said Hals. 'This lot'll do for us.'

Reiner looked behind him. All the men on the hill had turned at the explosion. The gun crews were leaving their cannon and advancing on them, and Lady Magda, Erich, and his swords were staring at them.

'Scum!' cried Erich, stepping toward them. 'Do you still plague me?'

'No,' said Lady Magda, holding him back. 'The banner must stay here.'

'As you wish, lady,' said Erich, shrugging off her hand. 'There is no need to move. Back to your cannon!' he called to the gun crews. 'I'll handle this rabble.'

The artillerymen obeyed like sheep.

'Shoot him!' shouted Reiner, drawing his pistols, as Erich started to turn the banner. 'Kill him!'

Franka and Giano raised their bows as Oskar aimed his handgun by laying the long barrel across the splint of his broken wrist.

'Hold your fire!' Erich commanded, and to Reiner's chagrin, he found it impossible to disobey the order. He could not force his fingers to squeeze the triggers. The others were similarly affected, shaking with the effort to shoot.

Hands shaking, Giano finally fired his crossbow, but the bolt flew off at an angle. 'Curse it!' said the Tilean, frustrated. 'My hands no listen!'

'It's the banner,' said Franka, her arms trembling as she held her bow at full draw.

Erich laughed and raised the banner, pointing at them with his free hand as his six swordsmen advanced. 'Kneel, soldiers! Listen to your leader. I am your rightful captain, You must follow my orders. Kneel and bow your heads.'

To Reiner's left and right Pavel, Hals and Oskar fell to their knees. Their chins dropped to their chests, though he could see them struggling to raise them. Reiner felt an almost unconquerable urge to follow suit. Erich *was* their rightful leader. He was the most senior officer now that Veirt was dead, and he was so strong and brave and had so much more experience than Reiner. It would be such a relief to let the mantle of command slip from his shoulders and let someone else lead again. Reiner's knees bent, but as he looked up to his beloved leader, he paused halfway to the ground.

Erich's face was twisted in a smug sneer, a jarring discontinuity with the noble image of him Reiner held in his head. He froze as his mind fought to reconcile the two pictures. To his left he saw that Giano and Franka were similarly halted in mid-genuflection.

Erich's swordsmen were closing, moving not like soldiers of the Empire, but like apes, hunched and menacing, eyes blank, mouths slack. Reiner tried to move, but his limbs couldn't answer the conflicting commands his mind was sending them.

The first swordsman reached Franka and raised his sword like an executioner. Franka shook with the effort to leap away, but could not. The sword was coming down.

'No!' barked Reiner, and fired his first pistol without thinking, blasting a ball up through the swordsman's jaw and out of the top of his head. The man dropped, gouting blood and spilling brains, and Reiner found that this small disobedience had broken the banner's hold on him. He could move.

The pistol's report had freed Franka and Giano as well. They stumbled back from the attacking swordsmen, gasping and cursing, but Oskar, Pavel and Hals were still frozen, sagging bonelessly to the ground. The swordsmen closed to cut them down.

Franka, Reiner and Giano jumped forward again to defend their comrades. Franka lunged under a swinging blade with her dagger, but was clubbed to the ground by the swordsman's elbow. Reiner blocked a sword that swung for Oskar's head, then shot its owner through the heart with his second pistol. Giano threw his crossbow in a swordsman's face and stabbed him through the heart with his sword.

'Kneel, curse you!' Erich bellowed, but they were too busy to listen.

'Hals! Pavel! Oskar!' cried Reiner as he parried two blades. 'Wake up!'

Franka stumbled up, dazed. A swordsman pulled back his sword to hack at her. She dodged unsteadily to the side and he missed. Reiner chopped through the man's shoulder to the bone. He looked up dully and stabbed at Reiner as if he hadn't felt the blow at all.

Surprised, Reiner forgot to parry, and had to drop desperately to the ground to avoid the thrust. The swordsman raised his sword for the killing blow, but suddenly a spear thrust up into his ribs. Reiner glanced to the side. Pavel clung to the spear like a lifeline.

'Thankee, lad,' said Reiner, rising. He hamstrung the swordsman and turned to face another.

Pavel was still too muddled to answer. Beside him, Hals was slapping himself in the face and cursing, fighting the banner with all his will. Reiner and Giano guarded them. Oskar crawled away from the melee, dragging his gun.

Three swordsmen remained. They fought with crude strength, but little finesse. If Reiner and his companions had been in good health and in full possession of their faculties they would have made short work of them, but dazed and wounded as they were, they were nearly as ungainly as their mesmerized opponents. The swordsmen's attacks smashed into their parries with numbing force, and they shrugged off wounds that would have had normal men screaming.

Franka helped Reiner kill another sword, cutting his throat with her dagger from behind while Reiner kept him busy.

'Go on, captain,' called Hals as the swordsman fell. 'We've these last two. Go teach that brainless jagger a lesson.'

Reiner looked to where Erich and Lady Magda watched the fight with anxious eyes. He didn't want to face von Eisenberg one on one, especially when the knight had the power of the banner giving him strength. But someone had to do it. With a sigh he plucked a pistol from the belt of a fallen swordsman and started up the hill as his companions fought on behind him. Smoke and sparks blew all around him as the woods that surrounded the hill burned like brittle hay. It was almost impossible to see the battlefield through the flames.

Erich thrust the banner at him. 'Kneel, dog! As Baron Albrecht's vexillary, I command you! Do as he ordered! Obey me!'

Lady Magda smirked as Reiner staggered, the force of the order like a yoke on his neck, bearing down on him. The urge to kneel and kiss the ground was nearly overpowering. But having fought it off once, it was easier to disobey a second time. He kept walking, shaking his head in an attempt to clear it.

'Sorry, von Eisenberg,' he said, forcing the words through his lips. 'You've picked the wrong troops to try your sorceries on. Brig scum are terrible at following orders.'

With a squeak of fear, Lady Magda backed away, then turned and ran to the edge of the cliff. She snatched up a yellow flag from the ground and began to wave it vigorously over her head.

Reiner paid her no mind. He raised his pistol and aimed at Erich.

'Put it down, Hetzau,' called Erich. 'I command you.'

Reiner fought the order and kept hold of the gun, but only just. Firing it was out of the question. His fingers would not obey him.

Erich laughed and slashed at him with his free hand. The knight was unarmed, and ten paces away, and yet Reiner flew back as if punched in the chest with a battering ram. He crashed to the ground, gasping, a fiery pain burning his ribs and abdomen. He looked down at himself. His leather jerkin was untouched, but blood was seeping through his shirt. He tore it open. Three deep gashes had opened the flesh of his abdomen. He could see the white of his ribs through one. He winced in agony.

'The claws of the manticore. he croaked.'

'The claws of the *griffin*,' said Erich, smug. 'To rend the enemies of the Empire.'

He slashed again. Reiner rolled to the side and claw marks appeared in the turf where he'd lain.

'If you still think you're fighting for the Empire, you're more of a fool than I thought,' grunted Reiner. 'And griffin or manticore, it's still an unfair advantage.'

'Unfair?' said Erich, offended. 'This is a holy weapon.'

Reiner tied his jerkin as tightly as he could against his wounds. 'And I have only this sword.' He climbed unsteadily to his feet, hissing with pain, and glared up at Erich, who looked like a hero in a painting, his head haloed by the sun. 'I thought you were a man of honour, Erich. A gentleman. What's has become of level ground? Of fair play and a choice of weapons?'

'Why should I play fair when you cheated in our last encounter?'

'I did not cheat. Hals acted on his own. I was perfectly willing to fight another touch with you, only fate intervened.'

'A likely story,' sneered Erich.

'Think what you like,' said Reiner, 'but here I am, ready to go again, to prove who is the better man, and you attack me with invisible claws and muddle my mind with the power of the banner. Dare you call that fair? Dare you call yourself a gentlemen?'

'You question my honour, sir?'

'I do until you put down that banner and fight me man to man.'

'Don't listen to him, you fool!' cried Lady Magda, hurrying back from the cliff-edge. 'You must not put down the banner.'

'Lady, please,' said Erich. 'This is a quarrel between men.' He glared at Reiner. 'How do I know you won't cheat me again?'

Reiner put his hand on his heart. 'You have my word as a gentleman and the son of a Knight of the Bower. I will fight you in accordance with the rules of knightly combat. May Sigmar strike me down if I lie.'

Erich hesitated, frowning.

Lady Magda balled her fists. 'You clothheaded infant, I order you to hold fast to the banner and kill this man instantly.'

This seemed to decide Erich. He raised the banner high over his head, then jammed it savagely into the ground so that it stood on its own. He turned to Reiner, removing his sword belt and drawing his beautiful long sword. 'So,' he said. 'To the death this time?'

'Oh yes,' said Reiner, and shot him in the face. The ball smashed through Erich's nose and exploded out the back of his head with a spray of gore. The knight folded like a house of cards, an expression of surprise frozen on his ruined face. He was dead before he hit the ground.

'You were right after all, Erich,' said Reiner as he threw the pistol aside. 'I *am* a cheat.'

# CHAPTER NINETEEN
## I WILL NOT FAIL AGAIN

REINER LOOKED FROM Erich's lifeless body to Valnir's Bane, stuck in the ground beside it. The banner was within his grasp, all he had to do was to throw it into the burning trees below and it would be destroyed, yet he hesitated to touch it. He forced his hand to reach for it.

'No!' Lady Magda shrieked and launched herself at him with a stiletto. He cuffed her to the ground and turned on her, raising his sword. 'Fine, I'll finish you first.'

She rolled out of reach, then laughed and pointed behind him. 'You insect. Turn and face your doom!'

Reiner looked over his shoulder. Bursting out of the wall of fire that cut off the base of the hill was Baron Albrecht and ten of his knights, their steeds mad with fear, manes and tails smoking.

Reiner's men, standing over the bodies of the swordsmen they had only just defeated, turned as well and stared at the squadron of knights advancing up the slope toward them. Hals lay on the ground, clutching a wound in his good leg, no longer good. Reiner noticed with superstitious dread that sparks from the burning trees had set the little shrine of Sigmar on fire and it burned like a torch. Not a good omen.

The knights lowered their lances and charged the companions. They stepped back wearily, too dazed to run. There seemed no way to prevent them from being run down. Unless...

Suddenly inspired, Reiner snatched up the cursed banner and ran forward, his slashed ribs screaming in protest at the awkward weight. The haft bit his hands with crackling black energy. It surged up his arms and made his joints throb in agony.

'Stop!' he shouted. 'Albrecht! Knights, I command you! In the name of Valnir, stop and turn back!'

Albrecht and his knights reined up hard, their chargers rearing and plunging, as if suddenly faced with a stone wall. One fell from the saddle.

Albrecht forced his horse down and reached for his sword.

'Fall back!' bellowed Reiner. 'Turn about! Down the hill.'

Albrecht froze, his hand halfway to his hilt, fighting the banner's influence with all his concentration, but his knights obeyed the order without a fight, wheeling their horses and starting down the hill again. At the base, the horses shied from entering the burning woods again, and would not continue. The knights spurred them savagely. The horses wheeled and bucked, throwing off their riders, who, horribly, picked themselves up and walked into the burning trees. Through the flames, Reiner could see their cloaks and tabards catching fire as the flames leapt at them. Reiner winced. It was horrible death.

Albrecht remained where he was, visibly shaking as he tried to ignore Reiner's order.

'Turn about, baron!' called Reiner. 'I am your leader now. I command you to charge down the hill!'

Albrecht began haltingly to turn, cursing and sweating as his hands jerked the horse's reins to the right against his will.

Reiner laughed. Baron Albrecht was obeying his commands! What a delicious joke. A giddy thrill ran up his spine. With the power of the banner coursing through him, he could make anyone do anything. A vision of ordering his father to kiss his own arse flashed across his mind, but that was mere childish vengeance. With power such as this he could do great things. It was a dark power, true, but if a man was strong enough to control it, it could be made to work for good. He could right grievous wrongs, depose cruel despots, force evil men to lay down their arms. Or better yet, he thought with a chuckle, he could turn them against each other, make evil fight evil for once, and slaughter each other to the last man. Wash the world clean with their blood. He would be king! Emperor! He would remake the world in his...

A searing pain erupted in his back. Something sharp ground between his ribs. He shrieked and dropped the banner. The here-and-now snapped back around him. Magda was drawing back her stiletto to stab him again. He backhanded her across the mouth. She fell on top of the banner.

Hissing in pain, Reiner turned, raising his sword, 'You should have cut my throat, sister.'

'Stand, villain!'

Reiner looked over his shoulder. Albrecht had returned to himself, and was dismounting his charger.

'Touch not the lady!' he said, striding forward and drawing his long sword. His blue-hued plate flashed darkly in the sun.

'The lady is a conniving seductress who has turned you against your brother and your homeland,' said Reiner, stepping back. But despite his brave words, he felt like a rabbit in the path of a chariot. Albrecht was stronger, fresher, better armed and armoured – not to mention a head taller. He braced for the baron's swing.

A shot rang out. Albrecht staggered as one of his shoulder pieces spun off, holed and twisted. Behind the baron Reiner could see Oskar, kneeling near the unconscious Hals, lowering his smoking handgun. Franka and Giano fired as well, but their missiles glanced off Albrecht's armour. Pavel was shambling forward, dragging his spear. Reiner's heart swelled. He had forgotten. He was not alone.

Albrecht recovered and closed with Reiner, swinging mightily. Reiner ducked and stepped past the baron to hack at his back. His sword bounced off the shining plate, ineffectual, and he had to twist away as Albrecht lashed out behind him.

'Hold him, captain,' called Pavel. 'We're coming.'

Oskar had dropped his gun and Giano his crossbow and they were limping after Pavel, swords drawn. Franka was circling wide, nocking another arrow.

'Lady Magda,' Albrecht shouted. 'Take cover. I will deal with these traitors.'

'No,' said Lady Magda as she pulled herself to her feet. 'The banner must fly or the battle is lost.' With an effort she lifted the Bane and staggered with it toward the crest of the hill.

'Someone stop her!' called Reiner, dodging a thrust from Albrecht. 'Knock down that banner.'

Pavel and Giano turned, but it was Oskar who ran after the abbess. 'I have failed you too often, captain,' he cried. 'She will not escape me again!'

'Be careful!' called Reiner, but Albrecht's sword was in his face and he could spare Oskar no more of his attention. He parried and, with Pavel and Giano, began circling the baron like dogs baiting a bull... They lunged in with their swords and spears as he spun this way and that.

'Dishonourable knaves,' Albrecht gasped, his face red within his helmet. 'Three on one? Is this how men of the Empire fight?'

Reiner danced in and cut Albrecht across the calf. 'Do men of the Empire enslave their subjects with sorcery and pit them against their brothers? Do men of the Empire slay their own kin to win power?'

'My brother is weak!' said Albrecht. 'He does Karl Franz's bidding like a lap-dog, and refuses to join me in ridding the mountains of Chaos for good and all.'

'And so you bring a new evil to the land to fight the first?'

'You know not of what you speak.'

As he circled, Reiner saw, over Albrecht's shoulder, Oskar catch up to Lady Magda. The abbess turned at his approach, raising her hand to command him, but Oskar shielded his eyes and slashed at her with his sword. It was a weak strike, hardly more than a scratch across the back of Lady Magda's hand, but it was enough to cause her to yelp and drop the banner, which fell against Oskar's chest.

Lady Magda leapt at the artilleryman like a wild cat, stiletto held high. He blocked it with the haft of the banner and bashed her in the face with the pommel of his sword. She dropped like a stone.

'Magda!' cried Albrecht, as the sister sprawled limp on the grass. He started toward her, his own combat suddenly forgotten.

The three companions took advantage and lunged in together, but once again Albrecht's armour defeated them. Giano's sword caromed off his helmet. Pavel's spear pierced his leg guard, but not deep enough to wound him. Reiner's sword skidded off his chest plate.

With a howl of fury, Albrecht lashed out at them. He kicked Giano to the ground, cut a deep gash in Pavel's shoulder, then slashed back at Reiner and caught him a glancing blow to the scalp.

Reiner dropped, eyes unfocused with pain, the world spinning around him. He felt the ground hit his back, but wasn't sure where the rest of his body was. Albrecht was a blurry form above him, raising his sword over his head. Reiner knew this was bad, but couldn't remember why.

Franka's voice echoed in his ears. 'Reiner! No!'

The shaft of an arrow buried itself deep in Albrecht's armpit, sticking out of the gap between his breastplate and his rerebrace. Albrecht roared in agony and dropped his sword. It fell point-first, dangerously close to Reiner's ear. Reiner rolled up, weaving wildly, all balance gone, and stabbed blind at Albrecht with all his might. The tip impaled the baron's left eye. Reiner felt it smash through the back of the socket and enter his brain.

Albrecht dropped to his knees, wrenching the sword from Reiner's grip. He swayed but didn't fall. Reiner grabbed his hilt again, put a foot on the baron's chest and shoved. Albrecht's face slid off the blade and he crashed to the side like a wagon full of scrap metal tipping into a ditch.

'Cursed lunatic,' spat Reiner, and sat down hard, clutching his bloody, buzzing head.

'Reiner! Captain!' cried Franka, running to kneel beside him. 'Are you hurt?'

Reiner looked up. His vision cleared. The girl's face was so full of sweet concern that all at once Reiner wanted to crush her to him. 'I...'

Their eyes locked. There was an instant of perfect communication between them, where Reiner suddenly knew that Franka wanted to hold him as much as he wanted to hold her. This was followed by a second look, in which, still without speaking, they both agreed that this was neither the time nor the place, and that the charade must continue.

With a forced grin, Reiner broke eye contact and clapped Franka heartily on the shoulder. 'Why I'm fine lad, just fine. Nothing a needle and thread won't fix.'

Franka grinned in return. 'I'm happy to hear it.'

It sounded like bad acting in Reiner's ears, but Pavel and Giano were struggling to their feet on either side of them, so he carried on.

'And I am happy with your shooting,' said Reiner. 'You saved my bacon with that shot.'

'Thank you, sir.'

Pavel looked up the hill and groaned. 'Lady of Mercy, what's he done now?'

Reiner turned. At the crest of the hill, Oskar stood hunched, still holding the banner, his face twisted in a grimace of agony.

'Oskar!' called Reiner. 'Oskar! Drop it! Put it down!'

Oskar didn't move. He was frozen to the spot, shaking like a man in a high fever. His face was drenched in sweat, the yellow glow of the burning shrine of Sigmar shining upon it. He spoke through clenched teeth. 'I... cannot.'

Reiner and the others started toward him.

'No!' he cried. 'Come no closer! It makes me want to do terrible things.'

Reiner took another step. 'Come now. You must fight...'

Oskar swiped the banner at him. 'Please, captain! Stay back! I cannot control it!'

Reiner cursed. 'Oskar, you must put it down. While you hold it aloft it continues to control Albrecht's troops.'

'I know,' said Oskar miserably.

'I held it,' said Reiner. 'I know what it whispers to you. But you must fight it. You must...' Reiner trailed off as he realised that he hadn't been able to put the banner down of his own volition either. It was Magda's knife in the back that had saved him.

Tears ran down Oskar's frozen face. 'I cannot fight it, captain. I am weak. You know I am. I...' With an agonised cry he slashed at them again with the banner and staggered forward a few steps, then forced himself to stop. He looked like a man struggling to hold his ground against a giant kite. 'No,' he muttered furiously. 'I will not fail again. I will not.'

Straining as if he had the weight of a mountain on his shoulders, Oskar straightened and turned away from them.

He took a step toward the shrine of Sigmar. Then another. He moved like a man in quicksand.

'Very good, Oskar,' said Reiner. 'Throw it in the fire. That's a good man.'

Oskar closed on the shrine at a snail's pace, but at last stood mere feet from the fire. He reached out, and Reiner and the others could see his arms shake with the effort of trying to let go of the banner. It remained in his hands.

'Sigmar help me,' he wailed. 'But I cannot. I cannot!'

Reiner stepped forward again. 'Oskar, be strong!' he called. 'Be strong!'

'Yes,' hissed Oskar, through his teeth. He closed his eyes. 'Yes. I will be strong.'

And as Reiner and the others stared, aghast, he walked slowly, but deliberately, into the roaring flames of the burning shrine.

Franka screamed. Reiner shouted something, but he wasn't sure it was words.

'Oh, laddie,' murmured Pavel.

They could see, through the sheets of flame, Oskar standing in the middle of the shrine, shoulders back, burning like a candle, his clothes and hair charring, his skin crackling and bubbling. The flames raced up the pike and the banner caught, first only at the edges, which burned with a weird purple light, then all at once. There was a sound that was more than the roar of flames, a deep rumbling howl of inhuman fury that made Reiner's hair stand on end, and then, with a deafening crack, the banner exploded.

Reiner and the others were knocked flat by a blast larger than all the battle's cannon shots put together. A huge ball of purple flame erupted above the shrine as its splintered timbers spun past them like straw in a tempest. The last thing Reiner saw – or at least thought he saw – as he lost consciousness was a daemonic face, screaming with rage, boiling out of the fireball. Then it was gone, lost in billows of thick, grey smoke, and the blissful black of concussion.

# CHAPTER TWENTY
## YOUR GREATEST SERVICE

REINER OPENED HIS eyes. Thick smoke was still rising around him, so he couldn't have been out long. Groaning like an old man, he sat up and looked around. There was no trace of Oskar or the shrine of Sigmar except a patch of burned earth. Franka was getting to her hands and knees beside him. Giano was hissing as he pulled a dagger-long splinter of wood out of the meat of his arm. Pavel sat with his head between his knees, holding his face.

There was an irregular thumping behind them. They turned. Hals was crutching their way, the sleeve of his shirt tied around his head. 'So, we're alive then,' he said. 'Who'da thought, hey?'

'All but Oskar,' said Franka.

'Aye,' said Hals. 'I saw the end of that. Braver than we gave him credit for, I reckon.'

The boom of a cannon made them look up. Manfred's gun crews were at their pieces again, firing down at the battlefield below. Reiner and the others levered themselves to their feet and limped to the cliff edge, and discovered to their great relief that the crews were firing at the Chaos troops again.

'That's the stuff, lads!' cried Hals, waving his crutch. 'Give 'em some pepper!'

The same thing was happening all over the field. Though the battle was such a jumble that it was difficult to see what was happening, at last it became apparent that, Albrecht's troops, finally free of the banner's evil influence, were coming to their senses and joining their brothers in Manfred's army in attacking the Kurgan and driving them back toward the castle. Where before there had been tangled knots of frightened men fighting any who approached them, now the clarion calls of horn and drum were rallying the men of both armies into cohesive units which attacked their common foe with renewed fury. The pall of gloom was lifting from the field with the clearing smoke. The sun shone brightly on the burnished helms and breastplates of the Imperial knights and the ranked spear points of the state troops. The Kurgan, who seconds ago had had the upper hand, now found themselves outnumbered, and fell back in confusion. All over the field, companies of marauders were breaking and fleeing before the newly ordered ranks of the Imperials.

Franka, Pavel and Hals cheered.

Giano gave a satisfied grunt. 'We do our job, hey? They paying us now? Give us reward?'

Reiner nodded. 'Aye, I hope so. We've done the hard work. Killed Erich and Albrecht and...' He stopped, then spun, cursing. 'The witch! Where is she? We've forgotten the evil harridan who was the cause of it all.'

The others turned as well, looking for Lady Magda. She was no longer where Oskar had laid her out. They looked down the slope. She was nowhere to be seen.

'Curse the woman,' said Reiner. 'She's as slippery as an Altdorf barrister. Find her.'

But though they combed the hill all the way down to the smouldering woods, Lady Magda was nowhere to be found.

'She's flown the coop, captain,' said Pavel as they all gathered at the crest again.

Hals spat. 'Wouldn't I have liked to have seen her burn at the stake?'

Franka nodded. 'Better her than poor Oskar.'

They surveyed the field again. While they had searched, the battle had come to an end. There was still some mopping up going on, but for the most part the Kurgan had retired from the field, scrambling into the hills above Nordbergbruche castle and back into their holes. A large force of Empire troops was marching up the causeway to the castle gates and meeting little resistance.

Reiner turned away from the scene with a weary grunt, looking for a place to sit and tend his wounds, when he saw movement at the bottom of the hill. Knights were advancing up toward them at a walk, supported by a company of greatswords. It was Manfred.

Reiner sighed. 'Here comes his nibs. Time to face the music.'

He tried to brush the soot and dirt from his jerkin and tidy up his kit as best he could. The others did the same. It was pointless. They all looked like they'd been dragged through a briar patch backwards.

Manfred reined to a stop before his brother's body, his generals around him. He gave the corpse a long, sad look.

Reiner swallowed, nervous, and saluted. 'My lord. I can explain. It is as I said before. The banner, which you must have seen, gave Albrecht…'

Manfred held up his hand. 'There is no need to explain, you blackhearts. 'Tis obvious what happened here. You have disobeyed me by escaping from the confinement I put you in, and you have killed my noble brother.' He turned to the captain of the greatswords. 'Captain Longrin, fetch a litter for my brother's body and bring him to his rooms in

Nordbergbruche once they have been prepared. Be sure to drape the banner of our house over him, that all may know that a hero died today. Then arrest these men and see that their wounds are seen to. It wouldn't do for them to die before I had the pleasure of hanging them. When they are presentable, have them brought to me. I wish to interrogate them personally.' He reined his horse around. 'Now let us hurry. I want to see what those animals have done to my home.'

The greatswords advanced on Reiner and the others, who stood open-mouthed with shock. They had expected angry questions, or an argument over whether they had done right or wrong, but this curt dismissal flabbergasted them.

'Y'ungrateful bastard,' snarled Hals at Manfred's retreating back. 'Y'bleeding boil on Sigmar's arse. Y'don't know when somebody's done ye a favour, do ye? Well I hope y'get the pox and it falls off.' He spit. 'I wish I had it to do all over again. I woulda' took the hanging at the beginning and saved myself the trouble.'

Captain Longrin slapped Hals across the face with a mailed glove, knocking him to the ground. 'That'll be enough of that, gallows bird.' He motioned to his men. 'Bind 'em, lads. They've still some fight in 'em.'

The greatswords tied the wrists of the company and marched them down the hill.

'Curse all counts,' said Reiner bitterly. 'Never will I trust another.'

'Hear hear,' said Franka.

BUT MANFRED WAS as good as his word, at least in one regard. Reiner and his companions received the best care. Their wounds were salved and bound, their broken limbs set and wrapped in plaster casts. They were fed and cleaned and dressed in plain, but well-made clothes, and then placed in an empty barracks tent to wait upon Manfred's pleasure, under a much more alert guard than before.

Pavel, Hals and Giano took advantage of the delay to lie on the cots and get some shut-eye, but Franka sat huddled in a corner, glaring at nothing. The company had been separated in the hospital tent as their various hurts had been seen to, and Reiner suddenly realised that Franka's masquerade might have been discovered.

He sat down next to her and spoke in a whisper. 'Er, has your, er, manhood survived?'

She shook her head. 'I fought them, but they gave me a bath.'

Reiner sighed. She choked out a sob and butted her head against his shoulder. 'I don't want to go back!'

He put an arm around her. 'Shhh, now. Shhh. You'll wake the others.' He chuckled bleakly. 'And there's no fear of you going back. They'll hang you with the rest of us.'

She fought to smile. 'Aye, there's a comfort.'

After another hour, as the sunset turned the walls of the tent a deep glowing orange, a captain of the guard opened the flap. 'File out, scum.'

They stood, hissing and groaning, their wounds stiff, and followed him out. A double file of greatswords flanked them as they marched through the camp and came at last again to Manfred's magnificent tent. The captain held the canvas aside and they entered one by one.

It was dark in the tent, only a few candles illuminating the rich fabrics and dark woods of Manfred's furniture. Manfred sat in a fur-draped chair. Three more men sat in the shadows behind him. All were dressed in fine clothes and fur cloaks. To Reiner's surprise, there were no guards present, and five empty camp chairs waited for them, facing Manfred.

The companions hesitated in the doorway.

'Forgive me for not seeing you in my home,' said Manfred. 'But the savages have made it unlivable. There is much cleaning to be done. Please sit.'

They sat, looking around suspiciously, afraid it was some new kind of trap.

'Gollenz!' called the count. 'Wine for our guests.'

A servant came out of the shadows with goblets of wine on a silver tray. Reiner and his companions took them as warily as they had taken their seats. Perhaps Manfred meant to watch them die in throes of agony from poisoned wine. Or perhaps he meant to drug them to make them talk.

When the servant had retired, Manfred leaned forward. He coughed, seemingly embarrassed. 'Er, I want to apologise for the deception I employed earlier. There was indeed no need to explain, for when that unholy banner appeared on the hilltop, I knew that you had told the truth, and that my brother did mean to slay me.'

'But then…' said Reiner.

Manfred held up a hand. 'I and the Empire owe you all a debt of gratitude that we can never repay. You, more than any others in my army, have won this day, and the destruction of the Bane has prevented its influence from spreading any further. You have saved the Empire from a long and fratricidal war.'

'So…' said Reiner.

Manfred coughed again. 'Unfortunately, in these troubled times, with the great war over but the cost not yet counted, and the rebuilding still to be done, the morale of the citizenry is low. It would not do for them to believe that their lords were so weak that they could be corrupted as Albrecht was corrupted. They must not learn of his betrayal and the falling out between us. It would shake their faith in the nobility just when they most need us to be strong.'

A cold coil of dread snaked around Reiner's heart. Something bad was coming.

'Therefore,' said Manfred. 'Though it pains me to do it, you will still charged with Albrecht's crimes.'

'What!' barked Hals.

'The public needs a villain, a focus for their hatred. A scapegoat who can be disposed of so that life can return to normal.'

'And we're it,' said Reiner hollowly.

Manfred nodded. 'It will be your greatest service to the Empire.'

Hals pounded the arm of his chair and rose. 'Y'twisty little worm! Y'admit we saved your skin, and the Empire's, and still ye mean to give us the drop? I'm starting to wonder if we're fighting on the right side!'

Manfred raised his hand again. 'I haven't finished.' He waited until Hals sank back into his chair. 'I said it will be your greatest service to the Empire, but it will not be your last. You will be hanged with great public spectacle in Middenheim in a week's time.'

Franka tried to hold in a sob, but failed.

'At least,' continued Manfred, 'the crowd will believe it to be you. In reality it will be some other garrison scum: deserters, saboteurs, the like.'

A spark of hope kindled in Reiner's chest. 'So you mean to free us after all?'

'You will be freed, eventually. But first you will have the honour of further serving your Empire.'

The spark of hope fizzled out, and the feeling of foreboding began to creep over him again. 'How so?'

Manfred smiled thinly. 'The more I thought about what you accomplished here today, and the lengths you went to achieve it, the more I came to believe that we could make use of you.' He leaned forward again. 'The Empire needs blackhearts like yourselves – men who will do things that would be beyond the pale to the average soldier, men who are not awed by rank or power, who think for themselves and keep their wits in desperate situations.' He took a sip of wine. 'Battles are not the only way the Empire stays strong. There are less honourable deeds that must be done to keep our homeland safe. Deeds no true-hearted knight could allow himself to undertake. Deeds only knaves, villains and dishonoured men could stomach.'

'Y'high-talking twister!' growled Hals. 'All yer fine manners and all yer asking is for us to do your back-stabbing for ye!'

'Precisely,' said Manfred. 'After your doppelgangers are executed, you will become invisible. No one in the world but myself and the men you see before you will know that you still live. You will be ciphers, able to enter any situation and become who we wish you to be. The perfect spies.'

'And what if your perfect spies decide they don't want to do your dirty work?' asked Reiner. 'What if they decide to slip their leashes? These brands are only a death sentence within the Empire.'

'Aye,' said Giano, crossing his arms. 'I be my own man. No one control me.'

'Do we not?' asked Manfred. 'My brother had the right idea, branding you, but his methods were crude.' He motioned to the man behind him on his left, a white-bearded ancient in the black robes of a scholar. 'Magus Handfort is a member of the royal college of alchemy. He has developed a poison that can be activated from afar, at any time he chooses. While the surgeons were tending to your wounds, they rubbed this poison into your cuts.' He raised his hand as Reiner and his friends began to stand and protest. 'Take your ease, please. The solution is perfectly harmless until the magus reads aloud a particular incantation. Only then will you die a horrible agonising death.' He smiled, as warmly as if he were wishing them a happy and prosperous new year. 'And he will only read the incantation if you fail to report back to me at the end of the assignments I shall give you.'

'You swine,' said Reiner. 'You're worse than your brother. At least he offered a reward if we completed our mission. At least there was to be an end to our bondage.'

'My brother never intended to honour his end of the bargain, as you well know,' said Manfred. 'And he used you for his own interests, whereas now you will be working for the good of the Empire.'

'He said that too,' said Pavel.

'You will be well rewarded,' continued Manfred. 'When duty does not call you, you will live well indeed, within the walls of my castle. And when this time of crisis is over and the terror is at last vanquished, you will be freed from your service and given riches enough to build entire new lives. In addition, as you have all died, all your crimes will die with you.' He gave Franka a significant look. 'Your secrets will remain buried in your past, and you may live as you choose, new men.'

Reiner and his companions looked blankly at Manfred as he sat back and folded his hands in his lap.

'So,' he said. 'What have you to say? Do you take my offer? Will you help the Empire in its hour of need?'

'I'll say what I said to your brother,' sneered Reiner. 'We haven't much choice have we?'

'No,' said Manfred. 'You have not.'

A SHORT WHILE later, riding toward Nordbergbruche castle in a coach with heavily curtained windows, Reiner and his companions looked at each other glumly.

'That some loads of horse mess, hey?' said Giano.

'Aye,' said Pavel. 'Until the terror is vanquished, he says. The Empire has stood for two thousand years and there's always been some terror or other banging on the gates.'

'We're in it for the duration all right,' said Hals.

'Isn't there anything we can do?' asked Franka.

Reiner shook his head. 'Not unless we can find a way to flush the magus's poison from our system. But until then…'

'Until then,' said Pavel, 'they have us.'

'Aye,' growled Hals. 'By the short hairs.'

Reiner laughed and couldn't stop. His life might have become a never-ending nightmare, but at least the company was good.

*Nathan Long* has worked as a screenwriter for fifteen years, during which time he has had three movies made and a handful of live-action and animated TV episodes produced. He has also written several award-winning short stories. When these lofty pursuits have failed to make him a living, he has also been a taxi driver, limo driver, graphic designer, dishwasher and lead singer for a rockabilly band. He lives in Hollywood.

# INFERNO!

Inferno! is the Black Library's high-octane fiction magazine, which throws you headlong into the worlds of Warhammer. From the dark, orc-infested forests of the Old World to the grim battlefields of the war-torn far future, Inferno! magazine is packed with storming tales of heroism and carnage.

Featuring work by awesome writer such as:

- Dan Abnett
- Ben Counter
- William King
- Graham McNeill
- Nathan Long

and lots more!

Published every two months, Inferno! magazine brings the grim worlds of Warhammer to life.

For subscription details call:

US: 1-800-394-GAME
UK: 0115 91-40000
Canada: 1-888-GW-TROLL
Australia: 02 9829-6111

For more information visi www.blacklibrary.com/infern